ROYAL REFINEMENT

THE KABIERO ROYALS BOOK TWO

EMMA LEA

Cover design by Michelle Birrell
Book design and production by Michelle Birrell
Cover photograph licensed by Adobe Stock

ISBN: 978-0-6488558-7-3

✿ Created with Vellum

OTHER BOOKS BY EMMA LEA

This is Emma Lea's complete book library at time of publication, but more books are coming out all the time. Find out every time Emma releases a book by going to her website (www.emmaleaauthor.com) and signing up for her Newsletter.

SWEET ROMANCES

These are romantic tales without the bedroom scenes and the swearing, but that doesn't mean they're boring!

The Young Royals

A Royal Engagement

Lord Darkly

A Royal Entanglement

A Royal Entrapment

A Royal Expectation

A Royal Elopement

A Royal Embarrassment

A Very Royal Christmas

A Royal Enticement

The Kabiero Royals

Royal Ruse

Royal Refinement

Bookish Book Club Novellas

Meeting Prince Charming

Meeting the Wizard of Oz

Meeting Santa Claus

SWEET & SEXY ROMANCES

In my Sweet & Sexy Romances I turn up the heat with a little bit of sexy. No swearing, or very minimal swearing, and brief, tasteful and not too graphic bedroom scenes.

Love, Money & Shoes Series

Walk of Shame

Standalone Novels

Amnesia

HOT & SEXY ROMANCES

Hot & Spicy Romances turn the heat way up. They contain swearing and sexy scenes and the characters get hot under the collar.

Recommended for 18+ readers

Brisbane City Hearts (formerly TGIF)

Love to Hate You

Want to Date You

Hate to Want You (coming soon)

Collins Bay Series

Last Call

The Christmas Stand-Off

Game Changer

ABOUT THIS BOOK

Duchess Sophia Dellis, *Archontissa of Kalon,* needed a date for the upcoming Kabiero Royal Ball. The man she planned to take as her date just dropped her for someone with a higher social media profile. Not that Sophia was heartbroken. Nico was a sweet guy, or at least he was until he turned into a fame monster—something that wouldn't have even happened if Sophia never gone out with him in the first place. Now she was left with six weeks to find someone to fill his place on her dance card and no prospects in sight...that was until she saw Ethan across a crowded club. He was completely unsuitable, but her best friend, Frankie, dared her to turn him into a *Duke Incognito.*

Ethan Samuels was minding his own business, working behind the bar in the hottest new club on Kalopsia when two members of the new Kabiero Royal court approached him with an outrageous proposal. How could he turn down a duchess? Plus, he would get an adventure that a simple guy from

Australia would never have even dreamed of; learn how to navigate the world of wealth and royalty, attend a royal ball on the arm of a beautiful woman, and get a foot in the door of a new career on a super yacht. It was a no-brainer as far as he was concerned.

They both knew what the deal was. Sophia would teach Ethan everything he needed to pass as a duke, and Ethan would get the experience he needed to break into a new career. It was a business arrangement. No one was supposed to fall in love.

AUTHOR'S NOTE

Raida is not a real alcohol :) Originally I was going to use ouzo as the national drink until I did a bit of research that I discovered ouzo can only be called ouzo if it is made in Greece. ¯_(ツ)_/¯ So I decided to use a fictional alcohol to go along with my fictional island and my fictional country and my fictional monarchy and my fictional...okay, you get the idea.

If *raida* was real, it would be just like ouzo :D

This book is written in AUS/UK English. This means words like 'color' and 'favorite' are spelled *colour* and *favourite* as is standard in UK English. Also *'storey'* appears instead of 'story' to describe the floors of a building.

Book one in the series was written using US English because both main characters were American. In this book, one of the main characters is Australian and the other is educated in the UK English style. It felt weird and inauthentic to have them speak in the US English style.

Also, I'm an Australia and writing with US English just feels...wrong. Call it a quirk of my writing style. We're all friends here and a few stray Us and Es shouldn't come between us <3

For anyone who has ever felt superfluous or has not yet found where they belong.

CHAPTER 1

Sophia

"Is this true?"

"Is what true, Mama?" I asked, trying to keep the exasperation out of my tone. I knew what she was asking, and I really didn't want to talk about—

"Nico," she said, and then sighed dramatically.

I rolled my eyes, thankful we were on a voice call and not FaceTime.

"Yes, I broke up with Nico," I replied. *Thank God*, I added silently.

"But why?" Mama asked, her voice whiny, as if she couldn't possibly understand why I would do such a thing.

"You obviously saw the Instagram story he posted," I said. "And the TikTok."

Mama was quiet for a moment and before I could say

anything to fill the void and hopefully head off any more whining, my father's voice came across the line.

"We liked Nico," Papa said.

I clenched my teeth to stop myself from growling. Nico was a worm, not that my parents had ever seen that side of him. I hadn't either until it was too late.

"He was The One," Mama said, her voice a loud, awed whisper.

I barely contained the snort, coughing to clear it from my throat.

"No, Mama, he wasn't The One."

He wished he was, but I knew even before I started dating him, Nico was not and never would be The One. I just wish I'd known what a worm he was before I took him from a zero to a hero. I thought Nico was sweet—not my type, but sweet nonetheless. He was a little shy and reserved and cute in a puppy dog kind of way. I thought I could date him for a few months, get my parents off my back, have a date for the big ball coming up, and then we could go our separate ways.

I knew being seen with me would raise Nico's profile. I was a duchess. I had an enormous social media following. I had influence. I was also aware of how incredibly arrogant that all sounded, but I was also a realist. These were just facts. Being a duchess or an Instagram princess or even an influencer were not *who* I was, none of them were personality types, they were just convenient labels hung around my neck so people could put me in whatever box they felt comfortable with.

Nico's profile was raised simply by appearing in a photo alongside me, and before long, I'd created a monster. I had no idea how hungry Nico was. He asked for a few tips to increase his following, asked me to mention him in my stories, asked me to give him some style and fashion hints, and before long he was Tweeting our dates and Instagramming every little thing we did.

"But he is so gorgeous," Mama said. "And look at his numbers."

By numbers, she meant social media followers across all the platforms. I was well-versed in the numbers game. It was my job, after all. Yep, I was a duchess, and I had a job, although the two of them went hand in hand. I was the social media manager for the palace. Not Buckingham Palace, no. The Kabiero Royals were a small court and Kalopsia was a small country, but I was a duchess and I was part of the king and queen's inner circle. I was a lady-in-waiting, which was just a fancy—and somewhat antiquated—term for an assistant to the queen.

Don't get me wrong, I loved my job, and I loved being a lady-in-waiting. It got me out of France and away from my family and gave me a little bit of independence and room to breathe. Of course, as long as there was internet and cell phone reception, I was never really free of my family.

"You need to settle down soon," Papa said. "It's not right that you are single while the rest of the court are married."

"Papa, I am not the only single member of the court," I said with a huff. "There are only two court members who are engaged, and they are engaged to each other."

I was talking about Lucas and Frankie, of course. I'd had a front-row seat to their courtship. They were best friends who pretended to be engaged and then fell in love for real and got engaged for real. It was all so romantic, and I was so happy for them, but that was not my destiny and Nico was definitely not the guy I would get my happy ending with.

"Which is all the more reason for you to find someone sooner rather than later," Papa said.

"What about Lord Dorian?" Mama asked, obviously already over my split with 'perfect Nico.'

I did snort then because Dorian Stamos? Ducas of Paralia? He was the very last man on earth who I would consider as a life partner. I'm pretty sure I would end up stabbing him in his sleep. Not really…but maybe? I shook myself. No, Dorian was not a candidate and never would be.

"No, Mama," I said. "Not Lord Dorian."

"I met this nice young man—"

"Papa, no," I said, putting my foot down. I had been on a handful of dates with guys my father deemed 'nice young men' and just…no. They only dated me to get on my father's good side, and I wanted more than that. I wanted to date someone who saw me as more than just a stepping stone to impress my father or a way for them to increase their social media profile. A cardboard cutout of me could achieve the same thing.

"You need a date for the ball," Mama said. "You cannot turn up alone."

"It's six weeks away," I replied. "That's plenty of time to find a date."

"You can't just pick someone up off the street, Sophia," Mama said. "You're a duchess. You need to find someone worthy."

I rolled my eyes again. What was 'worthy' anyway? It was just another label. I was really sick of labels.

"Sorry Mama, Papa, but I have to go. Talk soon."

"TELL ME *EVERYTHING*," Frankie said as soon as I opened the door.

"At least wait until we're inside," Elena grumped from behind Frankie.

"Pregnant lady," Meredith—*Queen Meredith*—said, elbowing her way past both Elena and Frankie before kissing my cheek and crossing to the overstuffed armchair in my suite.

The others followed her in; Frankie, Elena, and Elena's sister, Athena. Danika, one half of Meredith's security detail, stuck her head in the room for a quick look and then took up a position outside the door. Flint, the other bodyguard, positioned himself on the other side. I gave them a smile before closing the door and turning to look at my uninvited guests.

"I see Jamie has bumped up your security," I said to Meredith, crossing to sit in the only empty space on the couch beside Frankie. Danika was the head of the security team for the entire palace. That she was on Meredith's personal detail said a lot about how serious Jamie was when it came to protecting his wife and unborn child, especially since they were *inside* the palace and behind several layers of security.

Meredith pointed to her barely protruding belly. "Baby on board," she said, and then rolled her eyes.

The Kabiero royal court was not what anyone would call conventional. We used first names and didn't stand on pomp and circumstance when we were together. Of course, when there were outside visitors to the palace, the protocols and ceremony were what anyone would expect them to be within a royal court.

"I don't want to talk about me, or Jamie's paranoia," Meredith said, motioning to my lady's maid, Larissa, to order some food from the kitchens. "I want to talk about you and how you are and how much we hate Nico."

"I never liked him," Elena said, admiring her perfect manicure. Everything about Elena was perfect, from her flat-ironed straight dark hair to her flawless makeup and elegant style. I wanted to be Elena when I grew up.

"You don't like anyone," Frankie said.

I also wanted to be Frankie when I grew up. No, she wasn't put together like Elena was, but I liked that about her. Frankie was real and honest and hardly ever censored herself. That was what we all loved about her...okay, maybe Elena didn't love that about her. But the Varoni of Lethe (Baroness of Lethe) had definitely thawed toward Frankie since she'd come to live at the palace full-time.

"True," Elena said with a tight smile. "But Nico always struck me as..."

"A social climber?" I supplied for her.

"I was going to say leech, but social climber works," she replied.

"I thought he was gorgeous," Athena said dreamily.

Athena always spoke dreamily. The two sisters couldn't be more opposite if they tried. They were both gorgeous, but there was a severity about Elena that was missing in Athena. Athena's edges were softer, probably because Elena protected her like she was as fragile as hand-blown glass.

"Yeah, well, as good looking as he was—is—he decided I wasn't enough," I said, slumping back against the couch.

"What?" my three friends screeched in unison.

I shrugged. It didn't hurt, not really, not when I didn't have feelings one way or another toward Nico. Was I angry that he decided to go after the current reigning TikTok princess (not a real princess BTW. Not even a real title, but whatever)? Yes, I was angry only because I needed him to stick it out with me for just six more weeks. I just needed him to be my date to the ball, and then he could have gone off to do whatever—or whoever—he wanted. All that work for nothing. All those weeks of turning him into an appropriate date for the ball for it to amount to nothing as he sought more social fame than I could provide.

"That worm," Frankie spat. "What do you need? Ice cream? Chocolate? Pretzels?"

"Pretzels?" Elena replied with disdain.

"Oh my God! Pretzels," Meredith groaned. "Why did you have to say the P word, Francesca? Now I want a pretzel!"

Just then the door opened, and one of the palace servers wheeled into the room a tray.

"Do you have pretzels?" Meredith demanded of the poor man.

"Yes, your Grace," he replied and lifted a domed lid to reveal both salty pretzels and cinnamon ones.

Meredith made grabby hands and Frankie got up to get them both one of each. These were not the small pretzel crackers that were found in a nut mix, these were the large German style pretzels that made even my mouth water. I especially loved the sweet ones...they were deep fried and then coated in sugar and cinnamon, and they were...chef's kiss...perfection.

Elena didn't help herself to the pretzels, but took a small glass bowl of cut fruit. After a look at her big sister, Athena also took a bowl of fruit. I went for a pretzel.

We ate in silence for a moment and then Frankie spoke.

"We need to go out," she said, dusting her hands off. "We

need to get you out and about and seen to be living your best life."

I rolled my eyes. "I really don't care—"

"She's right," Elena said. "The best revenge is being seen not to care."

"But I don't care," I said. "I was only dating him so I'd have someone to take me to the ball."

"Even more reason to go out," Meredith said. "You need to fill that vacancy."

"Not you too," I groaned. "I just got off the phone to my parents, and they were saying the same thing."

"You misunderstand me," Meredith said. "I'm not saying you have to find someone to spend the rest of your life with. But you do want someone to dance with at the ball, right? You want some gorgeous hunk on your arm who will tell you you're pretty and knows how to show you off on the dance floor."

"Yeah, I do," I said, knowing it was shallow of me but not being able to deny the truth. Besides, my Instagram feed had been chock full of posts from Nico and *Carmelita* and it would be nice to have something to post in response.

"So let's go out," Frankie said, practically vibrating with excitement beside me. "A new club just opened near the resort. I bet we can get VIP tickets."

"I already have them," Meredith said. "But I can't go." She looked down at her belly, but she didn't seem too upset about missing out.

"I want to go," Athena said, but Elena was already shaking her head.

"There is no way I am going to be caught dead in a night-club," Elena said, and Athena pouted.

"Just you and me, then," Frankie said, turning to me and grasping my arm. "Please say yes."

I sighed and rolled my eyes and then nodded my head. "Okay. Let's go clubbing."

~

"I PROMISE YOU, I'M FINE," I said when Frankie pushed another cocktail in front of me and gave me sad, pitying eyes.

"You don't look like you're fine," she said. "You look like he really hurt you and to be honest, I didn't think you liked him that much."

"I didn't," I replied, swirling my straw through the frozen, neon-coloured drink.

We were seated in the VIP section and had table service as well as complimentary drinks. The bouncer on the door took one look at our tickets and then treated us as if we were queens. Okay, we were part of the royal court and our faces were pretty recognisable, especially since I'd been in charge of the palace's social media accounts, but I didn't expect to be treated like... well, royalty.

Ironic, I know.

"So why so sad?" Frankie asked. "It can't just be about the ball."

"Argh," I growled low in my throat. "I'm just annoyed," I said. "I made him, you know. He was nothing before he started dating me and now, look at him. He thinks he's all that. If not for me, he would still be a nobody."

"Whoa, arrogant much?" Frankie said, raising her eyebrows at me with a smirk.

"You know it's true," I replied. "I'm good at what I do. I know how to create a brand and promote it."

"Nico has a brand?"

"He does now," I replied. "Because of me. Do you think he would get anywhere near Carmelita if I hadn't godmothered him?"

"Godmothered him?"

"You know, like in Cinderella? Nico was a nice, sweet guy who Carmelita wouldn't have looked twice at. I think I understand how Dr. Frankenstein felt."

Frankie snort laughs, almost choking on her drink. "Sophia, the fairy godmother," she said. "I like it. It has a certain...*je ne sais quoi.*"

"I don't have a lot going for me, but that is one thing I know I'm good at."

Frankie reached over and covered my hand with hers.

"You have a lot going for you," she said. "You are smart and fabulous and not to mention beautiful."

"You just described every single influencer on Instagram," I said.

"You are my best friend," Frankie said. "And I don't say that lightly."

"Lucas is your best friend," I replied, dropping my head and feeling a little embarrassed by Frankie's words.

"Lucas is my fiancé," she corrected. "You're my BFF."

"You're my BFF too," I replied, squeezing her hand.

"Right, now that we got that over with, now let's talk about finding you a date for the ball." She scanned the club and then turned back to me. "Can't you just—" she made her fingers dance in some weird woo-woo way—"godmother one up?"

"I absolutely can," I replied. "But what if he abandons me too, just like Nico?"

"I don't think you can," Frankie said, smirking at me again. "I think you're all talk and no action."

"Please," I said, crossing my arms and giving her my best Elena stare.

Frankie shivered. "Don't do that," she said. "It's creepy."

I smirked but dropped the Elena-look. "I can godmother any guy here," I said.

"I'll take that bet," Frankie said with a grin. "Only I get to choose the guy."

"Don't be ridiculous," I replied.

"You just said you could turn any of these guys from a pumpkin into a prince—"

"I don't think that's how Cinderella goes."

Frankie waved my comment away. "Details," she said. "I bet you can't. I think you are all talk."

"And no action," I finish for her. "Right. You already said that."

"So prove me wrong. Take a guy and turn him into the perfect date for the ball. It's six weeks away. That's plenty of time for you to godmother him."

"You really don't believe that I turned Nico into the social media monster he is?"

"I mean, as your friend, I *want* to believe you," Frankie drawled, playing with the straw in her drink. "But how can I be *really* sure if the results can't be repeated?"

"You are ridiculous, you know that, right? This entire conversation is ridiculous."

"You can't tell me it doesn't intrigue you, though," Frankie said slyly. "I mean, you love this stuff. As you said, you're good at it. Aren't you just itching to get your hands stuck into another project?"

I huffed out a laugh because she was right. The more she goaded me, the more determined I was to prove her wrong.

"*Hypothetically,*" I began, and Frankie's smile widened. "If I were to take you up on this bet, who would you pick out for me?"

Frankie squealed softly and then turned to scope the club. "What about him?" she asked, pointing out a guy on the dance floor.

I stick my finger in my mouth and pretend to gag.

"What?" she asked innocently. "He's pretty to look at."

"Yeah, just ask him," I responded. "The guy hasn't looked at the woman he's dancing with for over five minutes. He's too busy checking himself out in the mirror."

Frankie grunted and then pointed to another guy. "What about him? He looks...nice."

"Yeah, he does," I replied. "Too nice. Elena would chew him up and spit him out. I can only alter someone's image, Frankie, not their complete personality."

"Yeah, but you don't have to impress Elena."

"No, but I do have to impress my parents, remember? I have to make this guy look like a viable alternative to Nico. I have to make him into some sort of titled gentleman. That guy would fold like a cheap suit."

"Okay, fine. What about him?"

"Him who?" I asked, trying to find the guy she was looking at.

"The guy at the bar."

"Which guy at the bar," I asked with exasperation. "There are lots of guys at the bar."

"The bartender," she corrected.

Just then he looked up as if he could hear Frankie talking about him, which was ridiculous because he was all the way across the noisy club. Our eyes met and a fission of...I didn't know what fizzled through my body. I wanted to look away, but I couldn't. I was trapped in his gaze and I didn't hate it...or at least, part of me didn't hate it, another part of me was freaking the hell out.

I licked my lips. "The bartender?" I croaked.

Frankie turned to look at me and smiled. "Oh yeah," she said, nodding with a smirk. "Him. He's the one."

"You think I can turn him into the Duke Incognito in six weeks?" I asked, breathless.

"No, but I think you'll have a whole lot of fun trying," she replied with a wink.

CHAPTER 2

Ethan

$\mathcal{J}$'d seen the two women as soon as they'd walked into the club. They were hard to miss, and not just because they were both gorgeous...although I was kind of biased. I thought all women were gorgeous, regardless of the societal conventions that dictated what was socially acceptable beauty. So yes, they were both beautiful, but that was not what caught my attention. No, that honour went to the way people treated them. The crowd actually, *literally*, parted for them like the Red Sea. People watched them as they crossed the club, led by none other than the owner of the club himself. Mr. Lykaios rarely came out from his office, or at least not while the club was open. There was a large one-way window on the floor above the club, and behind that window was Mr. Lykaios' office. He could see just about everything that went on in the club from up there and what he couldn't see from the window, he could see on the monitors set up with the security camera feed.

That's all to say, to see Mr. Lykaios personally escort two women through the club obviously meant that they were of some importance.

I hitched my chin toward the two women who had taken their seats in the VIP section and raised my eyebrows at my bar tending partner for the night. Sonny just grinned at me. He obviously wasn't going to give me the gossip, although I couldn't exactly blame him. The patrons were three-deep at the bar and we were getting smashed. Not much time to chat.

Mr. Lykaios came to the bar and set up a tab for the two women himself, telling both me and Sonny that the ladies' drinks would all be comped. He never did that. This was a guy who short poured drinks to save a few extra bucks…not every shot, just when the customers were already three sheets to the wind. He also made us use the less expensive brands when we determined a customer was too drunk to notice. It wasn't ethical, hell; it wasn't legal, but I'd worked in worse places. At least *Mr. Wolf* was clean and safe and paid well.

My eyes were continually drawn to the two mystery VIPs, despite how busy it was. After their arrival, the club seemed to swell to capacity, and I didn't know if it was because of them or just the regular Saturday night crowd. I had my suspicions that the two brunettes had definitely had an impact on the increase in patrons, which meant they had to be famous, right? They looked sort of familiar, but I couldn't put a finger on how I knew them, or at least where I'd seen them because I definitely didn't know them. I would absolutely remember them if we'd ever been introduced.

I expected them to get absolutely slammed, especially with

all the free booze on offer, but they drank moderately and spent most of the time talking or dancing. They didn't interact with the other patrons, and although they were definitely the centre of attention, no one actually approached them. In fact, the two VIPs barely even noticed the people gawking at them. It was almost comical to watch the club patrons make a long detour to the bar just so they could walk past where the two women sat. And it wasn't just the men checking them out. The other women in the bar were just as captivated by them.

"Seems like we have some famous faces in the club tonight," I said to one customer as I handed over her order.

She grinned at me. "The two princesses? Isn't it amazing to see them here? And no security detail either."

She picked up her drinks and sashayed away. Another eager patron quickly filled her spot at the bar and I smiled and mixed drinks, but all the while my head was spinning.

Princesses? I knew Kalopsia had a royal family, but to my knowledge there were no children yet. The queen was pregnant —that wasn't something I could have missed considering the papers covered her pregnancy with all the anxiety of a first-time parent—but there were no 'princesses' that I was aware of. Which made me wonder, were they from another country? Or was it an honorary title? Were they like, social media princesses? Or actresses who played princesses in a movie I hadn't seen? Or maybe mafia princesses? I doubted that last one, although I wouldn't put it past Mr. Lykaios to have ties to a criminal organisation. (That was unfair of me. Just because Mr. Lykaios was a nightclub owner didn't mean he had to have criminal associations.)

Needless to say, that little tidbit of information only left me with more questions rather than giving me any answers. But it did not deter me. One of my favourite pastimes was figuring out who a person was, and I was pretty good at determining someone's personality simply from the drink they ordered.

My skill was failing me tonight, though. The two mystery guests were ordering different drinks for every round and they were weird, obscure drinks that only someone who had worked in the industry would know. These were not the usual *Cosmopolitan* and *Margarita* drinkers, not that I had anything against those drinks. I loved a good margarita now and again.

I looked up, my eyes going straight to the couches where they sat, and for the first time that night, they were looking directly at me in return. My eyes snagged on the one with long hair and…wow. Just wow. What a rush. My entire body lit up, and I sucked in a breath from the force of it.

Her eyes were dark, although I couldn't make out the exact colour from where I was. Plus, the lighting in the club didn't make it any easier. I expected her to look away or smile at me or…something, but we were both frozen, or time stopped or…I didn't even know what. Maybe I'd fallen over and hit my head and this was some coma dream because nothing like this had ever happened to me before. Sure, I'd made eye contact across a crowded room with a woman I wanted to hook up with, but I'd never felt the connection like a physical punch to my gut.

She licked her lips and then said something to her friend, all the while never taking her eyes off me. Her friend replied, or I assumed she did. I didn't really know because I hadn't taken my eyes off her. She said something else and then the two of them were walking toward me and my heart very nearly beat right out of my chest.

~

DID TIME JUST SLOW DOWN? What the hell was happening right now? Nobody existed in the club except her…and her friend, obviously. The two of them were walking toward me and it was as if everything, and I did mean everything, just faded away. It was like some weird movie action hero shot thing and was it just my imagination or did the club lights turn to follow their progress, lighting them up as if they were parading down a catwalk? Was there wind blowing through the club to make her hair swish that way?

I blinked a couple of times and shook my head to clear it, and the noise and reality of the club came rushing back in. The patron who had been trying to get my attention for service turned to look at where my attention was, and then he moved aside in understanding, letting the two VIPs approach the bar.

I cleared my throat. "What can I get for you?" I asked.

They shared a look and the one with shorter hair smirked. Nobody said anything for a long time, and then short hair rolled her eyes.

"What's your name?" she asked.

Her accent was American, if I wasn't mistaken. I was pretty good with accents, a side effect of travelling so much.

"Ethan," I replied and smiled.

I didn't know why I was so nervous. I shouldn't be, I mean I'd worked in clubs with famous clientele before, but there was something about these women, one of them in particular, that had my body responding in crazy ways.

"Hi Ethan," short hair replied. "I'm Frankie. Nice to meet you."

She put her hand out across the bar and I shook it automatically, but my eyes were on the other woman, the one who hadn't spoken yet.

Frankie nudged her companion and the other woman blinked like she was coming out of a trance. I understood the feeling.

"My name is Sophia," she said, also reaching out to shake my hand.

I couldn't place her accent, but it was definitely European; a mix of accents if I wasn't mistaken, but I couldn't identify their origins.

I took her hand in mine, and I was not prepared for that initial contact. I should have been. Just locking eyes with her had done irrational things to me. Shaking her hand compounded that tenfold. I sucked in a breath and she jolted as if I'd electrocuted her. Both of our wide eyes met again and I could finally see she had chocolate brown eyes shot through with gold.

We shook hands for too long. I knew it was too long, but still I couldn't pull my hand away. We were stuck in a stasis, our hands moving up and down slowly as we continued to shake hands and it was…odd.

"So you're Australian," Frankie said, breaking the weirdness.

I slowly pulled my hand from Sophia's and turned to Frankie with a smile. "I am," I replied. "And you're American."

Frankie smirked. "I am, or was. I live here now, so I guess that makes me a Kalopsian?"

"And you?" I asked, turning to Sophia. "I know you are not American."

"No," she said with a shake of her head. Her cheeks flushed, and she shot a look at Frankie before speaking. "I am actually Kalopsian, although I lived in Greece and then France for most of my life."

"And now you live here?" I asked, not so subtly fishing for information.

"I do," she replied.

We stared at one another for a long moment and Frankie must have gotten bored because she spoke again, breaking the moment yet again.

"So Sophia was just dumped—"

Sophia glared at Frankie, and I frowned. Whoever dumped Sophia must have rocks in his head.

"I wasn't dumped," Sophia said. "*I* dumped *him*."

"Details," Frankie said with a wave of her hand. "It all amounts to the same thing, which is you don't have a date to the ball."

"The ball?" I asked, looking between the two of them. Why did I suddenly feel like I was the punchline for some fairy tale?

"The State Ball to welcome The Queen and her family from Merveille?" Frankie said, quirking her eyebrow at me. "You have heard about the ball, haven't you?"

"Um, no, actually," I replied.

"Seriously?" Frankie asked.

They were both looking at me like I should've known about the ball, but I didn't. I shrugged.

"So, there's a royal ball? I don't see how that has anything to do with me. It's not like I would be invited to a ball at the palace."

Frankie smirked. "But what if you could be?" she asked.

I looked between the two women. "I don't understand."

Sophia sighed. "As Frankie is trying—unsuccessfully—to say is, would you be interested in taking part in a little social experiment?"

"A social experiment that involves attending a royal ball?" I asked with a grin, thinking for sure they were pulling my leg.

"Exactly," Frankie said. "Sophia here thinks she can turn any guy in this place into a duke. I don't think she can do it."

"I did not say duke," Sophia replied. "I just said that I could turn any guy into an acceptable date for the ball."

I quirked an eyebrow. "You do know how rude that sounds, right? And condescending?"

"Ugh, of course I do," Sophia replied, rolling her eyes. "But it is true, nonetheless. Nico was nothing before I took him under my wing."

"So you're looking for another project?" I asked, offended on behalf of all the men in the club. Why were women always looking to change a guy? What did I look like, some renovation project in need of some TLC? A renovator's delight?

"No," Sophia said, staring daggers at Frankie. "Frankie made the bet and then chose you as my vic…I mean, test subject."

"Well, I mean…" Frankie raised her hands in a 'what are you going to do,' kind of way. "Sophia was making some grand statements and I, who has a doctorate in sociology, psychology, and anthropology, could not let the statement stand without some demonstrable proof."

"I honestly don't know whether to be flattered or offended," I said, looking between the two of them. I was offended, and a little flattered as well, if I was honest.

"Be flattered," Frankie said easily. "Sophia here is offering to turn you into a *duke*. She is going to godmother you so hard that even the queen will think you were born with a royal silver spoon in your mouth."

"Godmother me? I don't think that's a thing."

"Of course it's a thing," Frankie said. "Have you never read Cinderella?"

"So I'm Cinderella in this instance?" I asked.

"Cinder-*fella*," Frankie said, and then cracked up at her own joke.

Sophia rolled her eyes and then turned to me. "Ignore her," she said.

"So you don't want to take me to the ball?" I asked.

Sophia smirked. "Look, as unconventional as it sounds, I can do what I said. Nico was nothing before I started dating him. I've grown up in a royal household—or as close to one as a royal in exile can get. I know everything about how to act like a royal. I can have you looking, sounding, and acting like a duke in six weeks."

"And what do I get out of it?" I asked.

"What do you want?" she asked. "I can pay you, if that's what you mean."

I shook my head. "No…that's sounds a little too…off."

"Okay, so what do you want?"

There was something I wanted. Although I loved working in the bar, I had my sights set on something new, but I couldn't ask Sophia to help me with that.

"Nothing," I said. "There is nothing I want. I have everything I need."

Sophia looked me dead in the eye and I had the uncomfortable feeling she could see right through my lie. I didn't flinch or look away or react, though. Let her think whatever she wanted to think. I would probably never see her again, and I could chalk this up to one of those weird moments that happen in life. I could practically write a memoir about all the weird stuff that had happened to me while travelling.

Instead of saying anything, Sophia opened her clutch and slid a business card across the bar to me.

"What's this," I asked, picking it up.

"My card," she said.

I read her name and her title and swallowed.

"You're a duchess?" I asked.

"I am," she replied with a feline smile. She tapped the card with a perfectly manicured nail. "Call me if you change your mind."

I looked from the card up to her face. "You're serious? This isn't some sort of joke? You're not trying to punk the foreign guy?"

"I'm serious. I need a date for the ball. A date my parents and the queen will approve of. If you change your mind, then call me, but don't leave it too long. We're on a truncated time frame."

I slipped the card into the pocket of my shirt.

"Thanks anyway," I said. "It was nice to meet you, both of you, but I don't think I will be taking you up on that offer."

"Suit yourself," Sophia said with a one-shouldered shrug.

"So this means I win," Frankie said. "I win the bet?"

Sophia rolled her eyes. "You can't win the bet if he didn't agree."

Frankie turned to me. "Please say yes," she said. "I want to win this bet."

"You want to bet against me?" I asked with raised eyebrows. "I thought we were friends?"

Frankie laughed and pointed at me. "I like you," she said as they walked away.

❧

I WATCHED THEM WALK AWAY, my world a little rocked by the conversation. It wasn't every day that I was offered the opportunity to become a duke. I mean, I knew I wouldn't actually become a real duke, but still...no one had ever offered to godmother me before.

I shook my head and looked around the club. It was still busy and Sonny was swamped. Since Sophia and Frankie had been such important guests, I'd gotten away with ignoring all the other customers while I spoke to them, but now they were gone, I needed to get back to work.

I loved the energy of a busy night. Maybe I'd once fantasised that being a bartender would be like being Tom Cruise in that old movie *Cocktail*. It wasn't. Most of the time it was just yelling to customers over the loud music and hoping you heard their order correctly. Not to mention going home smelling like a brewery and the genuine problem of bar rot. Technically, it was called *paronychia* and was an infection in the cuticles and nail beds on the fingers. Not nice and a hell of a thing to get rid of. But I loved my job, despite the downsides of working behind a bar. I got to meet lots of interesting people and I'd travelled to well over fifty countries paying my way with the very transferrable bar skills I'd learned back home in good old Brisbane, Australia.

I'd only been in Kalopsia for about four weeks or so, but I'd scored this bar tending job in the brand new nightclub that was currently the hottest thing on the island. I didn't know how long I would stay; I had plans to move on, but not just yet. There was something about this small island nation that made me want to sit a spell and just be. I'd been on the move since I was twenty and I'd never, not once, felt the desire to stay. I'd seen some of the most spectacular places on the earth, and yet...

the wanderer in me could never really settle. My mum called it a restless soul, and I supposed she was right. My father told me I was running away, and maybe there was a bit of that too. I was terrified of getting stuck, and my solution was to just keep moving. A rolling stone gathers no moss, or so the saying goes.

My last stop had been in Greece, which was where I heard about Kalopsia. I'd never even known the place existed before, and as soon as I could organise a visa and entry permit, I'd left Greece behind.

I had plans to move on, but they differed from what I'd been doing for the past few years. I'd come to the Mediterranean with the view to getting a steward's job on a luxury yacht. The marina on Kalopsia was chock full of the exact boats I had my sights set on, but getting a gig on one of them would take a minor miracle.

When Sophia asked me what I would want in return for being her 'test subject' I had very nearly asked her if she knew anyone with a yacht and if her 'godmothering' could turn me into someone who could get a job on one. I wasn't opposed to asking for what I wanted. I'd learned long ago that it wasn't what you knew, but who you knew that got you ahead in life. I wouldn't have gotten the job at *Mr. Wolf* if not for meeting someone in the backpacker's hostel in Greece who told me about it and gave me the name of the person doing the hiring. But asking Sophia to find me a job felt…wrong. The entire thing she suggested felt wrong to me, which was why I'd said no.

That should have been that, but I couldn't stop thinking about it…the offer or the woman. Sophia was something else; long dark hair, those chocolate and gold eyes, full lips and a smile that made my knees turn to liquid.

Besides, I had an interview for a steward's job in the morning. It wasn't my first interview, but it was one that I was most confident about. The yacht wasn't big, but that didn't matter. It was the perfect size to cut my teeth on. I didn't even know if I was going to like the job. I could get on the yacht and a few days out at sea and I could hate it. I didn't think I would, but there was always the possibility. So this job would be perfect, if I got it.

I didn't need Sophia or her fairy godmothering. I could do this on my own. I didn't want to be a duke, anyway.

CHAPTER 3

Ethan

The day was warm, and the sky was clear. Boats bobbed gently in the water as I made my way down the marina walkway toward the berth where my prospective new place of employment was moored.

I stopped before the gangplank and checked the details on my phone. I looked back up at the yacht and my stomach did that sinking thing. But I tried not to read too much into it. Yes, the yacht was smaller than I'd expected. Yes, it looked like it needed a bit of TLC. None of that meant that this wasn't still a really good opportunity for me. My goal was to get to head steward, but with zero experience on a yacht, I had to start at the bottom and that meant starting on a less prestigious yacht.

I ignored my trepidation and pressed the intercom on the gate to the gangway.

"Yes?" the disembodied voice answered.

"Hi, it's Ethan Samuels. I have an appointment with Ms. Caruso."

There was a buzzing sound, and then the gate unlocked with a click. It felt creepily like what I imagined walking into a prison would sound like...not that I had any experience with walking into a prison...

I crossed the gangway and stepped onto the boat where the head steward was waiting for me. His white uniform was neatly pressed, if a little worn, and the navy blue epaulets on his shoulders a little faded.

"Follow me, please," the steward said.

He didn't speak as we navigated the tight quarters. The yacht really was small. So small it surprised me there was a crew at all. To me it looked like it only needed a captain and one steward, but what did I know?

The steward opened a door and held it for me as I walked through into the cabin. It was set up like a sitting room...more of a snug than a full-sized living room. Seated on one of the couches was a woman who looked to be in her early fifties. She wore a long gold and brown caftan, and her blonde hair was swept up in an elegant hairstyle. She wore dark glasses and her lips were painted blood red.

"Ms. Caruso, this is Ethan Samuels," the steward said.

"Thank you, Henry," Ms. Caruso said with a tight smile. Her voice was light and airy, and her smile widened when she looked at me. Her smile was toothy and feline. I felt very much like I was prey. "Have a seat, Mr. Samuels."

"Call me Ethan," I said as I lowered myself to a couch opposite her. The cabin was small enough that my knees were barely centimetres from hers.

"I understand that you've never worked on a yacht before,"

she said once Henry left the room.

"No, I haven't," I admitted. "But I'm a fast learner and look forward to the opportunity to learn."

"Taking into consideration your lack of experience, I won't be able to offer you the advertised salary," she said.

I swallowed back my grimace. "Of course," I replied. I'd expected that, but I still didn't like it.

"Obviously, I will give you...ample...opportunities to grow your experience and thereby increase your value to me. We can review your wages on a month-by-month basis dependent on your...dedication...to the tasks I set you."

That feeling of trepidation in my gut rose up once again. I didn't want to think badly of Ms. Caruso—I'd only just met the woman—but it sounded a lot like she would expect me to do things that were not covered in the advertised job description. I could just be jumping to conclusions. It could just be me reading more into the situation because of my initial gut reaction to seeing the yacht in person.

Ms. Caruso leaned forward and patted my knee. She kept her hand on my knee for longer than was appropriate before squeezing lightly. Her long, gold-painted nails looking a lot like talons. Diamond encrusted rings glinted from every finger and there was a jangle of gold bangles on her arm.

"I think we are going to get along fabulously," she purred before leaning back in her seat with a smile that made me feel decidedly uncomfortable.

I cleared my throat and reached for the folder I'd brought with me. "Here is my resume and a list of my work history. As you can see, I've been travelling for a few years now and I have worked all over the world—"

"Yes, yes, I've read your application. I'm more interested in your willingness to start at the bottom," she said. "And learn some new skills." Ms. Caruso leaned forward again, but didn't touch me this time. "How do you feel about working under a woman? Taking orders from a woman?"

"I don't have a problem working for a woman," I answered.

She smiled, her teeth flashing white between her red lips. "Excellent," she replied. "There is no Mr. Caruso, so I will be in charge. Do you understand what I'm saying?"

She watched me intently, and I really wished I could see her eyes behind her glasses. It was an unnerving experience.

I nodded slowly.

"Does that bother you?" she asked, tilting her head to the side as one of her hands played with the deep v-neck of her caftan.

"As I said, I have no problem with working for a woman," I replied.

She smiled, and I again had that unnerving feeling of being prey. "Lovely," she replied. "When can you start?"

I cleared my throat again. "I—uh—I have to give notice to my current employer," I said, stalling. "And I have another offer on the table…may I have some time to think about it?"

The smile drooped on her face, but she held it in place even if it looked a little brittle now. "Of course. But I can't wait too long," she replied. "We are scheduled to leave in a week and I'd want you on board and familiarising yourself with your role before we leave."

"I understand," I said, standing. "I will let you know by the end of business tomorrow."

She nodded and flicked her fingers, and the door opened to reveal Henry waiting for me.

"Thank you for your time," I said as I made my escape.

Henry didn't speak to me as he led me back through the yacht and out to the gangway. He didn't even say goodbye as I disembarked.

It took everything in me not to run away from the boat. What the hell had just happened?

I COULDN'T SIT STILL. The room I shared with three other people in the hostel was too cramped to pace in, and I couldn't concentrate long enough to read or play video games. Instead of making both myself and my roommates crazy, I left the hostel and headed to my favourite place on the island.

One of the things I loved about Kalopsia were all the small little secret alcoves and caves that dotted the coastline. There was only one main beach on the island and that was also the lowest—topographically speaking—point and where the resort and most of the touristy things were located. But there was so much more to the island. The palace sat on the highest point and there wasn't a place on the island anyone could go and not see it, except, I supposed, when you were actually in it. It reminded me of a story I'd heard about a man who lived in Paris and hated the sight of the Eiffel Tower so much he ate lunch at its restaurant every day, just so he didn't have to look at it. Not that I hated the sight of the palace. I didn't. I thought it was spectacular.

From the beach and the resort, the island rose in terraces, a narrow road winding its way up through the different boroughs. There weren't a lot of cars on Kalopsia, people generally made their way around on scooters and bikes. I hoofed it whenever I could, but the steep climb to the top of the island was not an easy walk.

I hired a scooter and headed out. It was only a short ride, but I took the opportunity to let the sun and sea breeze ease my unsettled feeling. The interview had disturbed me more than I liked to admit. I'd worked in some dodgy places, but I'd never been stranded at sea in a job where I felt...I couldn't even put into words how being on that yacht had made me feel. Uncomfortable seemed like an understatement, but unsafe wasn't the right word either. I'd definitely felt apprehensive about accepting the job, and after being on my own so long and travelling to so many different places—not all of them safe—I'd learned to trust my gut.

I would have declined the job out of hand except...it was the only steward position I'd ever managed to get an interview for. I'd submitted numerous applications, but I'd never gotten an interview. I knew I needed experience, but how was I supposed to get that if no one would even let me get a foot in? It was the classic Catch-22 situation. I didn't really have any idea what that really meant, except I was in a no-win situation. I'd never read Catch-22...

Now I was rambling in my own head as I avoided the decision I had to make.

I could stay at *Mr. Wolf*. It was a good job. The money was decent, and the tips were excellent. It had a bit of prestige attached to it since it was the newest and hottest club on the island. There was no reason I needed to find a new job.

No reason, except the reason I came to the Mediterranean was to get on a yacht. It was how I'd chosen my next destination...it was how I'd chosen every destination. I didn't just travel the world for the sake of it. It was all about the journey, rather than a destination. The steps I took to arrive at any place were just as important as the place itself. The years I'd spent travelling had also been spent learning. New cultures, new skills, new experiences. Doing the yacht steward thing was my next step.

Using that logic, I should take the job with Ms. Caruso, but even thinking about it caused me to shudder. I did not want to work on that yacht, but what was the alternative? No other yachts were going to hire me.

I parked the scooter and climbed off. I walked to the edge of the sheer cliff and looked out over the cerulean sea. I wished I could paint. It didn't matter how many photographs I took, nothing could capture the exact shade of the sea and the feeling of being here and having it spread out below my feet.

I took a deep breath and with one last look at the view; I walked over to the narrow trail that led over the edge.

I'd discovered the secluded spot in my first week on the island. The trail was steep and probably dangerous, but I'd followed it, anyway. It led to a cave carved out of the side of the cliff by the ravages of time and wind and sea. I suspected it was a place teenagers came to drink and smoke and do whatever they could to rebel against their parents—the cave held the evidence of my theory—but I'd never actually come across anyone in the month that I'd been coming here. It was probably because I came here during the day and the others possibly came here at night, but I was just guessing.

I sat at the mouth of the cave, my feet dangling over the edge, the waves crashing against the rocks far below me. I liked to come here to think. Seeing how small I was compared to the rest of the world helped to bring things into focus for me. It was far too easy to become so entirely self-focused that I lost sight of the bigger picture.

I knew I couldn't take the job on the yacht, even if I'd been trying to talk myself into it since the interview yesterday. Throughout my shift the night before, all I could think about was the way Ms. Caruso had looked at me and…yeah, nah. I just couldn't do it.

But I was lying to myself, because Ms. Caruso's offer wasn't the only thing that had kept me distracted the night before. There was another woman and another ridiculous offer that had been keeping me company.

Sophia's card burned a hole in my pocket. I shouldn't even be considering the preposterous proposal but…what if, just for a moment, as a hypothetical exercise, I considered it?

Sophia promised to teach me everything I needed to know to navigate the royal scene. Those skills had to be transferrable, right? She could even give me a glowing recommendation at the end of the six weeks and with her connections, she could very well get me a position on a luxury yacht that was leagues above the one Ms. Caruso owned.

It wasn't as if Sophia was *propositioning* me. She was doing it as a purely scientific exercise. It was a *bet* with her friend. It had absolutely nothing to do with me as a person—should I feel offended by that? Probably not. I was a random guy picked out of the crowd. Sophia wanted to prove something to Frankie, and I was simply the vehicle for that proof.

Or it could have just been a drunken conversation that she wouldn't even remember. It had been three days.

I pulled the card out and ran my finger across the gold-embossed lettering. It was an opportunity that I may never have again. It was a chance to learn some new skills and hobnob with royalty. If nothing else, it would be an amazing story to tell my grandkids—if I ever had them. Plus, I'd get to go to a real ball… apart from one very drunken B&S Ball I attended years ago, I'd never been invited to a ball before. Did it even count as a real 'ball' if you had to buy a ticket?

I shook my head and pulled out my phone. How could I walk away from this experience out of hand? Part of my travel mantra was to say yes to surprising and unconventional opportunities when they presented themselves, and this was both surprising and unconventional. The least I could do was have a conversation before I turned my back on it.

I dialled the number and waited while it rang. By the third ring, I was ready to hang up, but then I heard her voice.

"Hello?" Her voice was cautious but friendly.

"Um Sophia?" I asked, even though I recognised her voice immediately.

"Yes?"

"This is Ethan. From the club?"

"Ethan," she said, and I heard a smile in her voice.

"You remember me?"

"Of course I remember you," she replied. "Have you reconsidered my offer?"

"Let's just say I would like to hear more about it," I hedged.

"That's not a no."

"That's not a no," I agreed. "So, can we meet to…talk about it?"

"What are you doing for lunch?"

I DRESSED like I was going to a job interview. What did you wear to meet a duchess for lunch to discuss her turning you into a fake duke? I didn't think even GQ would have an answer for that.

Sophia was already at the cafe when I walked in. She looked like she was preparing to do a job interview, so I felt more relaxed in my choice of attire. That's all it was, really. Maybe not a conventional job, but when it all came down to it, I supposed I was applying for a job...as her date...for a royal ball.

How was this my life right now?

The first rule of improv was to always say yes. It was the only thing I remembered from my one term of drama in high school. It was a rule I'd applied to my life...within reason. Saying yes had given me some incredible moments in my life... it had also gotten me into some scrapes, but let's not talk about those. In the big grand scheme of things, those...scrapes...had been invaluable learning experiences too.

Sophia looked up at my approach and smiled. I lost my breath for a moment. I'd thought that initial attraction I felt toward her resulted from...I didn't really know what. But I certainly hadn't expected it to hit me with the same force today as it had the other night. I'd thought it was a fluke, but if the way my heart was hammering in my chest was anything to go by, it wasn't.

"Ethan," she said, my name a purr on her lips. "I'm so glad you called."

I smiled because...what did I say to that? I hadn't agreed to anything yet, but...if I trusted my own intuition, I didn't think I'd be walking out of this cafe without saying yes to everything she wanted.

I sat down and smoothed the front of my shirt. I should

have worn a tie, but I didn't own any. I traveled light, and it was only because of my need to attend frequent job interviews I had the dress pants and button-down shirt. They were the same ones I'd worn to the job interview with Ms. Caruso. They felt tarnished now, but I'd had no other option. I'd need to buy a new interview outfit before my next job interview.

"Should we order lunch first before we talk?" Sophia asked.

"Sounds like a plan," I replied, picking up the menu and looking it over.

I'd never actually eaten at this cafe and to be honest, calling it a cafe was a stretch. It was a restaurant, regardless of what they put on their sign. And not just any restaurant, *Koúpa Kafeneío* (ironically, translated as Cup Cafe) was one of the most expensive restaurants on the island.

I tried not to baulk at the non-existent prices. What was that saying? If you have to ask, you can't afford it?

"Maybe I'll just have a coffee," I said, putting the menu down.

"Don't be ridiculous," Sophia said, ordering for both of us and sending the server off with instructions to bring them each a glass of wine.

"I can't afford—"

Sophia held up a hand. "I invited you here, I'll pick up the tab."

I nodded in acquiescence, even if it felt wrong to do so. I wasn't opposed to a woman buying me lunch per se...okay, maybe I was. I shifted uncomfortably in my chair and picked up the water glass to take a sip.

"What do you want to know?" Sophia asked, her face open and friendly. "You obviously have questions."

"I do," I said and then cleared my throat.

"Go ahead. Ask me anything."

"I suppose my biggest question is, what is in this for me?"

"That's not your biggest question," she said, and then thanked the server when he placed a glass in front of her and poured the wine. She took a sip and nodded to the server, and he poured a glass for me before leaving. "Your biggest question is why. Why would someone like me want to do this?"

I eyed her over the lip of my glass. "Yes, I suppose I am wondering that. You could probably snap your fingers and have any number of men as a date for the ball. Why go to all this trouble?"

She smiled. "Originally, it was because Frankie bet me I couldn't."

"And now?"

Sophia shrugged. "I suppose it is an interesting experiment. My job is to build and maintain the brand of the palace and the royal family. It would be interesting to see if I could do the same with a person."

"You want to turn me into a brand?"

"No," she said with a laugh and a shake of her head. "But the same principles apply, if you really think about it. The way you present yourself to the world is a kind of brand."

"So I'm a guinea pig?"

"Something like that," she replied as she sipped her wine.

We were quiet as another server placed our meals in front of us. It was fish and some blanched greens in a clear broth. It smelled divine.

"Okay, so back to my original question," I said after taking a bite and appreciating the taste. "What's in it for me?"

"What do you want?" Sophia asked. "I'm happy to pay you

for your time. You will need to give up your job, so I can't not compensate you for that."

"Money isn't really a motivating factor for me," I answered truthfully. Sure, I needed money to survive, but it was only a means to an end.

"So what does? Motivate you, I mean?"

"Experiences," I replied. "Learning new skills."

"Both of which I'm offering you, but there has to be something else, something you really want."

"There is," I replied. "I want to work on a yacht."

Sophia nodded. "Deck, engineer, interior, or galley?"

"Steward," I replied.

She nodded. "So…how can I help with that?"

"Connections," I answered. "Plus, I don't really have the necessary experience. I mean, I've worked in hospitality for years; bars, restaurants, hotels. But I guess it's not quite the same as working on a yacht. Not…posh enough."

"So you need refinement," she said, and it wasn't a question. "I can do that. I can give you that and I know quite a few people who may need an extra crew member." She looked up at me then. "So do we have a deal?"

"Not until I know exactly what it is you require of me," I said, leaning back in my chair.

"I need a date to the ball, as I already told you. As a duchess, my date has to be…appropriate. My parents—" she broke off and shook her head "—my parents are snobs," she finished and grimaced. "I need them to approve so I can get them off my back. If they don't think you're a suitable companion for me, they will set me up with someone they think is."

"O-kay," I said slowly. "So what does that mean for me? How do I become the 'appropriate' companion?"

"Leave that to me," Sophia said. "I'll teach you everything you need to know."

"And the bet?"

Sophia smiled. "If I take you to the ball and no one questions your pedigree, then I win."

"What do you win?" I asked with a grin.

"Bragging rights and the pleasure of telling Frankie she was wrong," she replied with a matching smile. "Now do we have a deal?"

I exhaled slowly. There was no warning check in my gut, and the trepidation I'd experienced the other day when I went to my interview was curiously absent. It appeared this entire experience would be relatively painless and might even be fun. Plus, I would be one step closer to getting the coveted steward job.

I reached across the table to shake her hand. "We have a deal," I said.

She clasped my hand, and that weird electrical spark shot up my arm. Her eyes widened as if she felt it too and then snatched her hand back.

"Perfect," she said. "Give me a couple of days to get everything set up and then we can meet up again. In the meantime, you need to resign from your job at the club."

CHAPTER 4

Sophia

$\mathcal{I}$ expected him to baulk at resigning from his job. It was a big leap of faith and I was asking a lot, but this wouldn't work if he was still living the life of a normal, average, everyday person.

"Okay," he replied, shifting in his seat.

"Okay?" I asked, a little surprised he gave in so easily.

He shrugged. "I know how a con works."

I frowned. "A con?"

He sat forward, leaning his forearms on the table. It was not proper etiquette, but…I couldn't deny I liked the look of his forearms. Who knew a man in a business shirt with rolled-up sleeves could look so delicious?

"You do realise that is what this is, right?"

"Um, what?" I asked, dragging my eyes away from his bare forearms and back up to his face. He really did have a nice face.

I wouldn't mind seeing what it looked like under the dark blonde beard. His hair needed a trim too, but again, the way it curled around his eyes and flopped over his forehead was...nice.

He narrowed his blue eyes at me. He had blue eyes...did I know that before now? The night in the club when we'd first met, I'd only really taken in the general look of him—he was attractive, that was undeniable; dark blonde hair, full beard, well-proportioned body—

"You're pulling a con," he said.

"What?"

He smirked and may have rolled his eyes at me. I frowned. "I'm pulling a con?"

He nodded slowly. "You want me to pretend to be someone I'm not to fool your parents and the rest of the royal court, right?"

"It's not like that," I replied, back peddling. "I don't want to con money out of anybody. We're not doing anything illegal."

"Maybe not, but the principle is the same. This is a con. You want me to convince the people around you I'm some duke, right?"

"Yes, but I'm not trying to hurt anyone."

"I get that," he replied, his gaze softening. "But you are going to be lying to people. You are going to be lying to *everybody* in your life. Are you prepared for that?"

Wasn't my entire life a lie, anyway? What would one more lie be? But I couldn't say that to him. I could barely even admit to myself that my own life felt as thin as the screen my Instagram posts appeared on.

"It's not lying like that," I said instead. "It's not really like a *con*. It's more like when you're organising a surprise party for someone. You have to lie to them then, right? This is the same thing."

"Are you going to get me to jump out of a cake at the big reveal?" he asked with another smirk.

"Now you're being deliberately obtuse," I replied, feeling my stomach erupt with a kaleidoscope of butterflies.

I shifted uncomfortably, looking away from him so I could take a breath. He was...a lot. I'd thought the whole 'eyes meeting across a crowded room' thing was a plot device for romcoms and when it actually happened to me, I wrote it off as a fluke and too much alcohol, but...when he looked at me across the table...phew...it was A. Lot.

"I just want you to be sure this is what you want to do. Wouldn't it be easier to just tell your parents to back off?"

I snorted. Not the most elegant response, but it was involuntary and quite appropriate for the situation. "My parents are very invested in my life," I replied, trying to be diplomatic. "They have big hopes for my future and I will eventually do what they want, but I just need some space...a bit of breathing room. The last eighteen months have been a big change, and I just need some more time to adjust and find my feet. If I can just get them off my back for a while, things will be easier for all of us." I snapped my mouth shut, not quite sure why I was revealing any of that to him.

He gave me a long look that felt like he was seeing into my very soul...which scared me because I wasn't sure he would find much there.

"Okay," he said.

"Okay? Just like that?"

Ethan shrugged. "I know what family pressure is like. I

understand the need for breathing space. It's only six weeks, right?"

"Six weeks," I agreed, relieved. "Yes. Just until the ball."

"And at the end of six weeks, you will have gotten your parents off your back and I will get to sail away on one of those super yachts. I suppose you have a plan for that?"

"A plan for what?"

"How to explain me leaving," Ethan said.

"Oh, right, of course," I replied, lying through my teeth.

He laughed and there went those butterflies again. Phew. His laugh was…dangerous.

"I'll think of something," I said. "I'll make up some excuse for you having to leave and then I can pretend we are still together even though you won't be here." I relaxed back into my seat and smiled. "I could drag it out for…months."

"Months?" he asked, one of his eyebrows quirking.

"My parents live in France. They will be here for the ball, but once they go home, I only see them over Skype. I can have a whole itinerary set up for you that keeps you out of the country."

"That doesn't sound like it will end in disaster at all," he drawled.

I smiled, confident. "I've got this. After a suitable time has passed, we will have a very dignified breakup. I can use your continued absences for why it won't work between us."

Ethan leaned back in his chair and did that long look thing again, and I tried hard not to squirm under his gaze.

"Okay," he said again.

"Okay," I repeated. "So let's meet again on…" I mentally flipped through my calendar. "Friday," I said.

"This is a disaster," Meredith said.

I slipped into the room where the entire court was apparently meeting. No one informed me there was going to be a meeting. Even the sullen and silent Evan was in attendance. I still didn't know what to make of him, but if Jamie trusted him then…who was I to cast aspersions?

Frankie met my eye and winked, patting the seat beside her. Lucas sat on the other side of her and they looked so good together, I felt weird breaking the tableau they made, but I needed to sit and there was nowhere else. Okay, there was. I could sit next to Dorian but…it was Dorian, and I really tried not to get too close to him if I could help it.

I slid into the seat beside Frankie and turned my attention to Meredith, who was pacing while she rubbed her pregnant belly. Jamie looked concerned but not alarmed, so whatever the disaster was, it wasn't a threat to his wife.

"It's not a complete disaster—" Lucas said, but cut off when Meredith aimed a death glare his way.

"It will be if we don't get it sorted," she growled.

"There is a simple solution," Dorian said in his bored and condescending way. The duke had a way of looking down his nose at everyone, even the current reigning monarchs.

Meredith swung around to face him. "Enlighten us," she snapped.

"You need to appoint a Lord Chamberlain," he said, flicking some non-existent lint off his perfectly tailored pants. "This is the kind of thing they take care of."

"Are you volunteering for the job?" Meredith asked, a dangerous edge to her voice.

Dorian chuckled like she had just made the funniest joke. "No. That's just...no."

"But you seem to know so much about it," Lucas said.

Lucas was the sweetest cinnamon roll of a guy, except when it came to Dorian. For some reason—probably Dorian's natural ability to enrage just about anyone he ever came in contact with—Lucas always showed his teeth and claws around Dorian. Not that Dorian cared. He treated Lucas like a puppy who was testing out his bark and his bite.

"Of course I know about it," Dorian replied. "But not because I would ever lower myself to take the position. I know we are a fledgling court and it will take a while to furnish all the required positions to give us the credibility of being an *actual* royal court, but a Lord Chamberlain appointment is beyond due, especially since we are about to host a foreign court."

"What's going on," I whispered to Frankie.

"Meredith is freaking out because the chef is throwing a tantrum, housekeeping is in an uproar, and there appears to be a few problems with proper *protocol*."

"We need Dom," Meredith said to Jamie.

Jamie smirked in return. "I don't think Alyssa will let you steal her Lord Chancellor, Mer."

"Surely I could convince Dom and Priscilla to defect?" Meredith whined.

"Or we could find someone to fill the position from here," Jamie said, and then he turned to Dorian. "Do you know of anyone who would be suitable for the position?"

Dorian adjusted his cuffs. "I know of a few people who might be interested."

"That's all well and good," Meredith said, finally sitting down. "But it doesn't help us right now. How can we possibly hire someone and get them up to speed in time for Alyssa's visit?"

"We can help," Frankie said, taking my hand in hers as if we were a team.

Meredith looked at us both. "You can?"

"Of course," Frankie said. "I can work with the household staff and Chef loves me, and Sophia knows everything there is to know about protocol and all of that other stuff. She can be the event planner."

"Oh, I—" I stuttered but stopped when I saw the relief on Meredith's face. I sighed. "Sure," I said. "I can help out."

Meredith smiled. "All of you can help," she said, eyeing each of the court in turn. "Dorian obviously has superior knowledge, so of course we will need his help, and Elena, I noticed you've been unusually quiet. Surely you have some insights that could help."

Elena looked like she was going to refuse, but instead nodded her head in acceptance. She might not want to get her hands dirty with the actual work, but she would not stand for our small royal court making fools of themselves. Elena and Dorian were cut from the same cloth, and I felt smaller whenever I was around them.

"I already have a budget worked out. It just needs to be signed off on and then implemented," Lucas said.

Lucas was the resident bean counter and really good at his job. In fact, he was really the only one of us who had a real job inside the palace. Frankie had a job too, but hers was a consultant job. She *consulted* with the palace on matters pertaining to the social welfare of the people of Kalopsia.

I wasn't really sure what anyone else did. Evan rarely graced us with his presence. Dorian was always around but never seemed to do anything except be a pest, and Elena...well, she did whatever she wanted pretty much. As for me, I'd appointed myself the position of social media manager and Meredith had just gone with it. It wasn't a real job, not like Lucas and Frankie, but it gave me something to do. Now I would have to take on the protocol duties of a Lord Chamberlain and coaching Ethan...oh crap.

"Oh, um..."

Everyone turned to me, and I swallowed. I hadn't thought this through, but now that everyone was looking at me and waiting, I had to come up with something.

"There is a...VIP visiting the island," I said, my brain scrambling to make up a backstory for Ethan to explain the time I would be spending with him.

"A VIP?" Jamie asked with an eyebrow lift and a quick look at Danika.

"He's, um," I cleared my throat. "He's travelling *incognito*," I said, knowing it sounded like a lie as soon as it was out of mouth. "He will be staying at my grandparents' villa—" a detail I hadn't yet told Ethan about, mainly because I'd only just thought of it, "—and he has asked me to host him." I hid the grimace, or at least I hoped I hid the grimace.

I could feel Frankie practically vibrating beside me with her restrained laughter.

"But I should still be able to help," I added quickly when Meredith looked like she was about to panic. "I just wanted you to know that you might see him around from time to time."

"Is he here to see us?" Jamie asked.

"Oh, no. Not at all. He's on vacation and didn't want a whole press contingent following him around." I swallowed, hating myself for how easily I was lying. "He'll probably stay in the villa most of the time, anyway."

"We should at least invite him to the ball," Frankie said beside me and I jabbed my elbow into her side. "He can be Sophia's date."

Meredith grinned. "Is he good looking?"

I rolled my eyes. That went…better…than I thought.

"WHAT THE WHAT, FRANKIE?" I hissed as I pulled my friend into my suite after dinner.

Frankie just grinned at me over her shoulder as she waltzed across the room and fell into one of my sofas.

"You should be saying thank you," Frankie said.

"Thank you? Really? How did you arrive at that conclusion?"

I joined her on the sofa and flung my head back against the plush cushions.

"I got Ethan an invitation to the ball," she said.

"He didn't need an invitation," I said. "He was going to be my plus one."

Frankie snorted. "That would have caused more questions. I like the backstory you came up with for him, though. A secret duke vacationing on our little island and wanting to keep his real identity a secret so the press wouldn't hound him. Nice. You should write romance novels."

I rolled my eyes at her. "I had to think of something to explain who is he and why I will be spending so much time with him."

"So I take it he agreed to the bet?" Frankie asked turning to look at me. "The last I heard, it was an unequivocal no."

"Yeah. He called me and we met for lunch today to go over the details."

Frankie waggled her eyebrows. "Go over the details, huh? Is that what the cool kids are calling it these days?"

I rolled my eyes again. "It wasn't like that."

"But it could be," Frankie said. "He's gorgeous, and I saw the way he looked at you."

I waved my hand to dismiss her comment. "It's a business arrangement. One *you* pressured me in to."

Frankie snorted. "You wouldn't have gone along with it if you weren't the tiniest bit interested in it."

"A chance to prove you wrong and get bragging rights? Of course I was interested." I bit my lip and turned to sit so I was facing her. "But am I really doing the right thing? I mean...I *lied* to Jamie and Meredith. I sat in that room with the king and queen and—"

"Lied your backside off," Frankie said with a laugh. "Can I just say how proud I was of you, by the way. That took guts."

I dropped my head into my hands. "I'm going to hell, aren't I?"

"Not hell, no," Frankie said. "Danika might throw you in the dungeon though."

I groaned. "I should just call the whole thing off."

"You could," Frankie said, far too casually. "But that means I win."

I ignored her, too focussed on my own misery. "What if we get to the ball and the whole thing is a complete failure? I mean, I know I'm good at what I do, but there's always the risk of it blowing up in my face and then what? My reputation will be ruined and then what little credibility I do have will be shredded like yesterday's newspaper."

"What are you talking about?" Frankie said, sitting up.

I lifted my head and gave her a look. "You know what I'm talking about."

"No, I really don't," Frankie said.

I sighed. "It's okay, you don't need to spare my feelings."

"Sophia, I literally have no idea what you are talking about right now."

"Come on, Frankie. I know I'm the least valuable member of the court. All I do is social media and branding. Anyone can do what I do. I'm not like you or Lucas. I don't have a 'thing.'"

"A 'thing?' What does that even mean?"

"You know, a 'thing.' Lucas is the numbers and money guy. That's his 'thing.' You're the sociologist and people person. You've done so much for Kalopsia since you've been here. You and Lucas both. I don't have anything like that. I only got the title because my father was the duke during Jamie's father's monarchy."

"That's the only reason any of us are here," Frankie said. "Lucas only got the title because of who his father was before the coup. And you are not the least valuable member of the court. That's ridiculous. What about Dorian? I love the guy, but what does he contribute to the royal court except for snark?"

I smirked. Dorian and Frankie were good friends. It shouldn't work, but it did. I think Dorian might even have had a little crush on Frankie when she first came to the palace. Frankie was probably the only person in the palace who liked the duke.

"Dorian is…Dorian," I said, as if that explained his value to the court. "He knows people. He knows stuff. He has money."

"Yeah, yeah, yeah, but he hardly contributes anything. You,

on the other hand, contribute a lot. I mean, could you see Elena doing anything useful except look disdainfully at us all?"

"She's like a female Dorian," I agreed with a sigh.

"And Evan?" Frankie snorted. "He barely attends meetings unless Jamie demands his attendance."

"Yeah, but he has his reasons."

"Still, his reasons don't negate him from contributing to what we're trying to build here. At least you have a vision and are working all of us toward it. You are a social media star. No. You are a social media queen."

"But that's all I am," I said. "I'm as fake as the things I post on Instagram."

"I take exception to that," Frankie growled. "You're my friend and you are the least fake person I know."

"Still," I said, exasperated. "If I turn up with Ethan to the ball and he doesn't fool anyone, then Jamie and Meredith will kick me out faster than you can say, 'I win.'"

Frankie flung an arm around me and pulled me into a hug. "No way. Meredith would be in on the bet if given half a chance. Look at me and Lucas. We pretended to be engaged, and they didn't kick us out."

Yeah, but Lucas and Frankie were valuable to the court and to Jamie and Meredith, I didn't say. It was the truth, even if Frankie refused to believe it. I was like one of the porcelain dolls my mother collected. Pretty to look at, but of no actual use. My mother had certainly treated me like that, like a doll she could dress up and style and trot out in front of her guests to show them how lovely I was. But as far as having any intrinsic value? Or any depth and substance? I had none. Being a duchess in the brand new Kalopsia royal court was a lot like being that same pretty doll. I was just there to look good and round out the court. Nobody actually needed me.

Frankie gave me a squeeze. "Come on. This is going to be fun. You get to spend time with a cute guy and you get a guaranteed date to the ball *and* you get your parents off your back for a while. This is a win-win-*win* for you."

"Unless you win," I said with a smirk.

"Well, there is that," she replied and then hugged me when my smile fell. "Besides, you do have a 'thing.'"

I frowned at her.

"Your 'godmothering' is definitely a thing," she said. "I bet you could use that for other things too."

"Hardly," I said with an eye roll. "Name one practical application for this very useless talent of mine."

"I know plenty of people who would benefit from a fairy godmother," Frankie said.

"You know I'm not *actually* a fairy godmother, right?" I said. "They don't really exist. I just know how give ordinary things a temporary makeover. I can't turn pumpkins into coaches or mice into horses or make princes fall in love with orphaned servant girls."

"Maybe not," Frankie said tapping her chin. "But I know there are heaps of other things you can do with your miraculous powers. Leave it with me."

"Whatever," I replied with a sigh. "I think I have enough on my plate right now with Ethan and the ball. This fairy godmother is all booked."

CHAPTER 5

Ethan

"Where are we going?" I asked as the car wound its way up the narrow switchbacks.

"You'll see," Sophia replied.

"I should probably tell you up front that I'm not a fan of surprises," I said.

"I find that hard to believe," Sophia replied. "You seem like the spontaneous kind of person."

I nodded. "That's true. I do like spontaneity, but it's more of a controlled spontaneity."

Sophia turned in her seat to frown at me. "That...makes little sense. Controlled spontaneity is an oxymoron."

I shrugged. "Not really, or at least not to me. Sure, I like to be spontaneous and live a life open to opportunity, but that doesn't mean I'm going to plow headfirst into every opportunity that comes my way. I take time to think about things, research, plan where I can. It works."

Sophia studied me for a long moment before she nodded slowly. "Controlled spontaneity…I can get behind the concept."

I laughed. "I doubt very much that you have ever done a single spontaneous thing in your life."

"What we're doing is pretty spontaneous," she replied, and I knew I'd offended her, which wasn't my intent.

I tilted my head and looked at her, channeling my best Thor. "Hmm, is it, though?"

Sophia rolled her eyes, but I saw the corners of her mouth want to tilt up in a smile.

"So where are we going?" I asked again.

"We're here," she replied as the car slowly pulled through a large automated gate.

I peered out the window. The driveway was circular, winding around a large, dry fountain. It was seriously huge and I could only imagine what it would look like in all its glory with water cascading down the three tiers. Three stone, robed ladies with big pots of water stood back-to-back on the apex, their pots tipped as if pouring water—which I assumed they would be if there was water in the fountain. Below them were three ornate bowls in cascading order to catch the water they poured, and surrounding each of those bowls were what I could only assume were pixies and fairies and other mythical creatures. It was a spectacular piece of art that would be at home in any museum.

Then I saw the house.

'House' didn't really do the building justice, though. It was huge. And old. It looked to have grown out of the very stone it was built on. Constructed of the earth it stood on. I'd noticed that most of the houses on the island were built that way, but this looked…almost like the hands of the ancient gods formed it. Obviously, it wasn't, but that didn't diminish the awe I felt looking at it.

The car came to a stop, and the driver opened the door for Sophia. It took me a little longer to climb out because I was too distracted by the house and the grounds and the view. The view was spectacular. The house-mansion was built on the very edge of the cliff or had been carved from the cliff. From where I stood on the driveway, I could see out to the Aegean Sea. It took my breath away.

"What is this place?" I asked when I finally found my voice.

"It's my grandparents' villa," Sophia said. "My villa now, I suppose."

I turned to look at her as she looked at the 'villa.' Villa was definitely not the right word, as far as I was concerned. The building in front of us looked less like a villa and more like a small palace.

"You live here?" I asked.

Sophia shook her head. "No. I could if I wanted to, I suppose, but no. I live in the palace. The king and queen have given all the members of the court suites in the palace and it's more convenient for me to stay there rather than out here on my own."

I turned back to look at the *villa* just as the front door opened and a man stepped out dressed in grey dress pants, vest, and long black suit jacket.

"Is that your grandfather?" I whispered.

She smiled, but it was a sad quirk of her lips. "No. My grandparents died a few years ago. That is the butler, Charles."

"Butler?"

"The villa has its own staff," she replied. "Cook, house-keeper, butler, driver, and valet. You should be quite comfortable here."

"Staff...wait, what? *I* should be comfortable here? What does that mean?"

Sophia turned to me slowly, her eyebrows pulled down in confusion. "You're going to live here."

"Me? Live here?" I started to shake my head as I took a few steps back, away from the villa and toward the car. "No. Nope. No way."

"You live in a backpackers' hostel," Sophia said as if it explained everything.

"So?"

She rolled her eyes. "So, a duke visiting from another country would not be staying in a backpackers' hostel," she said.

"I'll move into the resort, then," I said.

"And how would that look? Me going to visit you all the time? The gossips would have a field day with it. Not to mention the resort staff would know who you really were within five minutes. No, you need to stay here. I've already told the queen that you're renting the place for your stay."

"What? I can't afford to rent this place."

Again with the eye roll. "I said you were renting it, I didn't say you had to actually pay rent. Seriously, Ethan. Staying here won't cost you anything and I'll pay for all your expenses for the period of our agreement."

"You're giving me your house and you're going to pay for everything? I can't agree to that."

Sophia quirked an eyebrow at me, more in annoyance than curiosity now. "Do you have a problem with a woman paying for you?" she asked.

"No," I blurted. "It just feels wrong for you to have to foot the bill."

Sophia crossed her arms and glared at me. "I'm asking you to give up your life for six weeks. I told you to resign from your job and move out of the backpackers' and I'm going to be monopolising your time for the next month and a half and you think I would let you do that without an income? How heartless do you think I am?"

"But surely there's another way—"

"You're supposed to be a duke visiting from a foreign country. People would expect you to live a certain way. For this to work, you have to be above reproach."

"Okay, fine, I get that, but...a staff? Surely I don't need staff?"

"Of course you need staff. Besides, we have employed these people at this villa for decades and I refuse to turn them out just because you're uncomfortable with them doing the job they're paid to do. These people were loyal to my grandparents and they're loyal to me and I refuse to offend them by not returning that loyalty."

"I'm not asking you to fire them," I said. "Send them on vacation or something."

"You really don't get it, do you?" Sophia said. "A duke would expect staff. Dukes do not cook or clean or even dress themselves. Not only that, but this team of people can help you. Charles has been a butler since he was in his early twenties. He knows everything there is to know about running a household —knowledge you can learn from for your own career aspirations. You want a job on a super yacht as a steward? Who better to learn from than a man who has made it is career to look after the wealthy and privileged?"

"I see your point, but—"

"*AND*, you need to get used to having servants around. You will be socialising with people who have entourages and servants catering to their every whim. You need to get comfortable having people cook and clean for you. This is the life of a duke, and if you're not living it, then people will get suspicious. My reputation is on the line here and I have a lot to lose if you fail."

I exhaled roughly. I didn't like it, but she had a point. This was what I signed up for, but I was suddenly having second thoughts about the whole deal.

"I need to think," I said, stalking off toward the cliffs.

"Do your sulking while you tour the house, at least," she snapped after me.

"Fine," I snapped back and redirected my feet toward the entrance where Charles was waiting.

THE VILLA WAS...WOW. Just...wow. And Charles, who showed me around, was everything I wanted and needed to be for my change of career. Was it weird to call a man elegant? Graceful? He was absolutely gracious and answered my ignorant questions about the villa and the age of it and the many treasures it housed. I knew a little bit about the coup that happened over a decade ago, but I didn't know any particulars. I knew a lot of the royal families lost their properties and their possessions, but apparently Sophia's grandparents had been among the lucky ones. They hadn't supported the coup, but either because of their age or the fact that their son was the acting duke at the time and was out of the country, the dictator hadn't targeted them and their villa had remained untouched.

The villa was built originally from the volcanic rock of the island, but it was also supplemented by other building materials —wood and steel and other such building materials that needed to go into making a house on a cliff stable. The original structure was more than a hundred years old, although no one knew exactly how old it was. It could be far older for all they knew, but the official records only started a little over a century ago, so that's the only dating evidence they had.

It was three storeys tall... above ground. The villa also had floors below the ground—the kitchen and cellar, most notably. The staff quarters were also technically below the ground, but Charles assured me they had access to the outside world via a terrace built into the cliff itself and below the main entertaining terrace of the villa proper.

I wanted to ask him questions about Sophia, but I knew he wouldn't answer. He owed me no loyalty, and I had done nothing to earn his trust. As much as I wanted to get to know the real Sophia behind the title, I knew I wouldn't be getting anything from the man who looked at her like she was his favourite niece.

As for Sophia herself, I didn't know where she disappeared to. After introducing me to Charles, she'd escaped into the villa and I hadn't seen her since.

I felt bad about our earlier disagreement and really, what did I have to be offended about? She was pretty much giving me a six week free ride, and I was carrying on like she had injured my pride? It was ridiculous, and my only excuse—although not an excuse at all—was that my male ego was hurt. No excuse, and completely ridiculous. She was offering me access to something that would take me years to learn, and I was pretty much throwing the offer back in her face.

It was stupid, and I needed to make it right.

Charles left me on the large balcony overlooking the sea to make organise some refreshments. I leaned against the stone balustrade and sighed. My argument with Sophia was petty. I was being ungrateful and unfair. I still didn't understand why she even needed me. Sophia could just snap her fingers and have a dozen or more men willing and able to escort her to the ball. For whatever reason, she'd chosen me and instead of feeling affronted by her easy wealth and her willingness to pay my way, I should be grateful.

I felt her presence as soon as she stepped out onto the terrace. I didn't turn around, waiting to hear what she had to say. She could very well call the entire thing off because of my tantrum earlier, and she would be well within her right to do so.

"Have you decided to terminate our agreement?" she asked from behind me.

I turned slowly to look at her. She was the picture of poise and calm, but there was a tightness around her eyes and mouth that hinted at her uncertainty of my answer.

"No," I replied. "And I apologise for earlier. I was out of line."

She waited a beat and then joined me at the edge of the balcony, leaning her arms on the warm stone and staring out at the horizon.

"I love this place," she said.

I turned and copied her pose, looking out at the view and giving her the space to speak.

"I loved coming here in the summer, and not just because it gave me a reprieve from my parents. There was just something so…renewing about being here on the island. If I could have lived with my grandparents full time, I would have."

"You loved them," I said simply.

"I did," she replied. "It devastated me when they passed. We weren't allowed back on the island to attend their funeral. I hadn't seen them in years because we'd been exiled and when they died…" she paused and took a deep breath. "Anyway, I was so happy when the king contacted me and asked me to come back to the island and take up the position in the court. My father was offended, of course, but since none of the others of his generation were being recalled, he couldn't very well object."

"The king formed a new court?" I asked, not really understanding how royalty worked.

Sophia nodded. "He wanted fresh vision. I suppose he also wanted people who would be loyal to him, rather than just loyal to his father. Many of the court fled before the coup, leaving his father vulnerable. I can understand why he wouldn't want any of them back in their original positions."

Sophia pushed up from the balcony and turned to look at him. "So are we going ahead with this?"

I stood as well. "Yes," I replied. "And I don't think I've actually thanked you for the opportunity, so thank you. I am grateful."

She smiled, and it felt like the sun coming out after a storm. "I should be the one thanking you," she said. "You are doing me a huge favour."

I smirked. "I think we can agree that it goes both ways. We're each getting something out of this deal."

Her smiled slipped, just a bit, at the mention of the deal. But before I could say anything, Charles appeared with a maid and a tray of food.

~

SOPHIA DROPPED me off at the backpacker's and said she would send a car to take me back to the villa when I'd collected my stuff. I packed my bag; I didn't own much. What was the point of collecting 'stuff' when I was constantly travelling? I'd sent a few items home, but I was more about making memories than collecting artefacts.

The car was waiting for me, just as Sophia said. The driver introduced himself as Francis and told me he would be my driver for the duration of my stay at the villa. It grated against me—another way Sophia was providing for me—but I shoved the feeling down. This had to be more than just a male ego thing, but I didn't have the headspace to deal with it. It was only for six weeks and I could do anything for six weeks. I'd once worked as a ski instructor for kids…if I could survive that, I could survive this.

I didn't even get to unpack my own bag. Toby, my valet, did that for me and after he clucked despairingly over the state of my clothes the first few times, I had to walk away. I would need a new wardrobe, I knew that. It seemed a waste, though. I would only use them for six weeks, and then what? What need would I have for fancy clothes on a super yacht? I would have a uniform and probably wouldn't need civvies at all until we docked again.

But I was getting ahead of myself. I had to get through the next month and a half and win Sophia's bet, and *then* land a job.

I meandered through the villa, not sure what to do. There

was a media room and access to every streaming service known to man, but I didn't think I could sit still to watch anything. There was also a well-stocked library, but again, the whole 'sitting still' thing was beyond me. I contemplated using the treadmill in the gym, but I just didn't have the motivation. Besides, it was in the underground section of the villa and I was already feeling claustrophobic.

Was that really the word, though? I was restless, there was no doubt about that, but I didn't feel closed in, exactly. More, I felt, untethered. Having no fixed address wasn't new. I'd been travelling the world for years and rarely stayed in one place more than six months, so moving out of the hostel shouldn't have felt so strange, but it did. I was free falling, and I didn't like it.

Maybe it was the lack of...people? Although I travelled alone, I'd never had a room all to myself, let alone an entire villa. I was never really on my own, but this felt...isolating. I knew it would be frowned on if I headed downstairs and tried to strike up a conversation with one of the staff, but I was starved for conversation.

I headed back to my room to grab my laptop.

"Is there something I can help you with?" Toby asked.

"No, I'm fine...actually, maybe you can help me. Does the villa have Wi-Fi?"

"Of course," Toby replied, sounding offended that it wouldn't have.

"Would you be able to hook me up?" I asked with a smile. "Please?"

Toby got me set up in the small office area off the library and logged me into the villa's Wi-Fi. After a few minutes, I had Skype connecting and my mother's face beamed back at me.

"Well, this is a surprise," she said and then frowned. "There's nothing wrong, is there? Do you need money?"

I grinned. "I'm fine," I replied. "Just thought I'd check in and let you know I have a new address."

"You left the island already?" Mum asked. "I thought you had work there?"

"I do," I replied. "But I was offered another position. In a private house. It's a six-week gig, and it has the potential to lead into a steward's job on a yacht."

"So you're not planning on coming home any time soon, then?" she asked, and the guilt of her morose expression pushed down on me like a weight.

"Not for a while yet," I replied.

I didn't go home much. Australia was a long way away from the rest of the world and it cost an absolute fortune to travel to and from there. I'd gone home during the pandemic, but it had chafed at me and as soon as international travel was back on the table, I took off.

Not that I didn't love my family; I did. I just didn't want their lives. I didn't want to live my life small, the way they did. I had nothing against people who chose that life, but it wasn't for me. I couldn't think of anything worse than being chained to an office desk working at a job that sucked the life from me just so I could buy a house and a car and a television and...

Creature comforts were nice, but I thrived on adventure.

"Your brother's baby is due in a few months, do you think you could come home to visit then?"

I'd missed his wedding and the arrival of his first-born child. I didn't see the point of being there when the kid wouldn't even know if I was or not. And it wasn't like my brother and I were buddies. He looked down on me for my life choices. He was entitled to his own opinion, but this was my life and I would live it the way I chose, not the way society expected me to. Having a 'career' meant nothing to me. My idea of success was not tied up in how much money I made or how much prestige I had. Something dear-old Shane couldn't understand.

"We'll see," I replied, noncommittally. "It depends where I am when the baby comes."

Mum sighed, but didn't push it. I sometimes thought she wished she'd taken the opportunity to travel when she was younger. Mum and Dad married right out of school and Dad went to work for the phone company and Mum worked as a hairdresser. It was honest work, and they'd bought the house and the car and had two kids and paid for all the expenses that went along with that, but they'd never left the city they lived in. They'd never travelled overseas and had only travelled inter-state once or twice.

Living a life like that petrified me. It was why I kept moving, why I kept travelling. I never wanted to get 'stuck.' I saw what it did to my parents, and I refused to let it happen to me.

CHAPTER 6

Sophia

J grabbed a plate of eggs and avocado from the buffet and joined Frankie at the table.

"I need help," I blurted out before looking around to make sure no one could overhear us.

We were on the terrace off the dining room that served as a breakfast room. Yes, there was a room set aside just for breakfast. It wasn't as big as the formal dining room and it opened out onto a south-facing balcony which overlooked the sea. *All the balconies and terraces overlooked the sea; they built the palace on the side of a cliff, after all.*

Frankie turned to me and quirked an eyebrow. "Help?"

I looked around again and leaned forward to whisper. "I need to get some clothes for Ethan. You know all the local business people in the area, I thought you could suggest someone.

They need to be sworn to a vow of silence or this will never work."

"I don't think I should help you win a bet against me," Frankie said with a smirk.

"You got me into this, so you have a moral obligation to make sure I have the best chance of winning."

"Yeah, I don't think that's how bets work," Frankie replied.

"If Ethan doesn't have a decent wardrobe, then this bet will be over even before it starts. You do want him to make it to the end and be my date to the ball, right? To do that, I need to make sure that he presents as a duke for the next six weeks and that means he needs clothes."

I was close to panicking over this, and Frankie just sat there grinning at me. I'd barely slept as I went over all the things I needed to do in order to make Ethan into someone who people would see as royalty. The clothes he wore were the bare minimum.

Frankie must have seen the hysteria in my eyes because she rolled her own and patted my hand. "Just order some online," she said. "A visiting duke wouldn't be wearing locally made clothes."

I bit my lip. She was right, but getting clothes from the mainland would take far too long.

"That doesn't help with getting him some suits and a tuxedo for the ball," I said. "I can't just order one online."

"I would cease to acknowledge you if you dared to buy a tuxedo online," Dorian said stiffly as he took a seat beside Frankie. "Why do you need a tuxedo, anyway? I thought Frankie was organising gowns for the ladies from a local designer."

"It's not for Sophia," Frankie said. "It's for—"

"My father," I jumped in before Frankie could blow the secret. "My dad wants a new tux for the ball. I was asking Frankie about the local tailors."

Dorian frowned at me, his dark eyebrows pulling low over his dark eyes and his lips forming a flat line.

"You're asking Francesca about tailors?" The disdain dripped like syrup from his tone.

"Um…yes?" I said because Dorian made me nervous and I couldn't think of anything clever to say. I was pretty sure he saw me as nothing more than an empty-headed porcelain figurine… or I could be projecting.

"Why wouldn't she ask me?" Frankie asked, offended.

"Francesca, darling, you know I think the world of you, but you don't know the first thing about having an excellent tailor," Dorian said, adjusting his cuffs. "I, on the other hand, am an expert."

Frankie rolled her eyes. "I noticed you got your tailor to relocate to Kalopsia," she said. "How much did you have to pay him?"

"He was overjoyed to move to this delightful island," Dorian replied and bared his teeth at Frankie in a semblance of a smile. "He knows how much my business is worth, not to mention the chance to tailor a suit for the king himself."

When the ball was announced a few months ago, Meredith had made a proclamation that all the gowns, suits, food, decor, and everything else that a ball needed was to be provided by local businesses. Dorian had refused to relinquish his tailor and instead had the man move to Kalopsia so he wouldn't have to wear an 'inferior' suit (his words).

Dorian turned back to me. "I thought your father had his own tailor," he said. "In France." He narrowed his eyes. "And why would he be asking his daughter to find a new suit for him? Are you lying to me, Lady Sophia?"

I opened my mouth to say something...anything, but Frankie beat me to it.

"It's for her secret duke," Frankie said.

Dorian quirked an eyebrow, not moving his gaze from mine. "Secret duke? Do I know this 'secret duke?'"

Dorian was a duke, the *Ducas of Paralia,* and he knew *everyone.* I shot Frankie a panicked look, which Dorian saw because Dorian saw everything.

Frankie placed her hand on Dorian's arm, causing him to look her way. "Promise to not say a word," she hissed. "Not. A. Word."

He took a long moment before he nodded slowly.

Frankie took a breath. "Sophia and I have a little bet going," she said.

"Not what I was expecting you to say," Dorian said with a lift of his eyebrows. "I assume it has something to do with this 'secret duke' of yours. Go on."

"Frankie bet me I couldn't makeover a guy so that everyone would think he was a duke," I said in a rush.

"Why?" Dorian asked, looking between the two of us.

"Because of Nico," Frankie said like that explained everything, and apparently it did because Dorian's face relaxed and a sardonic smile lifted the corner of his mouth.

"Oh yes, Nico," he said. "He was a nobody until you, what was it you said? Did a 'makeover' on him?"

"She godmothered him," Frankie said with a wink at me. "And I bet her she couldn't do it to another guy."

"Godmothered?" Dorian said, looking at Frankie with that

expression a person makes after sucking a lemon. If he wasn't so intimidating, I might have laughed.

"Yes, like in Cinderella?" Frankie said with an eye roll.

"Right, so you are *godmothering* this 'secret duke?'" Dorian asked, looking back at me.

"That's the plan," I admitted. "Except he's not a duke, he's a bartender."

I expected Dorian to turn a stormy frown on me because I dared to attempt such a thing, but instead he looked interested. Too interested.

"You're trying to turn a bartender into a duke?" he asked.

"A bartender who is a backpacker from Australia," Frankie added, unhelpfully.

Dorian did frown at that. "An Australian?"

"I don't think she can do it," Frankie said, her voice sly. "Even with your tailor."

Dorian looked affronted. "My tailor could make even an Australian look like royalty," Dorian replied. "But as soon as he opened his mouth, everyone would know he was a fraud."

"Well, there is more to playing fairy godmother than just putting him in a suit," I said. "Obviously."

Dorian turned those too perceptive dark eyes back on me. "Okay," he said.

"Okay?" I asked, not sure whether he was agreeing with me or something else.

"I will help you," he said.

"I didn't ask for your help," I said, momentarily forgetting that this man frightened me more than the king did.

"Maybe not, but you are going to need it. My tailor would be delighted to work for this 'secret duke,'" Dorian said. "After I get a look at him first."

"The Duke Incognito," Frankie said.

"What?" Dorian asked, turning back to her.

"That's what we're calling him," she said with a grin.

"Surely you know the man's name, at least," Dorian said.

"His name is Ethan Samuels," I said. "I've moved him into my grandparents' villa and told everyone he is visiting from another royal court and wishes to stay anonymous."

"He's going to need a better back story than that," Dorian said. "It appears you really do need my help if you hope to win this bet."

"Hey," Frankie said. "I thought you were my friend? Why are you helping her?"

"Because I believe Lady Sophia *can* godmother this man into a duke," Dorian said. "And I wouldn't mind helping her win against you."

"No fair," Frankie said, crossing her arms.

I swallowed. Accepting Dorian's help seemed…dangerous. It kind of felt like asking a crocodile to help me cross a river.

"SO THIS IS THE LORDLING?" Dorian asked, walking a slow circle around Ethan.

"Really?" I hissed at him, surprised by Dorian's outright rudeness. Although, I probably shouldn't be, Dorian was rude to everybody.

Ethan looked at me with a questioning gaze, and I sighed.

"This is Lord Dorian Stamos," I said. "Ducas of Paralia. He is going to help me…us."

We were standing in one of the parlour rooms at the villa. The sun shone brightly in through the windows and if I let myself, I could fall into the memories of being in this room with my grandmother, but now was not the time for reminiscing, not when I had two tom cats circling each other...or at least one tiger sizing up the other one.

Dorian completed his circuit and crossed his arms as he continued to study Ethan. "I think you may have bitten off more than you can chew," he said to me.

"No one asked for your help," I retorted.

"I believe you did ask for my help," Dorian replied, his voice unruffled while I was trying desperately to control my nerves and the sudden rush of irrational anger Dorian had ignited in me.

"No," I said. "I was asking for a recommendation for a tailor, not for the great Duke Dorian to be my personal Tim Gunn."

Dorian turned to look at me with a blank expression. "I don't know who that is."

I rolled my eyes. "It doesn't matter. All that matters is whether I can use your tailor."

Dorian sighed wearily. "Fine. He is on his way and should be here any minute. I still don't think it will work."

"Um, hello?" Ethan said, waving at us to get our attention. "You know I'm standing right here, don't you? I'm not some mannequin you can just dress up and talk about as if I'm not even here."

Dorian winced when he heard Ethan's accent. "Oh, that will never do," he said.

"I'm sorry you find me so offensive, my lord," Ethan said with sarcasm dripping from the words. "Should I perhaps not open my mouth and speak? Should I not look directly at you?"

Dorian's lips quirked infinitesimally and I would have missed it if I hadn't been watching for his reaction.

"Maybe you'll do, after all," Dorian said. "And no, you should always look directly at the person you're speaking to. You're a duke, or at least you're supposed to be. We don't bow our heads to anyone save the reigning monarchs."

Ethan looked at me. "So all I have to do is act like an insufferable jerk like him, and people will believe I'm a duke?"

I grinned. "Pretty much," I replied.

Dorian huffed. "No one would ever mistake you for me," he said. "You could try, of course, but it would be a complete failure, which I presume is not what you're going for?" He quirked an eyebrow at me and then Ethan.

Chastised, I sighed. "Fine. You can help."

That's what he wanted, wasn't it? That's why Dorian had inserted himself into this project, right?

"I don't know if I want to anymore," Dorian sulked. "Not if I'm going to be treated so poorly."

Ethan rolled his eyes and I willed him not to say anything that would further offend Dorian. The last thing we needed was for him to go to the king with the knowledge that I was bringing a pretend-duke to the ball.

"I'm sorry," I said. "We're sorry." I shot a look at Ethan, who sighed but nodded. "Please, Dorian, we need your help. I don't know anyone else who has as much knowledge of being a duke as you do."

Dorian sniffed but when he looked back at Ethan, I knew he was back on board…even if I didn't know if I even wanted him on board in the first place.

Before we could get into any further arguments, Charles announced the tailor.

"Perfect timing, as always, Alphonso," Dorian said. "Now, I have some ideas for what this gentleman will need."

"Don't I get a say in what I wear?" Ethan asked, sounding like the injured party now.

"Of course you will," I said at the same time Dorian said, "Of course not."

I glared at Dorian and he sighed, relenting.

"Fine. You get the final say," he conceded.

"We're also going to have to decide on your every-day clothes," I said, sitting down on the couch and reaching for one of the fashion magazines I'd brought with me.

"What's wrong with my clothes?" Ethan asked.

"That you even have to ask that proves how much you need me," Dorian said, not looking up from the book of fabric samples Alphonso had brought with him.

"There is nothing wrong with your clothes," I said. "They're just not exactly suitable for a duke."

"You should burn them all," Dorian said, still not looking up from the fabric he was fingering. "And never buy off-the-rack again."

I rolled my eyes. Seriously, with all the eye rolling that was going on today, someone's eyes were going to roll right out of their head.

"We don't all have a bottomless wallet like you," I said.

"I can't imagine your clothes would be suitable to wear behind a bar," Ethan said.

Dorian looked up at that and shuddered. "You're right, of course." His face turned thoughtful. "What are your plans after all this? You're just going to go back to working in a bar? Or are you hoping Fairy Godmother Sophia can find you your own Princess Charming?"

Ethan clenched his jaw before speaking. "I'm not looking for a wife, princess or no."

"So what do you get out of this little arrangement?" Dorian asked before turning to me. "You're not paying him, are you?"

"She's not paying me," Ethan replied with a growl.

"But she is paying for all this," Dorian replied slyly.

"Stop," I said, before Ethan could reply or before Dorian drove Ethan away. "I am providing for Ethan just as any employer would provide for their employee," I snapped. "Not that it is any of your business." I took a breath. "I asked Ethan to give up his job, so it is my responsibility to subsidise him during this time. He will need suitable clothes, a uniform, to fit the position. I am the one asking him to give up a sizeable chunk of his life for this bet, so of course I am going to provide for him. And as for what he gets out of it, Ethan wants to work on a yacht. I will be giving him the experience and connections he needs to get such a position." I narrowed my eyes at Dorian. "Why do you even care?"

"I'm just looking out for you, Lady Sophia," Dorian said. "There are a lot of unsavoury people in the world who wouldn't batt an eyelash at taking advantage of a naïve girl."

"Sophia is a woman, not a girl," Ethan snapped. "Neither is she naïve."

I felt warmth bloom in my chest at Ethan's proclamation.

"And I am not taking advantage of her," he continued. "I would never do something like that."

"I approached him," I said. "Not that I have to defend myself to you."

Dorian put his hands up in surrender. "Fine. I was just doing my due diligence. Now, I think this is the perfect fabric for the tuxedo for the ball. And you will need four other suits in this, this, and these two."

"I REALLY AM SORRY ABOUT DORIAN," I said as we got out of the car and stood on the pavement in front of a menswear boutique Dorian suggested. "He can be a bit…"

"Of a jerk?" Ethan finished for me with a raised eyebrow.

"I was going to say difficult, but jerk works," I said, shooting him a small smile.

Ethan relaxed, and I breathed a little easier. The atmosphere between the two men had been tense, and I worried for Ethan's dentistry with how hard he'd been clenching his jaw, not to mention the tightness in his shoulders.

"I don't know how you put up with him," Ethan said, rolling his shoulders.

I shrugged. "I don't see him much. Besides, I've grown up around worse behaved men. At least with Dorian there is no artifice. If he doesn't like you, he's not backward in telling you."

"I suppose there is that," Ethan said, turning to look at the store. "Do we really need more clothes? From what you and Dorian ordered from the tailor, I didn't think I would need to buy more clothes for another six years."

"Those clothes are for when we are out in public. These are for more informal situations."

"Informal such as…?"

"When you're at the villa, for example."

"I can't even wear my own clothes when I'm alone in the villa?" Ethan asked, incredulous.

I sighed. "Think of it like this. You're playing a role. For the next forty days, or whatever it is, you have to play the role of a duke twenty-four seven."

"But why? Why can't I just be myself when I am at the villa alone?"

"Muscle memory," I replied.

"Huh?"

"The more you pretend, the more natural it will become. If you're only wearing the duke as a disguise when you leave the villa, it will always look fake. You need to be the duke all the time so that when you are out in public, it comes as naturally as breathing."

Ethan huffed out a breath, but said nothing.

"It's not for forever," I said quietly.

He nodded, but didn't speak.

"Come on, then. Let's get this over with."

I walked into the store hoping he would follow. I went straight to the salesperson who recognised me instantly, and I was pretty sure all they could see was a big dollar sign where my body should be.

"Hello, can we please have a change room setup?" I asked.

The assistant hurried off, and I turned to see Ethan standing inside the shop and looking around like he was standing on the gallows.

"It's all really...preppy," he said, his mouth screwing up on the last word.

I looked around to see what he was seeing. I supposed it was preppy, but Dorian had suggested this place and I was inclined to take his advice when it came to men's fashion.

"Please tell me you will not make me wear a sweater tied around my shoulders," Ethan said and the smile on his face took the sting out of the words.

"No, but I may very well pick out some cardigans for you. We are heading into autumn after all."

Ethan groaned playfully, and I ducked my head to hide my grin. I walked away from the rack of cardigans I was standing beside and headed for the underwear section.

"We should probably get you some new boxer shorts as well," I said.

"What?" Ethan asked, and I turned at the panicked tone of his voice.

"Boxer shorts," I said, using my hand like a game show host to indicate the shelf of Calvin Kleins.

"What if I don't wear boxer shorts?" Ethan asked with a raised eyebrow, and it took me a minute before a red-hot blush suffused my cheeks.

"Um, oh, well…I guess that's one way of getting around the VPL," I stammered.

"VPL?" he asked slowly, his eyes blazing bluer than the sky.

"Visible panty line," I replied breathlessly.

His eyes widened suddenly, and then he laughed, breaking the weird tension between us.

"Yeah, I don't think I have to worry about that," he said, and then he saw my wide-eyed look and he shook his head. "Not because of what you're thinking. Because I don't wear trousers fitted enough for it to be a problem."

"Right," I said, turning away to hide how flustered I was. "Still, we should get some." I picked up a black pair of fitted trunks. "How about these?"

Ethan stepped up beside me and took the coat hanger from my hand. I could feel the heat of his body as he crowded me, and his low voice sent shivers along my skin.

"I don't need you to pick out my underwear, Sophia," he murmured in my ear.

"Yes, right, of course," I said, shifting away from him and

walking away, toward the back of the store. "Let me just check how we're going with a changing room."

I was a coward, and I ran away. I was not prepared for the way Ethan made me feel when he stood that close to me. It could have been just because we were discussing the intimate subject of underwear—that was exactly what I wanted to tell myself—but I knew there was more to it. Ethan affected me in a way no one else ever had. I didn't understand it and because I didn't understand it, it petrified me. I lived a carefully controlled life, and these feelings threatened to derail that. Not to mention this thing between us was a business agreement that had an expiration date. No way did I want to explore whatever this weird tension was. That was a guaranteed way to get my heart broken, and duchesses didn't get their hearts broken. If there were any hearts getting broken, a duchess would be the one doing the breaking.

CHAPTER 7

Ethan

I felt like a fool.

It had been a couple of decades since anyone had chosen my clothes, let alone dress me. My valet, Toby—ugh, even just that phrase made me shudder—laid out my clothes for the day. He'd taken delivery of them from the boutique yesterday and then laundered them––or had them laundered, I wasn't really sure how that worked—and put them away and then chose what I would wear today. It was…weird and uncomfortable and just really, really strange to have someone do for me what I had been doing for myself since I was a small child. Did the great and mighty Lord Dorian have someone dress him every day? It appalled me that the answer might be yes.

And yet, even as I dismissed Toby—because I absolutely drew the line at having him actually dress me—Sophia's words kept going around and around in my head. I might find this whole bowing and scraping thing uncomfortable, but the people who were employed in this villa took pride in their jobs and who was I to disparage them? I didn't have a career, not in any proper sense of the word. Yes, I was a career bartender, but that was just a fancy way of saying I'd been tending bar since I was old enough to stand behind the counter. To me bartending was a means to an end, to Toby and Charles and Mrs. Volcom, the housekeeper, and Macy, the kitchen assistant, this was their chosen profession and meant more to them than just a pay cheque.

Something else that made me feel like an idiot? The clothes on my body. Seriously. I spent my life in jeans or shorts with the occasional dress pants for an interview. I was now wearing wool slacks. Slacks. The word was awful, not to mention how the pants felt on my body. Okay, that wasn't entirely true. They actually felt fantastic, but every time I caught a look at myself in the mirror, I had to give it a second look because I had never seen myself dressed this way and it was still…weird.

I felt like I'd fallen down a rabbit hole or tripped through an inter-dimension portal or woken up in an alternate universe. How was this my life right now?

"Lady Sophia is here," Charles announced to me as I stood on the balcony with a coffee in my hand and contemplated just how bizarre my life had become.

"Thank you, Charles," I replied turning, expecting him to lead me to wherever he'd stashed her but freezing when I saw her standing just behind him. "Lady Sophia," I said with a little bow and in my best impression of Lord Stick-Up-His-Butt-Dorian.

She smiled, and it hit me like a sledgehammer. Who knew a smile could pack such a punch?

"You've been practising," she said as she nodded to Charles and stepped toward me.

"Just trying it out," I said with a small grin. "Does this outfit make me look fat?"

She frowned and growled. It was a soft sound, and I didn't think she was aware that I'd heard it, and it was just as intoxicating as her smile was.

"I hate it when people say that," she said. "It's fat shaming and I'm not here for it."

Chastised, my smile dropped, and I bowed my head in apology. "Forgive me," I said.

She sighed and waved her hand, dismissing my words. "I know people say it as a joke, but I've never found it funny." She took another breath and forced a smile to her lips. "Let me get a look at you."

I stood still as she circled me, much as Dorian had the day before. When she came back around to face me, a genuine smile was on her face. I realised I no longer felt ridiculous in the clothes I was wearing. Seeing Sophia's approval went a long way to soothing my insecurities about the outfit.

"The clothes look great," she said.

"Don't you mean *I* make these clothes look great?" I said, striking a pose.

She laughed, and it was like gentle wind chimes on the breeze.

What?

No, her laugh did not sound like wind chimes.

It was just a laugh. A pleasant laugh, for sure, but in no way was it wind chimes. I looked down at my coffee. What had Macy put in my coffee this morning?

"Are you channelling Dorian again or is this your own ego?" Sophia asked, grinning.

"It's all me, baby," I said, and then we both froze as the words fell like stone between us. Had I just called a duchess 'baby?' Kill me now.

Sophia cleared her throat, breaking the weird tension, and looked over her shoulder toward the villa. "We should get going," she said.

"We're going somewhere?" I asked, surprised.

"Yes, we have an appointment in town."

"Not more clothes," I grumbled.

She smiled. "No, not clothes. It's a salon appointment."

I froze. "Salon?" I asked slowly. "As in *beauty* salon?"

"It's a men's salon," Sophia replied easily, oblivious to my discomfit. "You need a haircut and a shave. I've also booked a manicure and a pedicure and an express facial."

"Facial? Shave?" I swallowed and gritted my teeth. "I am not shaving off my beard," I said, and it was my turn to growl. "I will wear these ridiculous clothes and speak like Lord Muckity-Muck, but I absolutely draw the line at shaving off my beard."

Sophia turned back to me, her arms crossed and a stern expression on her face, but I refused to back down. I'd been growing my beard since I was seventeen years old. Sure, it had looked like a mangy dog for a long time, but it was full and luscious now and I would not shave it off, not even if this was just for six weeks—less now—no matter what Sophia demanded of me.

"Oh, my god. Anyone would think I'd asked to cut off your finger or demanded you hand over your first-born child," she said with a slow shake of her head.

She lifted her hand and ran it across my jaw and beard, and

I'd be lying if I didn't admit that I liked the way it felt, but I refused to give her satisfaction of seeing it on my face.

She slapped my cheek gently. "Don't worry, big guy, I was only talking about a trim and a clean-up, I wasn't going to rid you of your manly mane."

I released a relieved breath slowly, hoping that she wouldn't notice. "I don't think I need a manicure or a pedi-whatever or a facial—"

"They're non-negotiable," Sophia said. "Did you notice Dorian's hands? His skin? I swear that man has a better skin care regime than I do. Your hands are rough and calloused, which works for your former employment but will raise red flags among the social circles we will be traversing. I dare say, your feet won't be much better and as for the facial, apart from being one of the most relaxing body treatments around, your skin could use some work and you could use some pointers on how to look after it."

"You want me to put creams and mud and stuff on my face every day?" I asked, appalled.

"Cleanse and moisturise twice a day," Sophia said. "And add some sunscreen in the morning. The sun ages your skin faster than anything else."

"You're serious," I said.

"Deadly," she replied with a dangerous smirk.

WHO KNEW a salon appointment could make me feel like a new man? I certainly didn't. I had underestimated the power of the process, even if it took a heck of a lot longer than I'd expected.

Sophia was right. The facial was incredibly relaxing, so

much so that after, when the beautician was running through all the products I'd need for my new skin care regime—I now had a skin care regime *shocked face*—I'd just agreed to everything she suggested. That's how they made their money, I suspected. Lull the customer into a relaxed stupor and then get them to hand over their money with reasonable sounding suggestions of glowing skin and ageless beauty.

Okay, that was a bit cynical, even for me. But I had to grudgingly admit I felt and looked a million times better. My hair was shorter than I would have liked, but it looked...good. It suited me. And my beard...wow...just wow. It looked longer—how was that even possible when I'd seen the guy trim it?—and it was shaped and smooth and clean and the hot towel thing he did after he shaved my cheeks and neck? Nirvana. I would go back there just to get that hot towel thing again.

Even my hands and feet felt good. I couldn't exactly see myself making a regular appointment to have the mani-pedi thing again, but my hands and feet felt good. No bar rot in sight—a definite bonus when I was trying to impersonate a duke.

Sophia whistled as she approached.

"I almost didn't recognise you," she said with a wink, and I couldn't help grinning.

"I almost didn't recognise myself," I replied.

She cocked her head and crossed her arms. "So are you going to trust me now when I suggest things?"

"I wouldn't go that far," I said, winking at her, making her roll her eyes, but I saw the corners of her lips curl up in a small smile. "So what now?" I asked.

Sophia shrugged. "I have nothing else planned for you today," she replied.

"You're not just going to leave me stranded, are you? I mean

—" I spread my hands out so she could get a good look at me "—I'm all dressed up and have nowhere to go."

She snorted softly; her smile growing. "What do you want to do? Is there something you want to see or a place you want to go or anything you want to know about the island?"

"You've given me a heap of homework to do on the history of the island and all the places to see," I said. "I just want to relax and have a bit of fun. You do have time for fun in your life, right? It's not all godmothering reluctant fake dukes and attending to the queen in her castle?"

"I know how to have fun," she said. "I met you in a club, didn't I?"

"That doesn't count," I said, linking my arm through hers. "I'm pretty sure your friend dragged you there and you would have preferred to be anywhere else."

She sighed. "True, but I ended up having fun, even if Frankie had to drag me there."

"So let's have some fun now," I said, "unless you have some-where else to be?"

"I don't have anywhere else to be," she said with a shake of her head. "I took care of all my errands while you were getting pampered."

"Okay, so let's do something together," I said. "We could go surfing."

"I don't surf," she replied, "but I wouldn't mind going to the beach."

I turned us toward the boardwalk. "Let's go to the beach," I said, but she stopped me.

"We can't go to the public beach," she said.

"Why not?" I asked, confused.

"You're supposed to be a duke, remember? Can you see Dorian sitting on a public beach with all the *people?*"

"You have a point," I said. "So where do you suggest we go?"

Sophia bit her lip and my gaze zeroed in on it. I tried to drag my eyes away, but they were stuck there, watching as she worried her plump bottom lip.

"I have an idea," she said, and I managed to look up into her eyes before she caught me staring.

"Yeah?"

Sophia nodded. "Come on." Sophia took my hand and turned me back toward the car. "I just need to make a quick phone call on the way."

I eavesdropped on her conversation as she organised what sounded like a feast for a hundred people, and when she turned to me, her eyes were lit with a sparkle I hadn't seen before. It made something inside me clench and my mouth went dry and I had to cough to clear my throat and sit on my hands so I didn't reach out to cup her jaw. I didn't think she would appreciate it if I let myself get carried away.

"Where—" I cleared my throat again. "Where are we going?"

"You'll see," she said with a dazzling smile.

"Remember what I said about surprises?" I asked.

"Consider this some of your controlled spontaneity," she replied. "Only, I'm the one in control."

"That kind of discounts the whole 'controlled' thing, don't you think?"

Sophia only grinned at me in response. I wasn't really concerned. I trusted her, or at least I trusted she wouldn't do anything to blow the deception we were building.

"We're here," she said brightly as we pulled into the gate of the villa.

"You brought me home," I said, surprised to find that the villa had indeed started to feel like home even though I'd only been living there a few days.

"I have something to show you," she said as the car came to a stop. "You brought a bathing suit, didn't you? We didn't buy one—"

"I have some board shorts," I replied.

"Great. Go and get changed and meet me on the terrace."

Confused but willing to follow her directions, I went up to my room where Toby had already pulled out my board shorts and a t-shirt for me to change into. I thanked him and got changed before making my way back downstairs and out to the terrace. Sophia wasn't there, but it didn't take long for her to join me. She had also changed and was wearing a thin cotton cover-up over her own bathing suit. A bikini, from what I could see through the sheer fabric of her cover-up.

I once more dragged my eyes away from her and hoped she hadn't caught me staring. It was only then that I noticed Charles was behind her with an enormous picnic basket and a pile of towels.

"Thank you, Charles," Sophia said, reaching for the towels, but I beat her to it, taking both the towels and the basket from the butler's arms.

"Are we having a picnic on the terrace?" I asked.

"Nope," she said. "Follow me."

Sophia walked toward a small gate that led to the gardens. I hadn't explored much of the outside space yet, so I had no idea where she was taking us.

The path gently weaved its way down through lush gardens until we reached the very bottom terrace of the villa. There was another gate here and when Sophia opened it, I saw it led to a steep flight of stairs.

"This goes down to the beach?" I asked.

"Yep," she said. "A private little cove at the bottom of the cliff."

We didn't speak as we descended the stairs. They were steep and narrow but in good repair with a secure rail to hold on to— not that I could do that while carrying my load. Sophia turned around a few times to check on me, but I was fine.

Eventually we reached the bottom and Sophia kicked off her flip-flops to walk out on the sand. I followed her example and felt the warm sand squish between my toes.

"Over here is the best spot to set up," she said, leading me to a small little oasis with tall palm trees providing some shade from the heat of the day. "My grandparents planted these palms years ago," she said.

Together we set up the picnic. There was a large blue and white striped rug to spread out on the sand and then a couple of towels to dry off with.

"Swim or food first?" she asked.

"Swim," I replied, already reaching to take off my t-shirt.

Sophia's eyes widened as she saw my bare chest, and I couldn't deny flexing my pecs just a little under her gaze.

"Last one in is a rotten egg," I said, taking off toward the water.

"You should stay for dinner," I said, reaching out to take Sophia's hand.

We'd spent the afternoon on the beach swimming and

eating and lazing in the sun. It was...amazing. It felt like we were in another world, just the two of us, or on a deserted island. The water had been warm, but not too warm, and the waves gentle. It wasn't a surfing beach, that was for sure. The little strip of sand was in a naturally formed, protected cove with the huge cliffs behind and outcroppings of volcanic rock at either end. Our own little paradise where we spent hours together, uninterrupted by the demands of the bet or Sophia's royal duties.

I wasn't quite ready for our time to end.

Sophia looked up at me, her dark eyes searching my blue ones. She wanted to say yes, I could tell, but I could also see the reluctance.

"We could go over all the homework you've given me," I said, a small, encouraging smile tipping the corner of my mouth. "You can even quiz me on what I already know."

She bit her lip again in what I recognised as her thinking tell, but ultimately, she pulled her hand from mine and shook her head.

"I can't," she said. "I need to have dinner at the palace. They'll wonder where I've been all day."

"You could just tell them you've been entertaining the mystery duke," I said. "You could tell them he wouldn't take no for an answer when he proposed dinner."

She was considering it, I could tell by the way her eyes swept over me, but I also knew she was going to refuse.

I understood, I did. Things between us had changed, relaxed. We were almost becoming friends, or at least we were no longer just two acquaintances working together for a common goal. We'd learned more about each other that after-noon. I learned about her family and how she was glad to be away from them and how much she was not looking forward to seeing them again at the ball. I told her about my brother and his wife and his kid and about my mum and dad and the city I grew up in. We had lived such very different lives and yet, here we were, together on a tiny island in the Mediterranean. Our lives had been brought together in what I could only say was a stroke of fate, which Sophia strongly disagreed with. She didn't believe in fate and I couldn't say whether I had believed in it or not before I met her, but after meeting her I was open to the possibility.

"I can't," she said again. "As much as I've enjoyed our day together, I really need to get back to the palace."

"When will I see you again?" I asked.

"Next week," she said.

"Next week? It's only Tuesday, what am I supposed to do until then?"

"Learn all the things," she replied with a smile. "There will be a test."

"You can't leave me alone all week," I protested. "I will go insane and I will send everyone here in the villa insane as well. At least give me the weekend."

"The weekend?"

"The weekend," I said again. "Let's make plans for Saturday. You can show me around the island or teach me something or... I don't know, do your godmother thing and then Saturday night we can have dinner together, here at the villa, and you can quiz me on all the things about being a duke."

I hated to admit that I was desperate for her to say yes, but I was. And not just because I would be bored if left to my own devices for an entire week. I enjoyed spending time with her and at least if I had a concrete plan for the next time I would see her, I wouldn't go completely stir crazy.

"Saturday?" Sophia asked.

I nodded. "Or Friday night—"

"Saturday," she repeated. "I'll plan something for Saturday."

"And you'll stay for dinner Saturday night," I said.

She was quiet for a long moment before she finally nodded. "I'll stay for dinner Saturday night," she replied.

I grinned. I couldn't help it. The smile bloomed across my face and she returned it with one of her own.

"I had a really great time today," I said.

"So did I," she replied softly, and then she was pulling her hand from mine and walking out the door.

I wanted to call her back, but for what? She had to go, and I had to let her go. I'd never felt the weird separation anxiety that was churning inside me, not when I said goodbye to a date, not even when I said goodbye to my parents on my first overseas trip. I felt off-kilter with it. It had to be because of the situation I was in. I was practically under house-arrest in the villa until she came back. That had to be the reason it felt so odd.

Sophia looked back once before she climbed into the black car and I watched her drive away, feeling her absence keenly. I watched until I could no longer see the car and then turned and walked back into the villa that felt entirely too empty without her in it.

CHAPTER 8

Sophia

"Sophia, you remember Callie?" Frankie asked as she presented one of the local women she had befriended.

"Of course I do," I said, reaching out to shake Callie's hand. "It's good to see you again."

"Callie has come to look at the space for the flowers," Frankie said. "I told her to talk to you."

"Me?" I asked.

"Didn't Meredith appoint you as event planner for the ball?" Frankie asked.

"Event planner?" I asked again, stupidly. Meredith had asked me to help out, but event planner? I wasn't any good at that sort of thing.

Callie looked between us with a frown. "Should I speak to

someone else?" she asked. "Someone who knows what's going on?"

I swallowed and straightened my shoulders. Fake it until you make it, right? Hadn't I been doing exactly that my entire life?

"No, no, it's okay. I'll walk you through the space and we can discuss what we need," I said smiling at Callie.

"Excellent," Frankie said. "I have to go, but I'm sure the two of you will be fine. Just avoid Dorian, if you can."

"Avoid Dorian?" I asked, but Frankie was already walking away and waving at us over her shoulder. I turned to Callie, but she just smiled tightly at me.

I took a breath. I could do this. I styled photos all the time, and I'd attended many formal events in my life. I knew how they were supposed to work; I knew how all the moving parts were supposed to come together, I'd just never been in charge of putting them together before.

"So…the space?" Callie asked.

"Right," I said. "But first, let's go and see Lucas. He'll have a rundown of all the events happening and the budget. Then I can show you which spaces will need decor and how much money you have to work with."

"Spaces? As in more than one?"

"Of course," I said. "For the ball, there is the ballroom and the dining room and the retiring room and the entrance, of course. We will need some decor on the balcony off both the dining room and the ballroom as well. And then there are the other days and events for the rest of the visit."

"It's not just the ball?" Callie asked.

"The ball is the main event," I replied, leading her toward the wing of the palace where the offices were located. "But the queen and her family will be here for a couple of weeks and there will be various functions they will be attending."

"O-kay," Callie said slowly. "Frankie didn't mention all of that."

I snorted softly. "Of course she didn't," I replied. "Frankie only told you enough to get you to agree. She has a special gift of getting people to do things they don't want to do." *Look at what she got me to do*, I thought but didn't say. And I didn't mean the event planning thing, I meant the thing with Ethan.

Ethan, with his sparkling blue eyes and easy laugh and the way he looked at me sometimes. I'd been so very close to staying for dinner the other night. I'd wanted to. It had been such a great day with him and I hadn't been ready for it to end, but...but I couldn't let myself get too close to him. I couldn't act on the feelings that were developing between us. Hence why I'd put a few days between us, to give us both breathing space, or rather, cooling off space.

We reached Lucas' office, and I knocked before opening it. Lucas looked up at me and smiled, and even looked a little relieved to see me. I stepped through the door and opened it for Callie to follow me.

"What are you doing here?" The growl didn't come from Lucas, but from the couch on the wall of his office. I turned to see Dorian sitting there, but he wasn't looking at me, he was glaring at the woman behind me.

"She's with me," I said. I didn't know what was going on between Dorian and Callie. I hadn't even known they knew each other, but I would not let him bully her. I needn't have worried, though.

"I'm working," Callie said. "What are you doing? Sitting around watching other people work? Why am I not surprised?"

Dorian scoffed, but for the first time in all the time I'd known Dorian, he looked like he didn't know what to say.

I turned my attention to Lucas. "Hi Lucas," I said, drawing his attention. "I was hoping you had a run sheet of the events for the state visit and the budget for each event. Callie is going to be working with us on decor and we need to go over the spaces today to give her some idea of what we're going to need."

"Of course," Lucas replied with a smile. "Let me just print it out for you."

He clicked around on his keyboard while Callie and Dorian alternately scowled at and then ignored each other. I didn't know what was going on there and I didn't want to know or get involved, but now I knew why Frankie told us to avoid the duke.

"Also," I said to Lucas, taking a step closer to his desk. "I'm probably going to need some sort of office or whatever while I organise the visit. Who do I talk to…?"

"You should just take the Chamberlain's office for now," he said. "You will be basically doing the job until we find someone to fill the position."

"O-kay…" I didn't know how I felt about using the office of a member of the court, even if no one had been appointed to the position yet. It felt a little like walking around in my mother's shoes and hoping I didn't get caught. Plus, I didn't even know where the office was.

"It's down the end of the hall," Lucas said, as if reading my mind. "I'll give Felix in IT a call and let him know you will need access to the computer and printer and all that stuff."

"I have a palace login," I said.

"That's your personal one. You'll need one set up just for

this. No way do you want all your business email and everything else going to your personal account."

"Okay, great," I said as the printer stopped whirring.

Lucas turned in his chair and reached for the stack of papers he just printed out, handing them to me.

"If there is anything else you need, just let me know," he said. "I'll email you a copy of all this too as soon as we get your email accounts set up."

"Great, thanks," I said with a tight smile. It suddenly felt like I was wearing a coat made of metal and the weight bearing down on me was too much. Not that I'd let Lucas or Dorian or Callie see it. I was the master at making things look effortless. My mother had drilled into me the importance of letting no one see me sweat—also, don't sweat because ladies *glowed*, they didn't sweat.

I turned to Callie, giving Dorian a quick smile, and motioned for us to leave. Lucas had handed me almost an entire ream of paper—I may have been exaggerating, but it was the most paper I'd ever held in my life that wasn't a book—so I figured our best course of action was to go to my new office and at least familiarise myself with the plans before traipsing all over the palace with Callie.

That reminded me, I was probably going to need a floor plan of the rooms we were using for the various events and I didn't know the first person to talk to about getting one of those.

Why had I agreed to this? Why had I let Frankie talk me into it?

"You look petrified," Callie said as we walked down the hall.

I forced a smile to my face and laughed it off. "Just thinking about how many trees had to die for all this paper," I lied.

"Besides, I think the real conversation should be about what is going on between you and Dorian?"

Callie harrumphed but said nothing more.

We reached the office and I opened the door timidly, expecting someone to yell at me from the other side. No angry voice came so I straightened my shoulders and stepped into the office. It was larger than I expected with a wide, heavy wooden desk topped with a computer monitor. Aware that Callie was watching me, I stalked across the floor and around the desk to sit in the office chair and dropped the ream of paper Lucas had given me on the desk top.

Callie took a seat opposite me and cleared her throat. "I thought I was just here to do the flowers," she said.

I smirked at her. "You should know Frankie better than that by now," I replied. "When she said 'flowers' she meant decor."

Callie bit her lip. "I'm going to need help."

"Of course you are," I replied. "Some of the palace staff will be made available to you but if you can organise a workforce from the village, that would be great. They will all be paid." Or at least I assumed they would be. Jamie was not the kind of king to require his subjects to do unpaid labour.

"I'm going to need some help from you too," Callie said.

"Me?"

"Frankie told me you're like a fairy godmother who can turn frogs into princes." Callie smirked at me and I felt my cheeks colouring.

"Of course she did," I muttered. "Are you looking for a frog?"

Callie barked out a short, sharp laugh. "Not in the least," she replied. "But I have some women in the village who need some help. I think you could help them." She made woo-woo motions with her fingers. "Fairy godmother them, if you will."

"I think Frankie has overstated my abilities," I replied gruffly.

"Don't get me wrong," Callie said, sitting forward. "I'm not trying to get you to set them up with wealthy men. That's not what this is about."

"Then what is it about?"

"A few of the women I help have never worked outside the home, but with the way Kalopsia is changing, more and more of them want to work. They need money to support themselves and their families but they need help with learning how to present themselves."

"Like…for job interviews?"

Callie nodded. "There are also a few fledgling cottage businesses that need some help with their social media profiles. Even just a few pointers about how to promote their businesses and build their brands would be amazing."

"You think I can do that for them?" I asked, a little taken aback.

Callie stood. "If you think it is beneath you—"

"No. No, that's not what I meant," I said, standing as well. "I just meant that, well, do you think I actually have the ability to help them? I mean…"

Callie sat back down and crossed her arms, looking at me with a critical eye. I lowered myself to my seat and wanted to look away, but didn't.

"I've seen what you do for the palace and I follow your Instagram feed. I even know the entire story of you and Nico—"

"Frankie," I growled softly and Callie laughed.

"Not Frankie. I knew Nico. I've known him for a long time. No way could he have achieved what he did without someone else's help. *Your* help. I just want you to do the same for the women in the village. Use your powers for good instead of evil."

I smiled. Could I really do that? Could I use this seemingly useless ability of mine to do some actual good in the world?

"How about this," I said, leaning forward. "Bring them to the palace as part of your workforce. I can meet them and work with them while we all work together to pull this state visit off. They'll get some work experience to put on their resumes and I can teach them anything I can."

Callie grinned and stretched her hand across the table. "Deal," she said.

"Deal," I repeated, shaking her hand.

THERE WAS no reason for me to be nervous. There was absolutely no reason for my heart to be pounding or my breathing to be shallow.

This was not a date.

The car pulled up outside the villa and Ethan opened the front door as if he had been standing beside it waiting for me. I swallowed thickly. He looked good. He was wearing the approved 'preppy' clothes, but somehow, they didn't look preppy on him. They looked...far better than they should for my sanity. Not that I didn't want him to look good...I was just struggling to remember that I shouldn't see him as anything other than a project.

Ethan didn't wait for my driver to get out and open the door for him. He slid into the back seat beside me with a big grin.

"So, where are we going?" he asked eagerly.

I chuckled. "You're really enthusiastic this morning," I said.

"Are you kidding? I've been cooped up in that villa for three days with nothing but YouTube videos about table manners and the right way to use cutlery. I am dying to get out and go somewhere and actually talk to someone."

"You could talk to your staff," I said as the car pulled away.

"I've tried, but they seem scandalised that I would even approach them for conversation."

I frowned. "Do you need me to talk to them?"

He shook his head, his hands running up and down his thighs. "No, it's fine," he said. "I understand they have their jobs to do and talking to me isn't one of them."

"But if you want to learn about being a steward, Charles and Toby are the perfect people to talk to. I'll have a word to them."

"You really don't have to," he said, his cheeks colouring. "I'll talk to Charles myself."

I looked at him, looking for…I didn't know what. Maybe to see if he really was okay. He seemed kind of jumpy and on edge and I wanted to believe that it was just cabin fever, but I didn't know him well enough to be completely sure.

"If you're sure," I said carefully.

"I am," he replied with a big grin. "Now tell me where we're going. You obviously have a destination in mind."

"Have you ever tried raïda?" I asked.

He smirked and pointed to himself. "Bartender, remember. I've tried everything."

"Right," I said with a smile. "So I'm taking you to a local raïda distillery."

"*Andino Raïda?*" he asked.

"It used to be owned by *Andino Raïda*, but is now run by a local co-op. *Kalopsia Raïda* is a new initiative to help rebuild our industry. They partner with *Andino Raïda* for international distribution, but they are significantly different…or at least their flavour profiles are different. They only use botanicals grown on the island and whatever is in season. It makes each batch a limited edition. They are getting ready to release their first batch in time for the state visit."

"It's just the ball, right?"

"It's the ball and a few other engagements with high-ranking officials."

"But I only have to attend the ball…don't I?"

I bit my lip. "Um…well…maybe?"

"What do you mean, maybe? Our deal was for me to be your date to the ball."

"It will look strange if I show up to the ball with you when you haven't been to any of the other events." I turned to look at him. "Are you scared? Are you worried you won't be able to pull it off?"

Ethan scoffed.

"Have you been doing any of the homework I set for you?"

"Of course I have," he replied, offended. "I know what a salad fork is and even how to use it."

"And what about getting to know all the royal families and their courts? Have you been doing that homework?"

He bit the corner of his mouth. "Ah…not so much."

I rolled my eyes. "Okay, so you do know that Meredith is our queen and Jamie is our king."

"Yep, got that," Ethan said with an eye roll.

"Alyssa is the queen of Merveille. Have you heard of Merveille?"

"I already told you I did, and I've even been there," Ethan replied.

"Right so, Meredith's father is the Prime Minister of

Merveille and her brother is a duke in Alyssa's court. Meredith was Alyssa's closest friend and companion growing up. And then Jamie and Meredith were both guards in Alyssa's royal guard."

"Wait. The king and queen were body guards for another queen?"

"The king was in exile. Merveille took him in and hid him, and he grew up in the royal guard. Which is where he met Meredith and where they fell in love. When Kalopsia needed its king to return, he came and brought Meredith with him."

The car stopped out the front of the raïda distillery and the driver opened our door.

"Surprise!"

I looked up to see Frankie and Lucas waiting for us. I tried not to groan, but I must have made some sound because Ethan placed his hand on my arm and looked at me questioningly. I gave my head a small shake and smiled. I didn't have a problem with Frankie and Lucas being here to tour the distillery with us, I just wish she'd told me she was coming.

"You remember Lady Francesca," I said to Ethan. "And this is her fiancé, Lord Lucas."

"Lord Ethan," Frankie said with a mischievous grin as she reached to shake Ethan's hand. "So nice to see you again."

"And you," Ethan said, shaking her hand before turning to Lucas. "A pleasure to make your acquaintance," he said to Lucas, hesitating before reaching out to shake his hand and using that weird Dorian-esque voice. "I apologise. I don't know whether I'm supposed to bow or to shake your hand or..." he looked at me.

"A handshake is fine," Lucas said. "I'm a marquess and lower on the food chain than you, so you don't need to bow."

Ethan shook Lucas' hand and then raised his eyes at me. I turned to Frankie.

"I assume Lucas knows what's going on," I said with a deep sigh.

"Of course he does," Frankie replied. "I wouldn't keep something like this from my future husband."

"But we're keeping it from the king and queen?" I asked with raised eyebrows.

"Well, duh, we have to. Otherwise, how would we be able to tell if you won the bet?"

I turned to Lucas. "I'm sorry she dragged you into this," I said.

"I'm not," Lucas replied with his amiable smile. "It's been an entire six months since we kept a secret from the king and queen. This will be fun."

I groaned inwardly. "I don't know about fun," I mumbled.

Ethan reached for my hand and squeezed it, drawing my eyes to his. "Of course it will be fun," he said with a twinkle in his eye. "I'll make sure of it."

"How did I do?" Ethan asked me across the candlelit table.

I smiled at him. "Your table manners are exquisite," I replied, truthfully.

He grinned. "It's amazing what you can learn on YouTube these days," he said, leaning back in his chair.

"It is," I replied, picking up my wine and finishing the last sip.

We were sitting on the balcony of the villa. The night was warm, autumn not yet reaching the little Mediterranean island,

and the sky was clear. A soft breeze whispered around us off the sea, and the full moon added to the delicate candlelight lighting the space.

Dinner had been lovely. I enjoyed spending time with Ethan, something I could no longer deny, as much as I wanted to. Our time together shouldn't be a chore, but I hadn't expected to enjoy it so much. I thought it would be more like a job—an enjoyable job, but still a job. But that wasn't how it felt when I was with him. Even earlier today when we were at the distillery, it felt normal, easy, like we were a couple of friends hanging out.

Ethan and Lucas seemed to get on like long-lost friends, which was so much better than the way Ethan and Dorian had gotten on…which was to say they didn't get on at all. I'd worried Lucas would treat Ethan the same way, but I should have known better. Lucas was nothing like Dorian, and he and Ethan seemed to have a lot in common.

I knew by the way Frankie kept glancing at me and Ethan that she was plotting something, but I refused to be taken in by it. She was newly in love and of course she wanted everyone else to be in love too. What was it about newly minted couples that they felt they had to play matchmaker to every unattached person in their friendship circle?

I was not opposed to finding my person, but I wanted to work out who I was first before diving headfirst into a relationship. And as much as I liked Ethan and enjoyed his company, he wasn't sticking around. He was a wanderer, a traveller, a nomad, and I was certainly not. I enjoyed having my own place, a home, the security of routine and consistency. The two of us were diametrically opposed, and as much as my heart might yearn to get to know him more intimately, it would only lead to heartache for both of us...or at least for me. He was leaving after the ball and it would be remiss of me to think there could be any future for us.

"So what's the next lesson?" Ethan asked. "I've got the table manners and cutlery order and use down. I'm delving into the who's who of the European royal set, and I even know how to dress and speak like Lord Muckity Muck. What else have you got in store for me?"

"Dancing," I replied, laying my napkin aside. "I'm going to teach you to dance."

His eyebrows lifted. "Now?"

"Why not?" I asked. "It's a lovely night and we've had a delicious meal. A little bit of dancing would be a pleasant way to cap it all off, wouldn't you agree?"

Ethan stood and then held his hand out to me. "Would you care to dance, my Lady?"

"I would love to," I replied, taking his hand and ignoring the warmth that shot up my arm with our contact.

Soft music floated out of the speakers hidden among the gardens, and I smiled. Charles was amazing at anticipating our needs, and I understood why he had been with my grandparents for so long.

I started to lead Ethan in a waltz, but he stopped me. I looked up at him, and his eyes sparkled with mirth.

"I think I'm supposed to lead," he said.

"Oh, I thought—"

Before I could finish my sentence, Ethan was moving me across the balcony, his steps true and sure, and I felt like I was walking on air. I looked up at him and blinked. He was an excellent dancer.

"How...?"

He smiled down at me, and my stomach flipped. "Five years of ballroom dancing," he replied.

"Five years?" I asked, impressed but also confused.

He shrugged. "I got into it because I thought it was a good way to meet girls," he replied. "I stuck with it because it was fun."

There was something unreasonably attractive about a man who knew how to dance. Sure, a lot of men in the royal circles knew how to dance, but most of the time it was little more than them just moving me around the floor, counting their steps as they concentrated on what their feet were supposed to be doing. That was not how Ethan danced. Ethan *knew* how to dance. Like, really knew. Like maybe he was even better than me.

"I see that dance lessons aren't needed," I said, a little breathlessly and not because of the dancing.

"I still enjoy dancing, even if I don't get to do it very often anymore, and I would never turn down a chance to dance with you."

My cheeks flushed with his compliment and I looked up into his eyes, hoping to see he was just joking with me but really hoping he wasn't. If the heat in his eyes was any sign, Ethan was serious. He pulled me a little closer as we danced, or maybe I moved a little closer of my own volition. At this point, I couldn't tell. I was far too lost in the feel of his arms around me and the way he was looking at me and the way he made me feel.

I took a breath, trying to find my equilibrium, but it was a mistake. All I managed to do was breathe him in. His scent. Yes, the fragrance I'd bought for him (and can I just say how good it made me feel that he was wearing it tonight) but also the very essence of him. It had become so familiar to me and I hadn't even realised it.

"Sophia," he said, my name on his lips low and rough and sending shivers through my body.

I looked up at him, but he wasn't looking at my eyes, he was looking at my lips and I couldn't help my own eyes falling to his lips in return.

Was he going to kiss me? Did I want him to kiss me? Yes. Yes, I did, but that didn't mean it would be a good idea. The very fact that I wanted his kiss more than I wanted my next breath only told me I was out of my depth. It took everything within me, but I stepped out of his hold and I saw a flash of hurt in his eyes before he hid it behind his genial smile.

"I should go," I said. "It's getting late."

He nodded, swiping his hand across his mouth and not speaking.

"I think you're ready for your first public appearance," I said, reminding us both the reason we were here.

He quirked an eyebrow at me, still not speaking.

"I think it's time we went out on a proper date."

"What?" he asked, surprised and, if I wasn't mistaken, a little scared. "In public? At an actual restaurant?"

"Yes," I said with an eye roll. "At an actual restaurant, in public where everyone can see us. How's next Friday?"

"What am I supposed to do until then?" he asked. "I can't spend the entire week locked up here."

"Of course not," I replied as I headed inside and gathered my things. "Go out, do some sightseeing. Just remember you're a duke. Oh, I have something for you." I reached into my purse and pulled out a credit card. "Use this for anything you need to buy."

He took it reluctantly.

"Do your homework and I'll send a car for you on Friday," I said as I escaped out the front door where my car was already waiting.

Ethan managed to capture my hand before I could escape. I stopped and turned to him.

"No," he said.

"No?"

"If we are going out on a proper date than I am picking you up like a proper gentleman."

Why did that make my heart flutter? Or was it the way he held my hand?

I swallowed and nodded jerkily. "Okay," I replied softly.

He held my gaze for a moment longer before letting go of my hand and I walked away, my heart pounding erratically in my chest.

CHAPTER 9

Ethan

The week dragged, but I tried to use the time wisely. I studied the list of royal and royal-adjacent people Sophia listed, and I found I had a bit of a knack for remembering faces and names. I suppose I'd always been able to—it was a skill I'd picked up working behind a bar—but I hadn't thought it would come in useful for something like this.

After I'd exhausted all the knowledge I could glean about the relevant people, I approached Charles and started quizzing him about his position as butler and what it entailed. He was reluctant at first until I reminded him I wasn't really a duke and that I hoped to one day secure a similar position to his, but on a boat. After his initial hesitation, Charles warmed to the questions. He obviously loved his job, and it showed in the way he spoke about it.

When I could no longer stand being in the villa, I took

Francis and the car and had him drive me around the island. We hit all the touristy spots first before I asked him to show me the places the locals went. The island was beautiful. Of all the countries I'd been to, I'd never stayed long enough to really get to know a place. Sure, I'd seen all the hot spots, but I'd never delved deep into a place and gotten to know it beyond just the surface.

Kalopsia had scars. After the extensive research I'd done— thanks to Sophia's homework assignments—I knew more about the coup and the ten years of dictatorship they'd laboured under. The more I explored the island, the more I saw how much the island had suffered. But I could also see how the people were healing and the country with them. I heard a lot of good things about the king and queen and Frankie, who was acting as an advocate for the people displaced by the troubles— as the locals called that sad time in their recent history.

It made me like the country more as I got to know it better. While I still wanted to find a job on a yacht, I didn't have the itchy feet that normally came after being in one place for an extended period of time. The island felt more like home than even my own home did, and it had been a long, long time since I'd felt that way about anywhere.

In the middle of the week, I had a visit from the tailor for a final fitting of all the suits Sophia had commissioned. I couldn't deny the quality of the fabric or the way they fit. Thankfully, Dorian hadn't felt it necessary to accompany his tailor. Despite Dorian's protestations that Sophia and I needed his help to pull off this deception, I hadn't seen him since that first time. Unless Dorian's idea of helping us was only about dressing me, then I had seen no evidence of his 'help.'

The finished suits were delivered on Friday, and Toby was

beside himself with excitement over seeing them. There was also another delivery. A small box came with a note from Sophia. It was the first I'd heard from her since our dinner on Saturday night, and just seeing her name on the package smoothed my ruffles.

There had been a moment between us and she had run rather than let it happen. I understood why she ran. I was hardly the type of person she could get tangled up with. But knowing that didn't stop the disappointment of seeing her walk away from me. There was something between us, an attraction for sure, but something else too. Something deeper that I wanted to explore but...but we both knew I was leaving and even beyond that, I was a nobody, despite the way she was dressing me up. Nothing real could ever happen between us. Sophia was a duchess, and she needed to be with someone who was her equal. She needed to be with someone who would stay.

For the first time in my life, I wished I was a guy who stayed.

I walked into my room, and Toby was waiting for me. He'd chosen the suit I would wear tonight, and I handed him the box from Sophia. It contained a pair of cufflinks. I'd never worn a cufflink in my life and didn't have the first clue how to put them on, but I knew Toby would know.

"These are exquisite," he said as he admired the cufflinks.

"They are," I replied, although I didn't know what made a cufflink exquisite. They were tiny little silver hip flasks with what looked like diamonds embedded in them. The diamonds couldn't be real, surely?

I showered and dressed and then handed myself over to Toby. He fastened the cufflinks to my shirtsleeves and then fixed my tie before slipping my coat on. I'd worn a suit before, but it hadn't felt like this. The suit was...everything. It was the most comfortable thing I had ever worn. I'd expected to feel restricted. I was forever seeing men tug at their ties and collars and tug at their suit coat sleeves as if wearing a suit was uncomfortable. Suits I'd worn in the past had indeed been uncomfortable and hot, but not this one. No wonder Dorian walked about in one without a care in the world. I probably would too if I was him and had access to this kind of tailoring on a regular basis. I didn't know how I was going to go back to wearing off-the-rack clothes from here on out.

I'd even gotten used to Toby helping me dress. It didn't feel nearly as awkward as it had the first time. There was something to be said about having someone who laid out your clothes and then tidied up after you and made sure your clothes were all washed and ironed and put away. Did it make me lazy to enjoy not having to worry about such things?

I reminded myself that it wouldn't be forever. Two weeks had already passed and in only four more, I would walk away from this life, or at least walk to the other side, and by that I meant I would be on Toby's side of this life of wealth and not Dorian's.

THE PALACE LOOMED ABOVE ME. I stayed in the car and waited for Francis to open the door. I'd gotten to know Francis over the past week, and I quizzed him about the palace as we wound our way up to it. A duke wasn't supposed to be so familiar with the 'help,' I knew that. I couldn't imagine Dorian engaging his driver in small talk, but it felt weird for me to sit in the car and not talk.

Were all dukes like Dorian? I'd met Lucas, but by his own

admission he was a marquess, not a duke, and he'd also been raised in America, which I assumed was the reason he was so down-to-earth.

The door opened, and I got out, straightening my coat and tugging at my sleeves like I'd seen Dorian do. I was doing it because I was nervous and trying to hide it. Coming to the palace was a big deal. It was like going into the lion's den. This whole thing could end tonight if I made a mistake. I could expose us all, and I worried Sophia would be the one to suffer the consequences.

Not being able to stall any longer, I walked up the stone stairs to the portico. The large doors opened before I reached them and a doorman stood waiting for me.

He nodded to me and it took everything within me not to nod back, but I couldn't imagine Lord Dorian acknowledging the man so, even though it felt like the height of rudeness, I ignored him as I stepped into the foyer.

I didn't know what I was expecting—opulence and grandeur for one—but the foyer was nothing like I imagined. It was beautiful, but far more modern than I'd thought it would be. A massive chandelier hung from the double height ceiling and some large pieces of artwork hung on the walls, but there were no gold statues or Ming vases or any of the things I associated with palaces and kings and queens. If I had to describe it, I'd say it had a very minimalist vibe.

"My lord," the doorman said, and when I turned to look at him, I glimpsed something pink on the massive staircase.

My breath caught. Sophia stood there in a pale pink dress, her hair curled softly around her shoulders and her pink painted lips curved up in a smile as she caught my eye.

I watched as she slowly descended the stairs, my heart

pounding harder and harder in my chest the closer she got to me.

"Lady Sophia," I said, inclining my head in a nod as she stepped up to me.

"Lord Ethan," she replied with a crooked smile and a hint of mischief in her eyes.

"You look..." I cleared my throat. "You look lovely," I managed to say, despite my throat being tight.

"You don't look half bad yourself," she replied softly.

I stood looking at her for a long moment. Too long. I knew it was too long, but I couldn't make myself speak.

"Shall we go?" she asked, breaking the spell I was under.

"Of course," I said, clearing my throat and offering her my arm.

Sophia curled her hand through my elbow and I led us out the door but before we could leave, the doorman stiffened and intoned, "Lord Dorian."

We froze, and I turned slowly to see Dorian walking toward us with a smirk on his face.

"What are you doing here, Dorian?" Sophia asked.

"I heard we were having a special visitor, and I thought it would be rude not to make time to meet with him." Dorian's smile was small and tight and I couldn't help but notice the way he glared at me and where Sophia's arm was hooked through mine.

"That's...unnecessary," Sophia said, and I felt the tension in her body.

"Not at all," Dorian replied with a sly grin.

"Dorian," Frankie said as she entered the foyer with Lucas. She looked between Sophia and me before smiling at Dorian. "I wasn't aware you were at the palace this evening."

"As I was saying to Lady Sophia, I heard about our guest and I thought it rude for me not to meet him."

Lucas muttered something under his breath that I didn't catch, but I got the impression he wasn't a Dorian fan. That made me like Lucas a little bit more.

There was a moment of awkward silence before Frankie spoke.

"I just wanted to see you before you left. And to see you again Ethan."

"Do you think this is wise?" Dorian asked.

"What?" Sophia replied, glaring at Dorian.

Dorian looked me up and down, and his jaw tightened. I didn't know if it was because I looked better than he expected or whether he thought I was going to embarrass the entire royal court.

"Do you really think he is ready to face the public?" Dorian asked. "I mean..." He trailed off with a look of disdain. He didn't articulate what he meant, but I knew an insult when I heard it.

"I don't really think it is any of your concern," I said.

"It concerns all of us," Dorian replied with a low growl.

"You're being ridiculous," Frankie said. "Ethan looks the part and sounds the part. Much better than I did when I got here and I didn't embarrass anyone...or at least I didn't do any lasting damage to the court with my...unorthodox behaviour."

"That's because you are delightful, Francesca," Dorian said and the, '*but he isn't,*' went unsaid.

"It's just dinner," Sophia said. "I doubt very much Ethan is going to cause any royal scandals with just dinner. Using the wrong fork does not an international incident make."

Dorian huffed but said nothing.

I had to admit, the entire thing stung. Even Sophia's defence of me was...a bit of a slap, as if she didn't think I could pull this off either.

I straightened my shoulders and gave Dorian my haughtiest look. "If you're quite done insulting me and disparaging my character, I think it's time we left. Lady Sophia?" I used my Dorian-voice and looked down my nose at him, which was hard to do since we were approximately the same height.

"Yes, Lord Ethan. I think it is past time we left. Have a good evening everyone."

I didn't say goodbye as I turned us and led Sophia through the door down the stairs to the waiting car. Francis opened the door, and I waited for Sophia to slide in before I went around the other side to get in myself. I took a moment to smooth my tie, adjust my shoulders, and take a deep breath. I couldn't let Dorian get under my skin. He claimed to be trying to help, but I wondered if he was actually trying to undermine us. I wouldn't put it past him, although I didn't exactly know what his problem with me was. Maybe it was because I was Australian, or not of royal birth, or...who knew with Dorian. He could have taken exception to the brand of my shoes for all I knew.

Regardless, I needed to prove to Sophia that I was up to the task and the only way to do that was to be the duke she wanted me to be.

As the car pulled away, she turned to me and smiled, and the past few minutes vanished from my mind. Sophia was beautiful, I'd known this from the very first moment I'd laid eyes on her, but tonight there was something more. Maybe because I'd gotten to know her.

"I'm sorry about that—"

"Don't be," I replied, taking her hand.

"It was unforgivably rude of Dorian—"

I smiled. "Dorian is rude all the time. I would think something was wrong if he didn't get his jabs in wherever he could. Honestly, I'm fine. Please don't worry about it."

She sighed, but gave me a small smile in return and squeezed my hand.

"So what did you think of your first glimpse of the palace?"

"It wasn't what I expected," I answered truthfully.

"Oh? In what way?"

"It seemed...bare." She frowned, and I hurried on to explain. "I expected it to be stuffed with art and statues and priceless dynastic vases. There was none of that."

Sophia sighed but smiled. "The palace was ransacked and most of its treasures sold off to pay for General Anastas' lavish lifestyle. He pretty much stripped the palace bare."

General Anastas was the dictator who orchestrated the coup. He bled the country dry and then disappeared. Of course he would have stripped the palace of its treasures, and it explained why it had a minimalist vibe.

"We're slowly rebuilding the collection, but Jamie is far more discerning than the previous monarchs. He doesn't just want to fill the palace because he can. He wants the palace to showcase the heart of the country, so he is chasing art and other items from local artisans and craftspeople. It has a two-fold affect; promoting our creative industries and injecting funds into our local economy."

It was all very interesting, and I admired the king for what he was trying to achieve, but I was only listening with half an ear because my attention was all on the woman herself and the warmth of her body where it touched mine as we sat close in the car's backseat.

"Here we are," Sophia said.

～

FLICKERING CANDLELIGHT, half-finished glasses of wine, and a plate of the most decent chocolate cake I'd ever tasted sat on the table between us. Time had stopped, and it was just Sophia and I on the balcony with the stars and the moon shining down above us and reflecting off the sea like diamonds on a spread of velvet.

I'd seen the restaurant before but had never gone in. It sat on one of the low cliffs that edged the crescent of the bay and was built in the traditional way—as almost all the buildings on the island were.

We'd been given a private spot on the balcony, away from the main dining room, but we'd still garnered stares throughout the evening. I knew without Sophia having to tell me that our photos would be on Instagram and all the other social media sites by the morning…probably before we even finished dinner.

But I didn't care about any of it. The bet and the situation and the fact I was pretending to be someone I wasn't were the furthest things from my mind. The only thing dominating my thoughts was Sophia and the way she looked and the sound of her laugh and the way her sweet lips curved into a smile when I said something that amused her. I was completely captivated by the dark chocolate of her eyes and the curve of her cheek and the way her thick hair flowed over her shoulders.

Sophia reached her dessert fork toward the slice of cake we were sharing and cut through it, lifting it to her mouth and closing her eyes as she hummed her delight. I could watch her eat cake all day long. If it wouldn't create some sort of 'international scandal'—as Dorian had been so paranoid about —I would have fed her the cake myself...and that sounded creepier than I intended it.

She blinked her eyes open and looked at me, a blush tinting her cheeks.

"What?" she asked.

I quirked an eyebrow. "What, what?"

Sophia rolled her eyes and reached for another piece of cake. "Why are you looking at me like that?"

"I happen to like looking at you," I said and then groaned. "Sorry, that sounded...weird."

She smiled. "Not as weird as you think," she replied. "I happen to like looking at you too."

That shouldn't make me feel so good, but it did. I wanted her to like looking at me...I wanted her to like me. I wanted her like me as much as I liked her.

"How do you feel about going for a walk?" I asked, suddenly eager to move. The balcony and the privacy of the nook where we sat felt far too close and confined, and I needed to move.

Sophia put her fork down and slid her napkin off her lap, placing it beside her fork on the table.

"I'd like a walk," she said.

"You can finish the cake first, if you like."

She groaned and looked at it mournfully. "As much as I would love to eat it, I am so full, I think it would make me sick and then I would forever associate chocolate cake with feeling ill and that would be the worst thing in the world."

I laughed at her candour. It surprised me, but then she had surprised me a lot tonight. I'd expected to see the same polished, perfect Lady Sophia that I'd seen each time we'd met, but tonight she had relaxed and let her guard down and it gave me a little peek into who she really was.

I understood the need for the mask. She lived a very public life and people could be brutal when they sensed any sort of weakness, so I felt privileged that she trusted me enough to show a little of her true self. I treasured it, in fact.

I looked up to get the server's attention so we could pay the bill, but Sophia shook her head.

"It's all taken care of," she said.

I frowned. "I thought this was a date?"

"It was, it is," she said. "But the restaurant wouldn't have taken your money, anyway. Jamie has an agreement with all the restaurants on the island to charge the palace whenever any of us eat out. He can't visit the establishments himself because of security and propriety reasons, so it's his way of supporting them."

That made me feel a little better, but still…it felt odd. I felt like I was taking advantage of the situation and I would have felt better to pay something toward my board and upkeep.

I shook it off, not wanting it to ruin the evening, and stood, holding the chair for Sophia as she stood as well. Arm in arm we left the restaurant, and it was only then I noticed we'd been the only ones left lingering over our meal. I had no idea what time it was, and I didn't particularly care. I wasn't ready for the night to be over yet.

"Rather than a walk, how do you feel about me taking you to my favourite spot on the island?" I asked as I noticed Francis and the car waiting for us.

"I'd love that," Sophia replied.

Sophia got into the car, and I whispered the location to Francis before joining her. I took her hand in mine and she didn't pull away. I needed to touch her, and I'd found myself doing so all night. If she'd pulled away or shown any reticence about me doing so, I would have stopped immediately, but Sophia had returned the gestures, linking her fingers through mine and placing her hand on my arm or hand throughout the night too.

The car slowed and pulled off the road and then Francis opened the door and I got out before turning to help Sophia out. I linked our arms as we walked to the edge of the cliff. It was too dark to take her down the narrow track to the little cave, and she was wearing heels, so it wouldn't have been safe even in daylight. We stood behind the little safety fence and gazed out over the sea, and I felt her take a deep breath and relax beside me, even going so far as to rest her head on my shoulder.

"It's beautiful," she said.

"So beautiful," I murmured, but I wasn't looking at the view. I was looking at her.

She turned her face up to mine, and the moment stretched out between us. I lifted my hand and slid some hair off her face before I cupped her cheek and slid a thumb along her bottom lip. I wanted to kiss her. It burned through me with an intensity that stole my breath. Her lashes fluttered, and she leaned into my hand.

It took the strength of the gods, but I pulled away before I could cross a line we would regret.

"I've had a wonderful time tonight," I said softly.

"Me too," she replied, looking up at me.

It took everything in me not to lean down and brush my lips across hers.

"We should go," I said instead.

CHAPTER 10

Sophia

I saw the sun rise, but not by choice. When I had managed to sleep, my dreams were filled with images of Ethan and the almost-kiss we almost almost shared.

I still didn't know if I'd wanted him to kiss me or not.

Okay, that was a lie.

I wanted him to kiss me, but I knew it would just complicate things, and my feelings for him were already complicated enough. The question wasn't whether I wanted him to kiss me; the question was whether I was prepared for the consequences of it.

I dragged myself downstairs to breakfast. I could have stayed in my room and called for a tray, but that would have raised questions I didn't want to answer. But I should have known I wouldn't get away with it that easily. Frankie was waiting for me when I walked into the breakfast room and so was Dorian, although he was trying to pretend he didn't notice my entrance.

Dorian had never paid much attention to me before, and I couldn't understand why I was suddenly in his crosshairs. Surely he wasn't so paranoid as to think this thing with Ethan would cause any real scandal? No one would even know the truth apart from those who already knew, so where was the harm, and why was he so invested?

I grabbed some food from the buffet, even though I wasn't in the least bit hungry, and went to sit beside Frankie, who was practically vibrating in her seat.

"Tell me everything," she said.

"There's nothing to tell," I replied, as I forked some scrambled eggs into my mouth.

"Liar," Frankie said good-naturedly as she stuck her phone under my nose.

I knew what she was showing me. I'd already seen the notifications on my phone and had spent far too long scrolling through all the pictures people had posted about my date with Ethan.

He'd looked so deliciously handsome in his suit and tie, and the way he looked at me over the table was enough to turn my knees to water. I was weak enough that I wanted to see that look in his eyes over and over again, which may have been why I screenshot every pic I found of the two of us. We looked like a real couple on a real date and…

And what? None of it was real. It was all for show, even if it hadn't felt like it at the time.

"The two of you looked mighty cosy for it being nothing," Frankie crowed.

"Shh," I hissed. "Does the entire palace have to know?"

"Oh, honey," Frankie said, patting my hand. "The whole world knows."

I rolled my eyes, even though I knew she was telling the truth. The photos hadn't gone viral, but I had a large enough social media following to know just how wide the reach had been. I was already anticipating the call from my parents to find out who he was. So far, no one had identified Ethan, although there was speculation about who he was. I just hoped none of Ethan's friends and family followed me on social media, or this whole thing could blow up in our faces.

I bit my lip. "Is that going to be a problem?" I asked Frankie. "Is his cover going to be blown?"

"It's possible," Frankie replied with a small frown.

"No one will recognise him," Dorian said, taking a seat beside me. "He looks nothing like the scruffy barkeep you bought home originally. My tailor is a miracle worker, after all."

"Barkeep?" Frankie said with a snort. "Who are you? An eighteenth century rake?"

Dorian ignored her and turned to me.

"Are you sure?" I asked nervously. "I mean, he looks the same to me, just with a bit of polish."

"Hardly," Dorian replied as he adjusted his cuffs. "He looks like a completely different person. Not even his own mother would recognise him."

I doubted that, but if Superman could get away with just a pair of spectacles as a disguise and Cinderella fooled her stepmother with just a new dress and a pair of shoes, I supposed it was possible. Besides, it wasn't as if it was on the mainstream news sites. I was only a minor royal and an even more minor celebrity. It was really only my followers and maybe the palace followers who would see the pictures.

"We could call the whole thing off," Frankie said.

"Oh, you'd like that," I replied. "Then you'd win."

Frankie sighed and crossed her arms on the table, turning her too-knowing gaze on me. "The two of you obviously like each other," she said. "Why not just forget the bet and try for a genuine relationship?"

Dorian snorted, and I just shook my head.

"He's not staying," I said. "He's leaving in a little over a month."

"You could ask him to stay," she said gently.

"And what would he do?" Dorian asked, butting in. "Go back to working in the club as a bartender?"

"There's nothing wrong with bartenders," Frankie replied hotly. "*I* was a bartender."

"Bar tending was a means to an end for you," Dorian replied. "Not your chosen career. Lady Sophia can't date a bartender. It wouldn't be appropriate."

"My parents would throw a fit," I agreed. "And I doubt Jamie and Meredith would want one of their court members dating a transient worker."

"I don't think Jamie and Meredith would care, quite honestly," Frankie replied. "They strike me as the kind of people who wouldn't stand in the way of true love. They may even offer him a job here in the palace."

Dorian scoffed. "Like that would be any better? What would he be? The sommelier? Lady Sophia can hardly be seen to be dating a royal staffer."

"No one said anything about true love," I mumbled.

"You clearly like each other," Frankie said, holding up her phone with the photo again. "Every person in that restaurant could tell there was chemistry between the two of you. Why not see where it leads?"

As much as I wanted to do exactly that, I knew I couldn't. Falling for Ethan would be so easy. I wouldn't even have to think about it. But then he would leave, and he would take my heart with him. I'd asked so much of him already. He was practically changing his entire life for me and pretending to be someone he wasn't. How could I ask him to give up his travelling as well? He would end up resenting me and I couldn't live with that.

"It would never work," Dorian said. "He's too...common."

"Wow," Frankie said with a shake of her head. "That has to be the snottiest thing I've ever heard you say. If I didn't know better, I'd think you were jealous."

"Jealous? Me? Hardly. I have nothing to be jealous about," Dorian said with a huff.

"Are you sure about that?" Frankie asked, with a gleam in her eye. "Maybe you want to be the one courting our fair, Lady Sophia?"

Dorian gave Frankie a flat look. "As much as I admire *our Lady Sophia*, I have no romantic interest in her whatsoever."

"Me thinks he doth protesteth too much," Frankie sing-songed.

Dorian groaned. "Please refrain from butchering Shakespeare." He turned to me. "While you are lovely, Lady Sophia, I assure you I don't have any interest in pursuing you. I hope you won't take that as an insult?"

"Of course not, Lord Dorian," I replied. "I could hardly feel insulted when I have no desire to be pursued by you."

Dorian looked a little taken aback by my announcement, as if it surprised him I hadn't considered him as a viable prospect.

Frankie laughed. "Oh, that was priceless," she said.

"Yes, well, thank you for your scintillating company," Dorian said, as he rose from the table. "I must be going."

We watched him walk away before I joined Frankie in chuckling. "I think I hurt his feelings," I said.

"Hardly," Frankie replied. "You might have bruised his ego, but I don't think anything could actually hurt his feelings."

"That's mean."

Frankie grinned. "I love Dorian to bits, you know that, but that man has a stone wall built around his heart so thick I think he's forgotten he even has a heart. When he falls in love, he is going to fall bad and I can't wait to see it happen."

"I'll bring the popcorn," I said.

"How goes the search for a Lord Chamberlain?" I asked, as we settled into the circle of chairs.

The entire court was present at our weekly meeting. I didn't know how other royal courts worked, but I didn't think they met weekly like a Fortune-500 company. I liked it. I liked the way our monarchs took the time to check in with us and to keep us updated on how things were progressing. We were still a fledgeling monarchy, struggling to find our way back from near-destruction, and I believed the relationships these meetings fostered would only make us stronger.

Meredith grimaced at my question. "Not well," she said, and blew out a breath as she massaged her growing baby bump.

I tried not to let my disappointment show. I was hoping—in vain—that Meredith would find someone to take over from me. I wasn't exactly enjoying my duties as the stand-in event co-ordinator.

"Does it have to be a *'Lord'* Chamberlain?" Frankie asked. "Could it be a *'Lady'* Chamberlain?"

Dorian scoffed, but it was Jamie who answered.

"Traditionally it was a man who held the position but there is no reason a woman couldn't be employed instead."

Frankie looked at me and widened my eyes.

"No," I said. "I don't want the job."

"It would make my life infinitely easier," Meredith said.

"And as much as I would like to make your life easier, I have other duties," I said, remaining strong. "I know nobody actually thinks social media is important, but it would surprise you just how important it is and just how much time it takes up."

Meredith groaned. "You sound like Jeanette."

"Lady Jeanette?" I asked. "From the Merveille royal court."

"Yes. She's Alyssa's media expert," Jamie replied.

I smiled and leaned back in my chair. "Then you must know how busy I already am without adding to my duties."

"I'm surprised you have any time to do anything while you are entertaining your duke," Dorian drawled sardonically.

"Your duke?" Meredith asked, turning to me. "What duke is this and why haven't I heard about him?"

"You have heard about him," I said with a glare at Dorian. "He is leasing my grandparents' villa while he's visiting Kalopsia. I told you about him."

"You told me he was staying at the villa. You didn't tell me you were 'entertaining' him," Meredith said with a gleam in her eye.

"It's nothing," I said with a wave of my hand, hoping no one saw how much it was shaking. "I'm just being a good host by showing him around."

"And going to dinner with him," Frankie said.

I turned to shoot her a glare.

"Is this the man you were seen with at the restaurant the other night?" Elena asked.

"The photos were all over social media," Dorian said.

"Could we perhaps get back to the business at hand?" Lord Evan asked and the entire room went quiet as we all turned to gape at him.

Lord Evan Anastas hardly ever spoke. He hardly ever even attending these meetings. Nobody really knew much about him —nobody meaning me or Frankie or anyone I'd spoken to. No doubt the security team had a full dossier on him, especially considering his last name. Not that he was directly related to General Anastas, the usurper. They were tangentially related, but Evan was the current *Komis of Alethia,* a count in his own right, and not from the same direct line.

No one really knew why Jamie had included him in the court. His name was certainly not well received by anyone, which was probably why he stayed out of the public eye as much as possible.

"Before we get back to business," Meredith said after a long moment. "I want to know more about this duke. No, even better. I want to meet him."

"What?" I asked, maybe shouted if the way Elena winced was anything to go by.

"He's a visiting duke. Why wouldn't we want to meet him?"

"Um…because…"

"Because he isn't here on an official visit," Frankie said, saving me. "He's *incognito.*" She whispered the last part like it was salacious gossip.

Meredith's eyebrows rose in interest. "Is he in hiding?" she whispered back, and I rolled my eyes.

"No," I said. "As I told you when I informed you of his visit, he's travelling anonymously so the press doesn't get a hold of his location," I said.

"And having photos of you and him splashed all over social media was going to help that how?" Elena asked.

"That was not intentional," I replied.

Dorian snorted. "And you call yourself a social media expert."

Jamie held up his hand before we could descend into a bunch of bickering siblings. "Invite him to the palace," the king said. "I'm sure we would all like to meet him. Nothing formal. Just a meet and greet over a family style dinner. Surely he won't object to that?"

"No, your grace," I replied. I may have been a lot more familiar in my conversations with Meredith, but the king was different. I wasn't close to him like I was to Meredith, and I was still working out where my place in the court was.

Meredith clapped her hands. "Excellent. Tomorrow night."

"Tomorrow night? I need to check—"

"I'm sure your duke can make time for our reigning monarchs," Dorian said, with an evil twinkle in his eye.

"Of course," I replied through gritted teeth.

As soon as the meeting finished, I flew out of the palace and had Deacon—one of the palace's drivers—take me directly to the villa. I didn't even stop to text Ethan and let him know I was on my way. I was too worried and nervous and anxious…and obviously repetitively redundant in my ruffled state.

Sure, Ethan had behaved perfectly politely with excellent

table manners when we'd gone out to dinner, but having dinner with the king and queen...I didn't know if he was ready for that. The fact that the meal was being served family style should lessen the pressure, but it only heightened it in my opinion. When the atmosphere was casual, it would be easier for Ethan to forget the role he was playing.

It was a good idea to see Jamie and Meredith before the actual ball, but I'd hoped it would be closer to the event and it would be in a more formal setting with other guests that would divert the focus off Ethan. As it stood, Ethan would be the guest of honour and the complete and total focus of the king and queen, and I wasn't entirely sure he would pass their scrutiny.

I didn't even wait for Deacon to open the door for me. I bounded out of the car and up to the door and I lifted my hand to knock, but Charles opened it before I could.

"Are you all right, my lady?" Charles asked with a frown.

"Is Ethan here?" I asked. "I need to see him—"

"Sophia?" Ethan said, coming into the foyer. "What's wrong? You look like the horde is after you."

"I need to speak to you," I said, stepping into the villa and taking Ethan's arm. "Now."

He let me drag him into one of the sitting rooms and I closed the door behind us, letting go of his arm and then leaning against the door for a moment before I said anything. I needed a second to gather myself. I didn't even know why I was so panicked, only that I was and I needed to calm down before I told Ethan or I would freak him out too.

"The king and queen want to meet you," I eventually said.

"O-kay," he said slowly. "I assumed they would."

I pushed off from the door and paced the room with Ethan's eyes on me the entire time. "So did I," I said. "I just thought it would be at one of the formal events to welcome the queen and her consort from Merveille." I nibbled at my thumbnail, something I only did when I was extremely stressed.

"But?"

"But that's not what they want. They want you to come to the palace for dinner tomorrow night."

"That doesn't sound too bad," he said, still not getting the seriousness of the situation.

I threw my hands in the air. "It doesn't sound too bad, but it is," I said…or maybe screeched—tomato-tomahto.

Ethan walked over to me and caught me with his hands on my upper arms, stopping my pacing and making me look at him.

"This isn't a problem," he said.

"It is," I insisted. "They want to eat family style, which means they will be laser focused on you and there will be no other guests to distract them."

"Are my table manners that appalling that you are ashamed of me?" he asked, and even though there was a smile on his face when he said it, I detected a note of hurt in his eyes.

I deflated and even leaned into him, resting my forehead against his shoulder. His arms slid down my arms, briefly clasping my hands before they settled on my hips. It felt good to be close to him like this. There was a steadiness about Ethan that made me feel secure…not that I felt insecure at other times…did I?

Not the most pressing matter at hand, so I wouldn't analyse it now. For the moment, though, I would soak up his warmth and his assuredness and together we would find a way out of this mess.

"I'm sorry," I said with a sigh.

His fingers tightened on my hips and pulled me closer. My arms went around his waist and I let him hold me...or I held him...or...

"It's okay. We can do this," he murmured in my hair.

I relaxed further into him. "I never meant for you to come under such close scrutiny," I said. "It wasn't part of our deal."

"It's fine," he said. "I was bound to meet them anyway and this way it happens in a less public affair so if I crash and burn, the humiliation won't be quite so bad."

I tilted my head up to face him and searched his eyes. "You won't crash and burn," I said softly.

"No? But wasn't that what you were worried about?" he asked with an adorably confused look on his face.

"I overreacted," I said, suddenly realising that we were so close that there was not even a breath of air between us and our faces were close enough that I just needed to press up onto my toes and and we would be kissing.

I sucked in a long breath and then stepped away before I could give in to the desire to do just that. He let me go, if somewhat reluctantly.

"You're right," I said, tucking a stray curl behind my ear. "You will be fine. I have every confidence in you."

Ethan smiled and slid his hands into his pockets. He looked every inch the duke in his 'preppy' clothes. He even looked comfortable in them.

"I just have to pretend I'm Dorian," Ethan said. "Piece of cake."

CHAPTER 11

Ethan

$\mathcal{I}$ was nervous, but I would never let on to Sophia. She was nervous enough for the both of us. So much so she looked very much like she wanted to throw up.

"Are you ready?" she asked when she met me at the door.

"Of course," I said, adjusting my cuffs as I'd seen Dorian do. I was wearing the cufflinks she'd given me. It was our own private little joke about my true origins. "I was born ready."

She shot me a distracted grin and smoothed her hand down her dress. It was blue tonight, the colour of the sea, and it set off her olive skin and dark eyes. She wore her hair up in a twist at the back of her head, with a few curls framing her face. She looked stunning, but she would look beautiful in a cloth sack, as far as I was concerned.

I offered her my arm, and she took it, leading me through the foyer and then out to a large balcony where a square table was set for dinner. People milled about, drinks in their hands—I recognised Frankie and Lucas and, of course, Dorian—who gave me a once over and sniffed before turning away. I didn't know if that was approval or dismissal. I could never tell where he was concerned.

"Would you like a drink?" Sophia asked. "Some wine, maybe?"

"Shouldn't you introduce me first," I murmured to her, although I wouldn't say no to some alcoholic courage.

"Yes, of course," she said.

Sophia was as ruffled as I'd ever seen her. Maybe not as much as she had been yesterday when she stormed the villa in a panic. Even so, it was unnerving to see her so…twitchy.

"Lady Sophia," a female voice said, and we turned to see the queen.

I knew it was the queen because I had researched her thoroughly—as per the homework assignments Sophia had set for me.

The queen's red hair floated around her face in wild curls and her long dress flowed from a criss-crossed fastening around her neck. She smiled at me and I smiled back, inclining my head in as regal way as possible.

"Introduce us to your friend," she said, speaking to Sophia but not looking away from me.

"Yes, your grace," Sophia said, her fingers tightening on my arm as she moved us closer to the queen.

I bowed low when we came to a stop before both the king and the queen.

"Your majesties," I said, hoping I was getting the title of address correct. I wasn't sure how formal to be since this was not a formal occasion and, according to Sophia, the court had fairly relaxed protocols.

"King Jamie, Queen Meredith, may I present Lord Ethan," Sophia said, her voice shaking only slightly as she introduced us.

"It's a pleasure to meet you," the king said, extending his hand. I shook his hand, unsurprised by the strength behind it. "Your accent is...unusual."

"Ah, yes," I said, recovering my hand and trying a haughty smile. "I have travelled extensively, especially in my formative years." It wasn't exactly a lie... I could class my early twenties as formative years, yes? "We spent a lot of time in Australia."

The queen was watching me with seeming casualness, but there was something in her eyes that told me she didn't miss much. Their previous security training was obvious in the way they looked at me, and I felt like I was going through a security checkpoint at an airport.

"And where is home?" the queen asked.

This was where things got tricky. I would have to outright lie to the king and queen or risk blowing everything. I opened my mouth to speak, but Sophia beat me to it.

"He'd rather not say," she said, her fingers digging into my arm. "Since this isn't a formal visit and if word got out, it could be...a problem."

Meredith didn't react, just smiled serenely, although her eyes sharpened on Sophia.

"Lord Dorian. Have you met Lord Ethan?" The king asked, as Dorian approached.

"Yes, I've had the...pleasure," Dorian said with a narrow-lipped smile. "We share some common interests."

Common interests? Was he talking about the tailor or

someone else? Sophia, maybe? Was Dorian interested in her? Was that why he behaved so confrontational whenever I was around?

"Nice cufflinks," Dorian said. "Very...appropriate."

I tried not to frown at him. What was he trying to do? Discredit me in front of the king and queen? I thought he was supposed to be helping us.

"They were a gift," I replied, shooting a quick look at Sophia whose cheeks had pinked.

"If you will excuse us, King Jamie, Queen Meredith, I should introduce Lord Ethan to the rest of the court," Sophia said, clutching at my arm like a lifeline.

"Of course," said the king. "I'm sure we will have plenty of time to chat over dinner."

"That's what I'm afraid of," Sophia murmured under her breath as we walked away.

"I don't think that went as bad as you thought it would go," I said quietly to her as she directed us toward a server with a tray of wine glasses.

"The night is young," she replied, reaching for a glass and downing it in one gulp before reaching for another.

I took a glass and steered us away from the wine. The last thing we needed was for Sophia to have too much to drink and then blurt out something that could ruin us. I didn't know what she was like when she was drunk, but I'd seen enough of it working behind a bar to know that if we were going to get through tonight, we needed to keep our wits about us. I now understood why Sophia had been so worried. The informality of the evening meant I had nowhere to hide.

I led us toward Frankie and Lucas and another woman, who I knew to be Elena Manolis, *Varoni of Lethe.* By all accounts she and Dorian would make a good match and, if the way she was looking at me as we approached was any sign, I think she disapproved of me as much as Dorian did.

"You already know Lord Lucas and Lady Francesca," Sophia said, and Frankie giggled at her title. "Let me introduce you to Lady Elena."

I took her proffered hand and bent over it, but I didn't kiss it. That just felt too weird.

"Lovely to meet you," I said. If I were a real duke I would outrank her, so I stayed aloof, trying to act like I thought Dorian would, but still be polite.

"And you," she replied, pulling her hand away and eyeing me cautiously.

Before we could get into conversation, a server cleared his throat and announced dinner was served. I patted Sophia's hand, which was still securely tucked through my elbow, and took a breath. Now the interrogation would really begin.

THE 'INTERROGATION' didn't actually happen, and I didn't know if they were just trying to lull me into a false sense of security so I would lower my guard or if they really had no intention of trying to find out everything they could about me. It unnerved me and I found it hard to relax, even though the mood around the table was just as described—family style.

"How goes the planning for the ball?" Dorian asked, turning to Sophia.

"Fine, thank you," Sophia replied, and I looked at her.

"You're organising the ball?" I asked, surprised. Didn't the palace have their own event coordinator to handle that sort of thing?

"Not on my own," she assured me. "The palace is a little short-staffed and I'm helping out, as are other members of the court, right Dorian?"

He huffed. "I don't see why I should be required to assist. You and that woman have it well in hand."

"That woman?" I asked.

Frankie snorted. "What is it with you and Callie?" she asked. "Is it because she hasn't fallen at your feet in adoration?"

Dorian sneered and then sipped his wine, refusing to answer.

"Who is Callie?" I asked.

"Callie is amazing," Sophia answered. "She has gathered together all these women from the village and organised them into these little cottage businesses like florists and seamstresses and cleaners. She's helping me with decor and has a team of people to help set up and pack down. Maybe she should take on the position of Lord Chamberlain...or rather, Lady Chamberlain."

"No," Dorian snorted. "That woman shouldn't be allowed anywhere near the palace and she definitely shouldn't be given a position in the court."

I shared a look with Sophia. I didn't know Dorian well, but I doubted he got his feathers ruffled over anything unless it was the vintage of the wine he drank. To see him so obviously disturbed by this person made me eager to meet her. Anyone who could get under Dorian's skin was someone I wanted to get to know.

"If you need any help," I said, "I have some free time on my hands."

"Oh, I couldn't—"

"No," Dorian said. "Dukes do not get their hands dirty."

"Seriously, Dorian?" Lucas said. "Not all members of the court are as opposed to working as you are."

"Besides, it could help me too," I replied, and then clamped my mouth closed as I noticed the attention we'd garnered from the king and queen. They would want to know how helping a foreign royal court would help me, a duke presumably with their own court. "It would be an interesting endeavour to see how other palaces work. Kalopsia has shown me it has a very modern approach to governing and it would be fascinating to see it at work." I really, really hoped that sounded sufficiently...duke-ish.

Sophia bit her lip as she looked up at me. "I'll think about it," she replied.

"I think it's a wonderful idea," the queen said. "Lord Ethan is right in his assessment of us being a modern monarchy and I think other royal courts could learn a lot from us and the way we do things."

"It's unseemly," Dorian protested. "Are you going to ask Queen Alyssa to wash her own dishes when she is here?"

The queen snorted. "Alyssa has washed dishes before," she said. "Although, no, I wouldn't expect her to do it while a guest in my house. But she isn't offering, and Lord Ethan is. We may learn something from him as well."

"Are you sure you don't mind?" Sophia asked me.

"Not at all," I replied. "I have been a little bored cooped up in the villa all day with no one to talk to. It would give me a chance to get to know Kalopsia better, and I'd get to spend some more time with you."

I hadn't meant to say that last bit, even if it had been the initial reason for offering my help. Besides, we were trying to convince Sophia's parents that we were an item, even if that wasn't the plan for the rest of the court. It couldn't hurt for people to see us together. It would reinforce the ruse for her parents if the other members of the court thought there was something going on between us.

A soft sigh came from across the table and I looked at Athena, Lady Elena's sister, as she looked between me and Sophia, with a love-struck expression on her face.

Elena rolled her eyes, and the queen smirked as she looked at us. I shifted in my seat. Maybe saying that had been a mistake after all.

"That's settled then," the queen said.

Frankie, who was sitting beside me and was suspiciously quiet, elbowed me in the ribs. When I turned to look at her with raised eyebrows, she grinned.

"You like her," she said, speaking softly enough that no one else could hear.

"Of course I do," I replied in a whisper. "Lady Sophia is a wonderful host."

Frankie rolled her eyes dramatically. "That's not what I meant and you know it."

She was right. I did like Sophia, but there was no benefit to me voicing it. Frankie knew I was only here because of a bet. In fact, Sophia and I had only met because of a bet.

Frankie nudged me with her shoulder. "She likes you too," she whispered, and then winked at me.

That shouldn't make me feel as good as it did, but it was nice to know I wasn't the only one having these conflicting feelings.

"So tell us more about those cufflinks," Dorian said. "They were a gift? From someone special?"

"Someone very special," I replied.

"And the significance?" Dorian persisted.

I shot a quick look at Sophia, who was studiously not looking at me.

"That's a private matter," I replied with a smug grin. "I'm sure you understand."

"You know you don't actually have to help me out with the ball preparations," Sophia said as we walked through the palace's terraced gardens after dinner.

"I want to," I replied truthfully. "I was being honest when I said that it would be a good experience for me. It would look good on my resume."

I rolled my lips together to stop speaking. It felt uncomfortable to talk about the eventuality of me leaving, and if the look on Sophia's face was any indication, she didn't like me talking about it either.

"I think tonight went well," she said, changing the subject.

"I think so too, except for Lord Dorian being a jerk."

Sophia grimaced. "Yeah, he was being particularly snarky tonight."

A companionable silence fell, and we wandered down the flagstone path with the sea breeze whispering gently around us and our hands occasionally brushing. We stopped at the end of a garden, where there was a stone bench and a stone balustrade that served as a lookout for the view. It was dark, but the sky was clear and the moon reflected on the ocean below us. There were boats out on the water, their running lights winking at us from a distance.

We stood side by side, barely a hair's breadth between us, and I took a chance and hooked my pinkie finger through hers. She surprised me by turning her hand and grasping mine, twining her fingers between mine.

"It's beautiful here," she said, her voice quiet.

I looked down at her and swallowed. "It is," I replied. "And so are you."

She turned to me then and tilted her face up to mine. I reached up, like I had wanted to do a hundred times, and slid a lock of hair behind her ear, taking my time to skim the softness of her cheek.

"I know things between us are...complicated," I said, my voice rough as I squeezed the words out through my strangled throat. "And this will probably complicate them even more but —" I skimmed my fingers under her jaw and tipped her chin up toward me. "I'd really like to kiss you."

She licked her lips, her eyes dropping to mine. "Yes," she whispered. "I want that too."

I slid my hand around to the back of her neck and weaved my fingers into her hair while I lowered my head to hers, torturing myself as I prolonged the moment. I would never get another first kiss from Sophia, and I wanted to relish this moment, draw it out, and make it last forever.

My lips met hers in a gentle caress. The touch ignited something inside me, and my heart felt like it was going to explode. Her fingers fisted in my shirt and pulled me closer, and my spare hand went to her waist.

We kissed again and again. Time stopped. Universes were born, expanded, and died. Stars exploded and supernovas were created. There was nothing and no one except the two of us.

It was perfect.

I reluctantly lifted my head and looked down at Sophia. She blinked up at me as if coming out of a trance, and I fully understood the feeling.

I hadn't expected our kiss to feel like that. I hadn't expected the simple coming together of lips to completely upend everything I believed about myself and my future.

"Sophia—" I started, not really sure what I was going to say, but before I could say anything more, a voice interrupted us.

"Here you are," Dorian said, striding into the small alcove where we stood.

Sophia jumped away from me; putting a distance between us that was more than physical.

"Dorian," she said, her voice shaking. "Were you looking for me?"

Dorian looked over at the two of us and smirked. "How... quaint," he said in that way of his that made me want to introduce him to my fist. "I hope I'm not interrupting." He quirked an eyebrow as if to show that he knew very well he was interrupting, and he didn't care in the slightest.

"Is our presence required?" I asked, feeling irrationally angry at the interruption.

"Lady Sophia's presence has been requested, yes," Dorian said, looking at me with a sneer. "You, however, are not required."

The blow landed as intended, and I took a physical step back with the force of it. Lord Dorian was putting me in my place and the thing that prickled more than anything else was, he was right. Dorian was right.

I didn't belong here.

I didn't belong in the palace, and I certainly didn't belong with a woman like Sophia.

Lady Sophia.

A duchess.

A lady-in-waiting to the queen.

Part of the royal court.

I was a no one in these circles, no one except for the flimsy lies we'd told. I was a house of cards that only needed one stiff breeze to be knocked over and destroyed, and Dorian had the position and influence to do just that. Not to mention he was full of hot air.

"Oh," Sophia said, looking up at me and something like regret flashed in her eyes, but was it regret that she had to go or regret that she'd kissed me? I couldn't ask and I doubted she would tell me the truth, even if I did.

Dorian held out his arm to Sophia and she took it, giving me one more look.

"Good night, Ethan," she said softly.

"Yes, good night, *Lord* Ethan. You know how to find your way out, don't you?"

Dorian smirked at me one more time before he led Sophia away, but most telling of all was that Sophia didn't look back.

CHAPTER 12

Sophia

I didn't sleep, and *that* had become a recurring theme since I'd dragged Ethan into this ridiculous situation.

I blamed Frankie.

It absolutely wasn't because of The Kiss. Yes, it deserved capital letters. It was the kind of Kiss I had only ever read about but never experienced. Oh, I'd been kissed before—definitely lower-case kisses—but nothing had prepared me for the feel of Ethan Kissing me. It was like sticking a fork in an electric socket but...in a good way.

Damn Dorian and his interruption. It wasn't even for anything important. In fact, Meredith hadn't even noticed my reappearance in the drawing room. Sure, the rest of the court had been in attendance, but it wasn't like we were having a meeting or anything. It was just the usual after dinner debrief.

Damn Dorian. He did it on purpose, I suddenly realised. I wonder just how long he'd been skulking in the bushes, waiting for the perfect moment to interrupt us?

I lifted the mug from my desk and grimaced when I saw it was empty. I'd already been to the breakfast room far earlier than anyone else. So early, in fact, that there had been no food ready, and I'd had to wait for the coffee maker to finish brewing before I could fill my cup. Racheal, one of the kitchen staff, had brought a tray of breakfast and another coffee to me in my office once there was food available, and I'd eaten it absently as I replayed The Kiss over and over *and over* again in my head. Hadn't I done it enough already? Why couldn't my poor, tired brain let it go?

It was just a kiss.

No. It wasn't just a kiss (lower case). It was a Kiss. It was The Kiss. The kind of Kiss that woke sleeping princesses from bespelled sleeps, and healed wounds, and broke evil enchantments and…

And I needed to get my head out of the clouds and back on the work in front of me.

There was a knock on my office door before it opened and Ethan walked in.

"What are you doing here?" I blurted out, my face flaming. His sudden appearance had me thinking for a moment I had conjured him from my obsessive thoughts.

He frowned. "You needed me to help with the ball," he replied, as if it was perfectly normal for him to walk into my office looking as good as he did.

"What?"

"The. Ball," he said slowly, enunciating each word carefully. "I'm here to help."

"No, Ethan. You don't need to help. It's fine. I'm fine. I have it all under control."

"That may be so," he said, his tone reasonable and irritating in its reasonableness. "But I want to help. I meant what I said. This would be an excellent experience for me."

"Right," I said, deflated. That's why he was here. Not because he wanted to see me again. Not because of The Kiss. Not because of me, only what I could do for him.

The story of my life.

"So put me to work, boss," he said with a grin, oblivious to the uncomfortable spiky feeling under my skin. "I'm all yours."

If only. I stopped the thought in its tracks. No. I didn't want to get involved with him, regardless of how epic The Kiss was. Regardless of how messed up I was today—or *because* of how messed up I was today—letting him in any further than he already was would be a mistake. He was leaving. Wasn't that why he was here? To get the experience he needed to walk out of my life without looking back?

"Okay, great," I said, forcing a smile to my face and pushing myself up from the desk. "Let me introduce you to some people."

I walked around the desk and stepped past him, but his hand shot out and gently grasped my wrist. I turned to look at him, hoping he would say something, hoping he would acknowledge The Kiss, hoping he would validate the tangle of emotions swirling inside me.

He looked like he wanted to say something, but then the look was gone and he smiled, dropping my hand.

"Lead the way," he said.

We strode through the palace and down into the very bowels of the place. It was more of a rabbit warren down there than it was above the stairs, but I knew where I was going. I'd been down there more times in the past two weeks than I had in the entire time I'd lived at the palace.

I knew I was throwing him to the wolves, but it was better than having him follow me around all day, and this—whatever it was—was getting more uncomfortable between us. If he was insistent on wanting to help and to gain some 'experience' then I would give him exactly what he asked for.

I stopped in front of a door and knocked, but didn't wait for a reply before opening it.

"Cirillo," I said to the man behind the cramped desk. "Let me introduce you to Lord Ethan."

Cirillo looked down his long, hooked nose at both me and Ethan, which was a feat considering he was sitting behind a desk and we were both standing.

I turned to Ethan. "Cirillo is the palace's majordomo," I explained.

"Majordomo?"

"I am in charge of the household," Cirillo said, standing. He was short, but that in no way robbed him of the authority that hung around him like a particularly prickly aura. "What can I do for you, Lady Sophia?"

"Lord Ethan is here to help," I replied.

Cirillo cocked an eyebrow. "Help? I don't need any help."

"Oh, I disagree," I said, not backing down even though I found the majordomo exceedingly intimidating. "Have you and Chef Diakos come to an agreement, then?"

The majordomo snorted. "The woman is a hack. A short-order cook at best and—"

"Yes, yes," I said, holding up a hand to stop the familiar diatribe. "I know all the reasons you dislike Chef so much, but you need to understand we are not replacing her, so you need to learn to work with her. Now come along. I would like to introduce Lord Ethan to Chef."

"I cannot believe our esteemed queen wants that woman to cook for the Merveille queen. We will be a laughingstock," Cirillo muttered, but he followed me out of the office and down the hall toward the kitchens.

I headed straight for the coffee machine as soon as I entered the bustling kitchen and poured myself a cup before turning to get Chef Diakos' attention. Despite Cirillo's dislike of the chef, she ran her kitchen with military precision and, as far as I could tell, was an amazing chef.

"Chef?" I called out across the din to get her attention.

Chef Diakos was an older woman with dark hair streaked with grey that she wore up in a chignon under her *toque blanche*. She turned and smiled at me before catching sight of the major-domo. Her smile turned into a frown and she marched over to us.

"What are you doing in my kitchen?" she demanded of Cirillo. "I told you to never step foot—"

I held up my hand and to stop the chef's tirade. "Chef Diakos, I'd like to introduce you to Lord Ethan. Lord Ethan, allow me to introduce you to Chef Diakos."

Ethan nodded at the woman before looking at me, a question in his gaze.

I sighed. "Do you think you can run interference between the majordomo and Chef?" I asked. "Our menu has stalled because they refuse to come to an agreement and without a menu we can't decide on anything else to do with the state banquet or the ball dinner."

I sipped my coffee and sighed. I'd left Ethan with the chef and the majordomo and hoped it would scare him off. If not, maybe he could get the two staff members to work together instead of constantly undermining each other. I was at my wit's end with the two of them and if not for Meredith being pregnant, I would have dumped the entire problem at her feet and thrown up my hands in surrender.

Ethan hadn't even baulked. I'd asked him to do something with them, and he'd nodded once and then turned his charming smile on Chef Diakos, earning a scoff from Cirillo. I left and came here, bringing my coffee with me.

I wasn't hiding, although the little stone bench hidden amongst the royal gardens wasn't exactly near any major thoroughfare, and most people probably wouldn't even think to look for me here...but I wasn't hiding. Not exactly.

I just needed some breathing room. Having Ethan in the palace, even if he was down in the kitchens, had my blood pressure rising. Seeing him again after our Kiss hit me more forcefully than I expected. If I'd gone back to my office—which probably still held a hint of his aftershave—then I would have gone insane.

So I came outside to clear my head, and my nose, and to reset, but I couldn't stop thinking about him. I had a hundred and one things I needed to do and think about that didn't include him, and yet...he filled my mind. Him and his maddening smile and the twinkle in his eyes and the way his hand felt when it cupped my cheek and what happened when his lips touched mine—argh!

I banged my head with my fist a couple of times, urging the distracting thoughts from my mind.

"Returning to the scene of the crime?"

I looked up to see Dorian standing on the path that led to my little alcove and smirking at me.

"What?"

"Isn't this where you had your little...dalliance with *Lord* Ethan?"

Was it? I looked around and groaned. It was. It was the same place we came to the night before. The same place where Ethan kissed me. My subconscious brain must have brought me back here while I wasn't paying attention.

"Go away, Dorian," I replied tiredly. "I can't do this right now."

"Do what?" he asked, surprised, or at least acting surprised.

"Verbally spar with you," I replied. "I'm too tired."

Dorian stepped into the alcove, which was the last thing I wanted him to do, and came to sit beside me. "Dreams of living happily ever after with your duke keeping you awake?" he asked.

I groaned, but didn't answer. If only it was dreams of happily ever after, but no, that wasn't what had been keeping me up at night. That honour belonged to me anticipating the moment when Ethan walked out of my life.

"You are entitled to do whatever you like in privacy," Dorian continued. "But I don't think getting publicly involved with Ethan is a good idea."

"Why don't you like him?" I asked, squinting against the sun as I turned to Dorian.

"Liking him has nothing to do with it," Dorian said. "He's not like us. He doesn't know what it means to be one of us."

"That's really...an awful thing to say," I said. "Just because he's had a different life doesn't mean he is below us. If anything, he is better than us. He's seen more and done more and done it by himself without the backing of a family fortune or notoriety."

"I didn't say he was less than us," Dorian said with a sniff. "I just said he was different. He has freedom to come and go, to travel the world, to do whatever he wants, whenever he wants. You and I don't."

As much as I hated to admit it, Dorian was right. I didn't have the freedom to just pick up and leave. My money and position gave me other freedoms, for sure, but they meant nothing to someone like Ethan. For Ethan, the world was open to him and adventure was a call he could heed without consequences. It wasn't the same for me or for Dorian, or for any of us in the palace.

I didn't know if I envied Ethan, not exactly. I liked my life, and I was grateful for all the luxuries my status afforded me. I didn't mourn my inability to travel whenever I felt like it, but I knew Ethan would. He would chafe at the bonds if he stayed, if I asked him to stay.

"Why are you telling me this?" I asked. "What's in it for you?"

"I'm offended you think that," he replied in his duke voice. "I'm simply looking out for another member of the court. If you go down, then we all go down right along with you."

"Go down?"

"What do you think will happen if you and Ethan get together? He has no title. Would you walk away from all this to follow him? To work on a yacht or in a bar and live in one of those disgusting hostels?"

"He could stay—"

"And do what? Come on Sophia, you are smarter than that. Your parents would disown you—"

"Not disown me—"

"Okay, maybe not disown you, but they wouldn't be happy. And what about us?"

"Us?" I asked, confused. "What us?"

"Us," Dorian repeated. "The court. The monarchy. We are already on shaky ground. We haven't yet recovered fully from the events of the past. We would never survive a scandal like the one that would erupt if you started dating a commoner."

Of course. Of course Dorian was worried about his own reputation. It didn't mean he was wrong, though.

Dorian stood. "Just think about what I've said. You'll see I'm right."

"I don't think you're right," I blurted, the words forming before my brain could hold them back. "Maybe in years past it was like that, but that isn't the kind of society we're trying to build."

"If you think that then you're more naïve than I thought."

"Call it naïve if you want, but I'd call it hopeful. The world is changing. Social barriers are being torn down left, right, and centre. The world has become far more tolerant of the differences between us."

Dorian snorted. "Tolerant? You think the world has become more tolerant? A simple peruse of the various hate-filled comments on your much loved social media would prove otherwise. What do you think would happen to your own public profile if it was to get out that Ethan was a nobody? He would be torn to shreds, as would you. You would lose followers as quick as lightning. And so would the palace. All our reputations would suffer because of your childishly idealistic view of the world. People might say they want equality, but they don't, not really. All people really want is to protect what they already have and gain more so they can be above others and look down on those who once looked down on them."

"Wow," I said, glaring at Dorian incredulously. "Who hurt you so that you have such a jaded view of the world?"

Dorian's lips thinned and his jaw clenched. "I'm not jaded, I'm realistic," he said before stomping away.

I DRAGGED myself into the dining room, grateful that it was more of a 'help yourself' meal rather than a sit-down with the king and queen present. They were eating in their suite, which they were doing more and more as Meredith's pregnancy progressed, and that meant a far more casual approach to the evening meal.

The buffet table was set up with a range of salads and meats with chefs ready and willing to serve us as much as we wanted. I didn't pay much attention to what they piled on my plate before taking it to a table just out of the balcony doors on the terrace.

"Hey," Frankie said, plopping down beside me.

"Hey," I replied, before shovelling a forkful of food into my mouth so I didn't have to say anything else.

Frankie frowned at me. "What's going on with you?"

I chewed my food and looked at her pointedly, hoping she would get the message that I didn't want to talk, but no such luck. I should've known Frankie wouldn't be put off all that easily.

Frankie waited until I swallowed—I couldn't exactly keep chewing indefinitely—and then asked again.

"What's going on?"

"Nothing," I replied, trying to sound casual. "Busy."

I forked another mouthful up, but Frankie put her hand on my arm to stop me from putting it in my mouth. If anyone else had done it, I would have freaked out. But this was Frankie, and she was my best friend.

"There is something else going on," she said. "So spill."

I sighed and then groaned and then put my fork down because I wasn't hungry anyway, and then I hung my head.

"That bad, huh?" Frankie asked sympathetically.

"Worse," I replied. "I think...I think I'm—"

"Falling in love with Ethan?" Frankie finished excitedly, her voice rising as she jiggled in her seat. "Of course you are, I can totally see it—"

"What? No," I hissed, trying to stop her from blabbering. "I'm not falling in love."

"But you do like him," Frankie said, a lot more calmly.

I blew out a long breath. "Yes?"

"What? You don't know?" Frankie raised her eyebrows at me.

"No."

"No, you don't like him?"

I rolled my eyes. "Yes, I think I like him. No, I don't really know. I've never felt like this before."

"Do you like spending time with him? Talking to him?"

"Of course I do," I replied. "He's a great guy and we get on really well and...and well..."

Frankie leaned in closer. "And?"

I lowered my voice. "We kissed."

Frankie squealed softly and bumped my shoulder. "And it was good, right? I mean, you liked it? He's a good kisser? Then what happened? Tell me everything."

"There's not much to tell," I said and Frankie's face fell.

"He was a terrible kisser?" She asked.

I laughed. "No. God no. The kiss was amazing. But nothing happened after. We were…interrupted."

"Interrupted? By who?"

"Dorian came to get me for the after-dinner debrief."

Frankie frowned. "Why? You weren't required to be there."

"Dorian made it sound like I was being summoned. I didn't even really get to say goodbye to Ethan, and it wasn't until I was sitting in the drawing room and I discovered no one had actually requested my presence that I realised Dorian had done it on purpose."

Frankie frowned again, deeper this time. "Why? Why would he want to interrupt you?"

"Because he doesn't think Ethan and I should be together. And…maybe he's right."

"That's nonsense," Frankie said. "There is no reason whatsoever the two of you can't be together. I think Dorian is just jealous."

"No, I don't think it's that," I said with a sigh, rubbing my forehead where a headache had begun to form. "He's concerned about a scandal damaging the royal court and by extension Jamie and Meredith. He's not wrong."

"He is wrong. Why would this create a scandal?"

"Because Ethan isn't like us."

Frankie snorted. "I really hope you don't mean that the way it sounds," she said fiercely.

"I just mean that he has freedom now. He can go wherever

he wants and do whatever he wants. I can't. I need to stay here. I can't just pick up on a wild tear and go backpacking across Europe. I have a job and responsibilities here."

"So ask him to stay."

"I can't do that either," I said miserably. "I couldn't ask him to give up his life for me. We would end up resenting each other, and what would he do? I can't see him lounging around living off my money, he'd want to work and he can't exactly go back to his job at the club if he's involved with me."

"There's nothing wrong with being a bartender," Frankie said tightly. "I was one, or had you forgotten?"

"That's not what I mean," I said with a groan and rubbed my forehead again. "When Dorian said it, it all made sense."

"Dorian," Frankie called, and I looked up to see the very man in question had just entered the dining room. "Come over here and explain yourself."

Dorian sauntered over and then sat elegantly, gracing Frankie with a beatific smile. "How may I be of assistance?"

"You can start by explaining the nonsense you've been filling Sophia's head with," she demanded.

"What nonsense?" Dorian asked. "I have only ever spoken the truth to her."

"Really? You think Sophia and Ethan getting together would cause a scandal that would damage the monarchy?" Frankie asked with a scowl.

"I do," he replied, unruffled. "And if you stopped to think about it, you would too."

"I refuse to accept your reality, and I substitute my own," Frankie said. "I don't want to live in a world where true love doesn't win."

"No one said anything about true love," I muttered, but neither of them were listening to me.

I picked up my fork and ate, not tasting anything I put in my mouth, while Dorian and Frankie continued to argue. I thought talking to Frankie might actually help me figure things out, but it hadn't, and now I was more confused than ever.

True love?

I didn't think that was even a real thing. Sure, I saw the love Frankie and Lucas shared, and Jamie and Meredith, but that was just your everyday, normal, romantic love. True love was something from fairy tales, and I very much doubted I would ever experience it.

CHAPTER 13

Ethan

That was…exhausting.

I slumped into a chair in the living room of the villa and tugged at the buttons of my shirt. When I'd volunteered to help Sophia, it had been with the intent of spending time with her, not being shipped off to mediate a truce between warring factions.

Regardless of the exhaustion that permeated my body, I felt also weirdly energised…maybe energised wasn't quite the right word, but there was definitely a fission of something lighting me up inside.

I hadn't yet managed to get Cirillo and Chef Diakos to agree on anything, but I had managed to get them to stop insulting one another. And they'd agreed to a sit down meeting so we could hammer out the particulars. Neither of them wanted to embarrass the palace, but they both had very different ideas of what not embarrassing the palace would look like. Cirillo thought the menu choices of the chef would mark Kalopsia as provincial, and Chef thought Cirillo had an outdated view of what was modern and fashionable among the top rated restaurants of the world. They both agreed they wanted the palace to look good in front of the visiting Merveille court. Now I just had to get them to agree on how to make that happen.

"Dinner is ready," Charles said, coming into the room.

"Thank you, Charles," I replied, and pushed myself to my feet. "I was wondering if I could ask you a few questions."

"Of course, my Lord," Charles said. Even though he knew my true identity, Charles insisted on treating me like the very duke I wasn't.

"In fact," I said, "I'd love to speak to Chef Contos and Mrs. Galanis as well."

Charles' eyebrows popped up in surprise, a rare show of emotion from the normally stoic man.

"Of course," he said. "Is there a problem?"

"Sort of," I replied thoughtfully, but at the look on his face, I spoke again. "Not with the staff here at the villa," I said. "They have asked me to help out with the preparations for the ball at the palace and I find myself needing to negotiate a disagreement between the majordomo and the chef."

"Ah," Charles said, as if he completely understood. "I shall make sure they are assembled in the drawing room after dinner."

"There's no need for that," I said. "The three of you could join me for dinner and we can discuss it over the meal."

I don't think I could have scandalised Charles more, even if I'd suddenly stripped off all my clothes and run around the villa singing a bawdy drinking song.

"That wouldn't be proper," he managed to say.

I sighed. "Okay. In the drawing room after dinner," I said, feeling very much like I was solving a murder in *Cluedo*.

I hated eating alone, but it had become my norm. Usually I took my homework with me to the dining room, much to Charles' disappointment. Tonight I took the iPad Sophia had given me with all the details for the upcoming state visit. She'd only asked me to help with Cirillo and Chef, but it would be good for me to familiarise myself with the rest of the program. Maybe I could find other ways to help as well. And maybe I could find a way to spend more time with her.

Dinner was delicious, as usual. I hadn't yet had a meal in the villa that hadn't been wonderful, but still it dragged. I tried to lose myself in the mountains of information on the iPad, but it couldn't hold my attention. Sophia was all I could think about... and that kiss.

One of the reasons I'd gone to the palace had been to see her and talk to her about what happened. I needed to know where she stood and what she was feeling and whether all the things I was feeling were only one-sided. She'd acted weird when Dorian interrupted us and I'd had a bit of a wake-up call, but it hadn't stopped me from reliving the moment of our kiss over and over. Surely there was something more going on between us. Yes, I knew I wasn't someone her parents would ever approve of but...but what if I could be?

I didn't know what that would look like. I wasn't planning to stay in Kalopsia, but what if I did? What if I changed my plans and stayed and found a way to be worthy of Sophia? Would we have a chance?

"My lord," Charles said, interrupting my spiralling thoughts.

"Chef Contos and Mrs. Galanis are waiting for you in the drawing room."

"Great. Thank you," I said, getting up from the table and scooping up the iPad. "Lead the way, Charles."

Chef Contos and Mrs. Galanis sat awkwardly on the armchairs. Their backs were stiff, and they looked worried. I smiled, trying to put them at ease, but they shot concerned glances at Charles instead of relaxing. I motioned for Charles to take a seat and then sat myself.

"I need your help," I told them. They relaxed minutely, but still looked worried. I plowed on, hoping to put them at ease as quickly as possible and maybe get some advice for dealing with the squabble at the palace.

"I've been tasked with trying to settle a dispute between the palace's majordomo, Cirillo, and the palace chef, Chef Diakos. I was hoping the three of you could help me come up with a plan or at least give me some advice for dealing with the two of them."

Their shoulders inched down from their ears and their spines softened slowly as I explained the position I was in. When I'd finished, they nodded, looking at each other first before anyone spoke.

"Cirillo is very set in his ways," Mrs. Galanis said. "I don't think he has left the palace in fifty years."

That revelation surprised me. "He stayed through the occupation?"

Everyone nodded. "He wanted to preserve as much of the palace as he could," Charles responded. "He was also able to get information out of the palace to the rebels."

I exhaled roughly. "That's...kind of amazing."

"He took the destruction and theft of the royal artefacts as a personal affront," Mrs. Galanis said. "I think he is more loyal to the stones that make up the palace than the people who inhabit it."

"What about Chef Diakos?" I asked. "Did she also stay through the occupation?"

"No," Chef Contos answered. "She is only new to the palace. General Anastas executed the original chef. He didn't trust him not to poison the food, so he got rid of him and installed his own, loyal chef. The king and queen appointed Chef Diakos to the position when they returned to Kalopsia."

"Do you know much about her?" I asked.

"She's worked in some of the best restaurants in Europe," Chef Contos said, a touch of admiration in his tone. "I have heard her food is excellent."

"It is," I said absently as I stroked my beard. "As is yours," I said, hoping to reassure Chef Contos.

"They come from two very different worlds," Charles said. "I can see why they are at loggerheads."

"Right, but how do I get them to work together?" I asked, at looked around the room.

I spoke with my staff well into the night and thought I had a solution, but I wouldn't know until I presented it to the two parties involved. We had a meeting set for that day and I wanted Sophia to be there too, which was why I was knocking on her door first thing that morning.

"Come," she called through the door.

I opened it and stepped through, a smile on my face. She

looked up, and a smile crossed her lips before she controlled it, and gave me a pleasant but impersonal look.

"Lord Ethan. What brings you to my office today? Have you solved the War of the Roses downstairs?"

"Not yet," I said, stepping further into the room. "But I think I have a solution. I was hoping you could join us at our mediation meeting."

"Uh." Sophia looked around, as if she were trying to find a way to hide from my request. "I don't think I can," she said. "I've got a lot to do, and I have a meeting with Callie today, which is going to take most of the day..." She looked up at me. "I'm glad you have a solution, though. I hope to hear good news by the end of the day."

She smiled, and I knew I was dismissed. I smiled in return and withdrew from the office.

Lady Sophia was avoiding me. I frowned. Maybe she hadn't enjoyed the kiss? Maybe she didn't feel the same way I felt about her...not that I could actually put my finger on what I actually felt for her. There was attraction there, definitely. I *liked* her, even though that word was not enough to describe how I felt, but the other 'L' word was completely ridiculous and too soon, and certainly not something I was feeling. Not even a little bit.

I walked through the palace, back toward the room where I was to meet with Chef Diakos and Cirillo, nodding to the staff as I passed. I didn't know them all, but I'd met a few of them the day before, and I felt like it was important to acknowledge them. If I was going to spend the next few weeks working with them, then I wanted to know their names and positions, at least.

Sophia's decision to put distance between us played on my

mind. We'd gotten to know one another in the previous weeks, and I thought we'd at least become friends. I enjoyed spending time with her, and I assumed she felt the same. Would she have agreed to the kiss if she hadn't felt a little bit of something for me? It was confusing and yet...if I put myself in her shoes, I could maybe understand. I hadn't had a chance to tell her I was thinking about extending my stay here in Kalopsia. It hadn't actually become something I was seriously considering until the night before. Without that knowledge, of course she would be hesitant to start something with me. Yes, we had the whole bet thing, but that didn't require opening up to one another.

There was also the small—or not so small—matter of me being a common born tourist. I may dress like a duke and speak like a duke, and behave like a duke, but I wasn't a duke. It was just pretend and there was no way I could suddenly acquire a title. I didn't go to university or come from a family with wealth and prominence. My family were working-class, honest people who hadn't left the city they lived and worked in for generations. I was the only one who'd flown the coop and now I didn't fit neatly into any classification except maybe loser or vagabond.

Definitely not someone Sophia's parents would want hanging around with their daughter, and especially not someone her parents would approve of her being in a relationship with.

The odds were stacked high against me and I should just give in to the inevitable, but there was this little hitch inside me that kept me from just giving up. The thought of walking away from Sophia and never seeing her again caused a clench in my gut. I didn't know if that meant we were destined to be together —I didn't even know if I believed in destiny or fate—but I knew

I wasn't ready to walk away from the spark between us. I trusted my intuition. I'd been living on that intuition for the past decade and it had never steered me wrong.

I walked into the meeting room to find Cirillo and Chef Diakos glaring at each other across the table.

"Oh good, you're both here," I said, taking my seat.

"Of course I'm here," Cirillo said. "This is the most important event the palace will host. It will set the precedence for all other events that come after. I refuse to let *her* ruin it."

Chef Diakos huffed. "I don't intend on ruining anything," she said. "I only have the very best intentions for the palace. I want us to be seen as a sparkling jewel in the Mediterranean, just as the original explorers described us."

Cirillo rolled his eyes, but said nothing.

"I'm so glad we are all on the same page," I said with my most charming smile.

They gaped at me.

"We all want the same thing," I explained. "Now we just have to find a way to make it happen."

"How can we achieve anything but mediocrity when he refuses to embrace anything newer than the 1950s?"

"Tradition is tradition for a reason," Cirillo growled. "Monarchies are built on tradition."

"And we have an excellent opportunity to start some new traditions as we work together to rebuild this monarchy," I said.

Chef Diakos smiled smugly, and Cirillo glared at me.

"That's not to say we should throw the baby out with the bathwater," I went on. "Cirillo is correct in saying we need the traditions of the past." Before he could crow about his victory, I hurried on. "But not all traditions are appropriate or welcomed in this new and changeable era."

They both looked at me now, neither one happy. At least I'd united them in something, that it was against me maybe wasn't so great.

"Look," I said with a sigh. "All I'm asking is for us to find a way to observe the traditions and customs of the past while also introducing some new traditions. We want to reflect the current monarchy, and I know you can both agree with me when I say that the Kabiero Royal Court is a blend of both the old and new. The king specifically chose his court from the new generation but also honoured the titles of the past court. There has to be a way for us to do the same thing with the state visit and showcase the very best Kalopsia has to offer."

LIKE A BOOKEND to the way my morning began, I ended my day by knocking on Sophia's office door.

"Come in," she called.

I pushed open the door and stepped through into the office, lugging the massive picnic basket I was carrying with me.

Sophia looked at me and then down and then back to me and I could already see her refusal forming on her lips, but I spoke before she could.

"I have some samples for you to try," I said.

"Samples?" she asked, her brow furrowed.

"I got Chef Diakos and Cirillo to come up with some ideas for the menus, as you requested, but before I sign off on them, I wanted to get your opinion."

"You got them to work together?" Sophia asked, gaping at me. "For real?"

I grinned. "It was a challenge, but in the end I knew they

both wanted the same thing. They just couldn't agree on the way to get there."

Sophia sniffed the air. My mouth was already salivating with the tempting aromas, and I'd hoped it would sway her and get her to share the picnic with me.

"What's in there?" she asked, a hint of awe in her tone.

"I have no idea," I admitted. "They wouldn't tell me. They ordered me out of the kitchen while they brainstormed."

I'd spent the intervening hours helping where I could. I met Callie and was impressed with the workforce she'd amassed. I could see why Sophia and Frankie liked her so much. As soon as I told her I was at her disposal too, if she needed an extra hand, she assigned me work, saying it surprised her a duke would lower himself enough to get his hands dirty. I saw the reason she and Dorian didn't get on, and it not only made me smile, but it also made me like her that little bit more.

"It smells good," Sophia said, and I saw the yearning in her eyes as she stared at the basket.

"So come and share it with me," I said.

"Oh, uh, I…"

"Please?" I asked. "I want to talk to you about a few things, and we need to decide if the food is up to the standard you want. Why not take a break and join me?"

Sophia bit her lip and then nodded. "That sounds perfect," she said with a sigh. "I was practically pulling my hair out here, anyway."

"Oh? Anything I can help with?" I asked, as she gathered her things and joined me.

"Not unless you know who to seat with whom at the banquet," she said with a sigh as we left the office.

"I know a little bit," I said. "But only from the homework

you assigned me. I'm happy to be a sounding board though if you need to talk it out."

Sophia smiled at me. "Thanks," she said.

We walked in silence for a while, and then I frowned and looked around. "Where are we going?" I asked.

We were in a part of the palace I'd never seen before. I thought she would take me to the dining room or the garden terrace, but it didn't look like we were anywhere near either of those places.

"It's my favourite place in the palace," Sophia admitted shyly.

I smiled. I liked she was showing me her favourite place. I'd taken her to the clifftop I loved, but I hadn't expected her to return the favour, especially not since she'd been avoiding me.

We walked down a long, dim corridor and then through an old wooden door. Beyond the door was a paved area surrounded by foliage, with a spectacular view across the ocean. Although, to be fair, every view over the ocean was spectacular. This view faced the opposite way, though, with the city spreading out below us before the tourist beach and then the sea beyond.

There were no tables or chairs, and I was glad I'd thought to bring a blanket. Ideally, my idea had been to take her back to the beach below the villa, but with her reluctance to be alone with me, I'd been happy enough to eat in the palace. That she'd brought me to this spot said...I didn't actually know what it said about the state of our relationship. She'd been avoiding me, but now she was willingly spending time alone with me, in a secluded garden, no less.

I put the basket down and spread out the blanket and we got busy unpacking all the food and wine Chef had prepared under the cooperative direction of Cirillo. Sophia oohed and ahhed over everything. There were some things I recognised, but a lot of it was foreign to me...or at least I didn't know what it was called.

"There's a menu," I said, handing her the piece of paper Chef had tucked into my pocket. "With wine pairings," I added as I read it for the first time.

Sophia took it from me and scanned it. "Wow. This is...amazing."

"You're going to have to explain it to me," I said. "I know a few things on there but some of the traditional dishes I've never heard of."

As we ate, Sophia did just that. She explained each dish and the importance of it in Kalopsia's history. Even the more modern dishes were takes on traditional ones and proved that Chef Diakos and Cirillo really had worked together.

Sophia grinned at me over her glass of wine. We had finished the meal off with a healthy slice of an extra moist chocolate cake drenched in syrup and topped with chocolate ganache. The entire meal had been a feast for the senses, and I hoped it met with Sophia's approval.

"You did it," she said. "You got Majordomo Cirillo and Chef Diakos to work together to produce this amazing meal."

"It was just a matter of showing them they're fighting for the same thing. They want Kalopsia to thrive, and they want the Kabiero Royal Court to shine. I showed them they could do that if they worked together instead of working against one another."

"You're really good at this," she said.

"I've spent more than a decade in the hospitality industry," I replied. "I've dealt with snarky chefs and belligerent front of house managers too many times to count."

"Well, I really appreciate it," she said, setting her wine down and leaning over to brush a soft kiss on my cheek.

I turned toward her, our lips millimetres apart. The evening had been relaxed and cosy. It had been reminiscent of our previous dinners, and the tension that had been between us since the kiss fell away. Now I stood on a precipice. I wanted to kiss her again, but I didn't want her to pull away from me again. I didn't want her to go back to avoiding me.

I lifted my hand and brushed a curl off her forehead. Her lashes fluttered when my fingers brushed her skin.

"I really like you," I said, the words feeling inadequate and even childish, but I didn't know how else to express what I was feeling.

She blinked up at me. "I really like you too," she admitted in a whisper. "But…"

"But," I agreed before I lowered my head, going slow and giving her time to pull away.

She didn't pull away, instead meeting me halfway. Our lips touched and if I thought our previous kiss had been a fluke, this one disabused me of the notion.

CHAPTER 14

Sophia

I woke with a smile on my face. It was probably the best sleep I'd had in an age and thinking about the reason only made my smile bigger.

Ethan.

He *liked* me. It sounded juvenile to think of it like that, but I couldn't help it. I'd never really cared if anyone *liked* me before. Sure, I wanted people to like me, but there had never been a guy in my life that I wanted to *like me,* like me. Usually because I hadn't ever liked them in return. My past relationships had been little more than having someone to escort to various places and be seen with. They hadn't been real relationships at all.

It was different with Ethan.

It started out as just another arrangement. Mutually beneficial for sure, but still just another arrangement similar to those in the past. Not at all unlike the one I had with Nico before he defected. But things had changed between us. I hadn't noticed it at first. Or I did, but I didn't understand what was happening and it scared me. But now…

I sighed and sipped my coffee, leaning back from my desk and staring out the window. But now…

We'd kissed twice and admitted that we had feelings for one another, but did that really change the situation we were in? He was still completely unsuitable—not that I thought that, but I knew my parents would—and he was still leaving. He could have told me he was staying or he could have…I don't know, told me we'd work it out. But he hadn't, and I'd been too addled by his kisses to think to ask what it all meant. Or even if it meant anything at all.

There went my smile.

There went my light and happy mood.

Chased away by the gloom of reality. Because even if things had changed between Ethan and me, the reality hadn't. I was a duchess. My parents would still disapprove, and I didn't know how the king and queen would feel when they found out the truth…which they would have to if Ethan and I were to continue to see each other. The plan had been for Meredith and Jamie to never find out the truth. That's why I'd agreed to lying to them. Ethan would leave after the ball and they would never see him again, and hopefully Jamie and Meredith would forget all about him. But if Ethan and I decided to be together for real, past the ball, then I would have to come clean to the monarchs and I didn't like the thought of what that would look like.

A knock on my door made me turn and I would be lying if I said I wasn't hoping it was Ethan. I hadn't seen him that morning, and I missed him. Which was hard to admit, since I'd been doing my best to ignore him.

"Come in," I called, a smile already on my face.

But it wasn't Ethan. It was Callie.

"Good morning," Callie said, coming into the office and taking a seat.

"Good morning," I replied. "Did we have a meeting this morning?"

"No, but I was hoping you had the final count for the banquet and the ball so we could finalise the seating chart and decide on the table placements."

"Oh, right," I said, shuffling some papers around on my desk and then giving up, instead waking up my laptop and bringing up the completed spreadsheet. "We have one hundred and eighty guests confirmed for the banquet and three hundred and fifty for the ball."

Callie made a note on her tablet. "Okay, great. So I need to look at the China and glassware and choose which is going to go with which meal." She looked up at me, waiting for…what?

"Um, okay," I said. "Cirillo would probably be the best person to talk to about that. I know there's a storeroom for all of it, but I'm not sure where it is. In fact, I didn't even think about it."

"That's why you employed me," Callie said with a smile. "I haven't formally met Cirillo. You should come with me."

"Are you afraid of him?" I asked with a smirk.

"Of course not," she replied, her cheeks pinking. "I just thought it would be better if you introduced me."

I grinned. "Fine, I'll come. I wouldn't mind having a look at the China patterns as well. The ones we use every day are just plain dinnerware but I ve heard the palace has some really gorgeous China."

We wound our way through the palace and down into the service area. I stopped at Cirillo's office and knocked.

"Lady Sophia?"

"Cirillo, let me formally introduce you to Callie. I know you've seen her around because she's been helping with the preparations, but I thought it was time for a formal introduction."

Cirillo bowed his head to Callie and gave her a rare smile. "I knew your grandmother," he said. "Wonderful woman."

"Thank you," Callie said, obviously touched by the man's words.

"So what can I do to help you ladies this morning?" Cirillo asked, turning back to me. "The menu is finalised and Lord Ethan said you approved it last night."

"I did, yes," I said, my breath hitching with the sound of Ethan's name. Yes, I'd been looking for Ethan the whole way down here, but I would not admit that to anyone or ask anyone if they'd seen him. "Callie needs to decide on the China and glass—" I stopped when I saw the look on Cirillo's face. "What's wrong?"

"Yes, well, Lord Ethan also asked me about the China and… well…perhaps you should just come and look."

I didn't like the sound of that. At. All.

We followed the majordomo down the hall and then into a large room with a long table running down the centre. It was currently a hive of activity as people polished and cleaned and catalogued what looked like far too few plates and dishes and glassware.

"Where's the rest of it?" I asked. Sure, there was more than the usual twelve place settings, but from what I could see there was nowhere near enough matching pieces to serve either the banquet or the ball.

"Gone," Cirillo said.

"Gone?" I squeaked. "How can it be gone?"

He lifted a brow to me, and I knew. I knew how it had disappeared, or rather been stolen or even broken. General Anastas had managed to gouge even the very bowels of the castle.

"What are we going to do?" I asked, looking at Callie and then Cirillo, but it wasn't either of them that answered.

"I'm taking care of it," Ethan said, striding into the room like he owned it.

I SWUNG AROUND to look at Ethan

"You're taking care of it?" I asked. "How did you even know it was something we needed to take care of?"

Ethan smiled. "Yesterday, when Chef and Cirillo were deciding on the menu, I thought it would be a good idea to make sure the palace had everything we needed. I'd busied myself by inspecting the 'dish room.' According to the scullery staff, a lot of the original dinnerware has been lost or destroyed. They've preserved a small amount but there are nowhere near enough pieces for the banquet or the ball. No one knew if we had ordered any, and the entire department was in a bit of a tizzy. I spoke to Lucas, and he informed me no one had discussed the cost of buying new dinnerware and cutlery and so I made some arrangements to hire some. I didn't think it was appropriate for me to purchase anything and the king and queen probably want to pick out their own patterns or have patterns designed for them, but we needed to do something. I haven't chosen anything yet, but I have the catalogue and the company I spoke to said they would have enough to cater to our needs."

"I…" I didn't know what to say. I sent Ethan down here to solve one problem and he'd done that and more. He was actually saving my bacon. I hadn't even given the dinnerware more than a passing thought. I'd never considered there wouldn't a be a storeroom full of all the pieces we needed. But Ethan had. He had the forethought to check and…and I wanted to kiss him.

I swallowed and turned back to the activity going on around us. "You're cataloguing what we do have," I said, stating the obvious.

"I thought we could see if we had enough of each dinner set to use for the more intimate dinners," he replied. "I also wanted to see if some of the patterns could be topped up, if they're still in circulation. I know a couple of the Royal Albert patterns are discontinued, but we might get lucky with the Noritake or the Villery & Boch."

I'd heard of Royal Albert, but the other two names meant nothing to me. I was gaping at Ethan. I thought he was a bartender? How did a bartender know anything about China patterns? But he'd said he'd worked in restaurants too, hadn't he?

"Um, wow, okay," I said, still not sure what to say. "Callie?" I turned to her to see she was looking at Ethan with interest. That made my gut clench, but I tamped it down. Now was not the time to let my confusing emotions about Ethan cloud my judgement.

"I can sit with Ethan and go through the catalogue," Callie

said. "Once we have a list of the remaining dinner, glass, and silverware, then we can decide on what we can use where."

"Okay, great," I said, disappointed that they didn't seem to need me to help.

"Once we have a final count on what we have in the store, I'll look online to see if we can purchase anything to build up the stocks again and email you a report," Ethan said.

"Great," I said again, feeling superfluous. "That's great." Ethan and Callie walked up to the large table and sat. Ethan was showing her something on his iPad, and Callie was nodding while she scrolled. I looked at Cirillo. He was looking at Ethan like a proud parent. I looked around the room to see how the scullery staff deferred to him, accepting him as their superior— and not in the way that he was a duke, but in the way of a boss with his employees.

It did something weird inside me. It was like watching a ballet dancer on stage or a footballer on the pitch. Ethan knew what he was doing, he was in his element; he was good—no, great—at what he did. It was attractive. I don't think I'd really appreciated the work that went on behind the scenes. I was more aware than some of the court—Dorian and Elena came to mind—but I'd also grown up having everything done for me. I knew about protocols and obligations and court gossip. I knew about the infighting and machinations of the former royal court and the power struggles that went on even after the court had run from the usurper. I'd learned it all at my mother's knee. It was the reason they tasked me with the seating arrangements and overseeing the event planning. I knew all about how to make something *look* good. I knew how to put a perfect sugar coat on things...but Ethan...Ethan knew how to make something work. He knew about all the cogs in the wheel and how to get them to turn in unison. I was useful for making things pretty, but Ethan made things functional. There was something really irresistible about that.

It was hard not to draw parallels with our lives. My life was as insubstantial as the images I posted on social media—images that were carefully crafted to look just right and to hide anything less than perfect. I was the veneer, as thin as the makeup I wore, whereas Ethan was the substance. Ethan knew who he was and what he wanted, and he worked to achieve it. He cared more about the journey than the destination. He *lived* rather than just drifted through life trying to live up to the expectations of others.

I wanted to be more like him. I wanted to not care so much about the visuals and focus more on the intent but...but a life of lessons drummed into me about appearing perfect and hiding weaknesses was a lot to throw off in a matter of weeks. My parents had indoctrinated me to believe perception was reality. Learning that maybe that wasn't true would take time to assimilate...if I could do it at all.

"I HEARD your duke saved the palace from a crisis today," Meredith said as she eyed me over her soda and lime.

"He's not my duke," I replied, gulping my wine.

We were gathered in the queen's sitting room. It was just her ladies-in-waiting, and Athena, of course. Athena was always there, like an extension of her sister.

"Nevertheless, I've heard good things about him," she persisted.

"He mediated the dispute between Cirillo and Chef Diakos,"

Frankie said with a mischievous grin in my direction. "And he even charmed Callie, and you know how prickly she is with anyone with a title."

"Not anyone with a title," Elena said. "Just those with the title of duke...or more specifically, a certain duke of this court."

"Yes, she does have a specific aversion to Dorian," Frankie said, "but she is still standoffish with everyone else. I'm surprised to see her and Ethan working so closely."

I gritted my teeth as I poured more wine into my glass. I did not want to talk about Callie and Ethan and how well they were working together. No, I wasn't jealous...okay, maybe I was. But he was supposed to be *my* date to the ball, and it wouldn't look good if he seemed to be cozying up to Callie.

Meredith waved her hand. "I don't see Callie and Ethan having anything more than a working relationship," she said.

I turned to her and raised my eyebrows. "How would you even know? You barely know Ethan."

Meredith looked directly at me, and a small smile tipped the corner of her mouth. "Because I've seen the way he looks at you," she said.

"Um, what?"

"Oh yeah," Frankie said, grinning evilly. "I saw the way he looked at her too. He definitely has a thing for our dear Lady Sophia."

"No, we're just friends," I argued. "It's not like that between us." *Even if I wanted it to be*, my brain added silently.

"He wasn't looking at you as just a friend," Elena said.

"Yeah, that definitely wasn't a 'friend' look," Frankie agreed.

"He's in love with you," Athena said in her dreamy way.

Athena was always looking at things through a soft-focus

lens, so I put little stock in her pronouncement, even if it made my breath hitch.

"Hardly," I said, taking another gulp of wine. "He's only here for a short time and I'm just being a good host by showing him around."

"A good host?" Meredith said with a quirked eyebrow. "Putting your guests to work is being a good host? Maybe I should try that."

I rolled my eyes. "You know very well he volunteered," I snapped. "I told him no but he wouldn't listen and you all encouraged him."

"Mm hm," Meredith hummed, sipping her drink.

Frankie winked at me and Athena looked over at me with hearts in her eyes, and my stomach rolled over. Yes, I liked Ethan, and he liked me but that didn't mean anything could come of it. I'd gone over these arguments ad nauseam, and I hadn't yet found a solution. I couldn't go with Ethan when he left, and I would never ask him to stay. We were at an impasse, no matter how much I wanted a different ending to our story.

"It doesn't matter, anyway," I said. "He's only here temporarily."

"I'm sure we could make room for him here in our court," Meredith said. "I like the way he has been working with the staff. He's very knowledgeable and polite and gets on great with everyone. Even Cirillo likes him, which in my opinion, is the highest praise. I know he's a duke..." Meredith hesitated as if she was waiting for me to correct her, but when I didn't, she went on. "But maybe he would be interested in making a move to Kalopsia permanent?"

Did she know how much she was breaking my heart right now? Meredith was saying all the right things, if Ethan really was a duke. It wasn't unusual for titled peers to marry into other courts—which is for sure what she was hinting at—but Ethan wasn't a peer and I couldn't imagine she would be quite so welcoming if she knew the truth.

"I don't think he's interested in staying," I said, trying to keep the sadness out of my voice, but if the way Frankie was looking at me was any sign, I wasn't doing a very good job of it.

"Maybe if I spoke to him," Meredith said and there was something cunning in her gaze. "Maybe if I asked him if he would consider it—"

"No," I said, cutting her off. "Ah, no, I don't think so," I said, trying for more casual and failing miserably. "I'm pretty sure he has his heart set on leaving."

I felt bad about outright lying to Meredith...not that I was lying about him wanting to leave. As far as I knew, Ethan really did have his heart set on leaving, but I felt bad about continuing to deceive her about Ethan's true identity. It was only for another couple of weeks, but still, I was suffering from a severe attack of the guilts. I wished I could tell her the whole sordid tale and ask her advice because I really did have feelings for Ethan that I knew wouldn't just disappear when he left. Meredith and Jamie had their own fraught romantic tale, as did Frankie and Lucas, so I knew they would understand, but coming clean would mean admitting I'd lied and I didn't want to do that. I didn't want them to see that side of me. I'd carefully crafted my perfect persona, and I was loath to let Meredith—a person I admired greatly—see behind the curtain and realise I wasn't as perfect as I pretended to be. If Meredith knew about the lie, it would destroy her perception of me. Perception was everything, as had been drilled into me my whole life. Without that perfect shell surrounding me, I was nothing.

"Callie told me you've been mentoring some the village ladies," Frankie said, changing the subject, much to my relief.

"I don't know if I'd call it mentoring," I said. "But I have been helping them in my own way."

Frankie knocked her shoulder into mine companionably. "Didn't I tell you there was more to you than just what you show on social media?"

"I don't know about that," I said with a shrug. "I am, after all, only showing them the same things I post on Instagram."

"Pfft," Meredith said. "You are helping those women find their own style and reach their potential. You need to have more confidence in your abilities. We wouldn't have employed you to look after our social media platforms if we didn't think you could do the job."

I shrugged, not used to the compliment. "I've never really felt like my particular brand of skill sets could have any real world applications. I just make things look pretty."

"You are doing more than just making those women look pretty. You're giving them confidence in themselves," Frankie said.

"Don't discount the impact you're having," Elena said in a rare show of support.

My cheeks flushed and I mumbled something unintelligible before taking another sip of my drink. I did feel proud of myself and the relationships I was building with the women from the village. I just didn't think anyone else had noticed or appreciated it.

CHAPTER 15

Sophia

A very unladylike squeal came from the queen as a cavalcade of cars drove into the palace's courtyard. The Queen of Merveille and her retinue had arrived.

Meredith, Jamie, and the rest of the Kabiero royal court stood on the steps of the palace, ready and waiting to greet the visiting monarch. Meredith could hardly keep her happiness contained, and even Jamie had a broad, bright smile on his face. I didn't think I'd ever seen the king quite so happy before— except, of course, when he was looking at his wife.

The cars pulled to a stop and Meredith—propriety be damned—ran down the steps to greet Queen Alyssa. The visiting queen clung to Meredith with as much desperation as Meredith clung to her. I knew about their close friendship, but I hadn't expected it to be so...effusive, especially when two queens were involved.

Jamie descended the stairs to greet the queen and her husband, Prince Will. Surprisingly, Jamie also shook the hands of several of the security team that had accompanied the royals. Of course I'd known he'd served in Queen Alyssa's royal guard, but it was still strange to see the king behave so familiarly with them. He always appeared so stoic and controlled around the palace. I understood the need for him to appear strong and confident after the troubles that had assailed Kalopsia during the occupation, but it was still a shock to see him so differently.

I wasn't the only one noticing, either. The other members of the court—namely Dorian and Elena—seemed just as surprised as me. Although Frankie, of course, took it in her stride.

Meredith cooed loudly as the young princess and prince—still just babies—were presented. The twins looked about curiously and smiled broadly, although the little boy seemed a bit more serious than his sister.

Meredith let out another squeal before running toward another man alighting from a car and jumped into his arms...or as much as she could, considering she was pregnant.

"Freddie!" Meredith squealed.

I had met the queen's brother, Lord Frédéric, previously, but it had been a while since he and his wife, Lady Alexandria, had visited. They also had a small child. The little girl with fiery red hair was younger than the twin princess and prince, but she already looked like she would be a handful.

Meredith plucked her niece from Lady Alexandra's arms and twirled her around, causing delighted giggles to erupt from the girl.

"Come and meet my court," Jamie said to the queen.

We all stood a little straighter, and I smoothed my dress and hair as the queen and her family approached us.

Jamie brought the queen down the line, introducing each member. The members bowed or curtsied in turn. Frankie's curtsey was still awful and I could see the queen hold in a laugh as they were introduced.

I took a breath and curtsied when my turn came. My curtsey may not have been as flawless as Elena's, but it was perfectly adequate.

"It's lovely to meet you, Sophia," the queen said. "Meredith has told me so much about you all I feel like I already know you."

"She speaks very fondly of you, as well," I replied.

The queen moved on to greet the senior staff of the palace and then we met each of Alyssa's court. There were a few more children and two other pregnant couples. I knew all this, of course. I'd assigned their rooms and knew each of the visiting royals from the bios I'd studied even before Jamie reclaimed his throne. My mother made sure I knew who every significant titled person was within Europe and beyond.

"Sophia," Meredith said, catching my arm as we all turned to troupe back into the palace. "I want you to get to know Lord Chancellor Dominique and his wife, Lady Priscilla," she said. "Also Lady Jeanette. I think they would be a great help to you. You might even consider introducing Lord Ethan to them." The last was said with a not-so-subtle wink and elbow nudge.

I didn't roll my eyes, even if I wanted to. I nodded and smiled as she moved away to slip her arm through Alyssa's. They bent their heads together like they were sharing a secret, and I wished I had a girlfriend I was as close to as that. Frankie was my best friend, but we'd only known each other less than a year, and the kind of companionship that existed between the two queens could only be achieved by spending years together.

Alyssa and Meredith grew up together, and back then Meredith had been her companion and personal guard. It made me sad that such a close friendship with someone my own age had never been fostered by my parents. They saw every other noble as potential competition, and they had trained me to see them that way too. I wasn't even that close with my siblings.

"Lady Sophia," a deep voice spoke from beside me.

"Lord Chancellor," I replied with a nod of my head. "Is there something I can assist you with?"

He smiled and shook his head. "No, but I wanted to speak with you. Meredith said you have been put in the position of event planner since the palace has not yet appointed a Lord Chamberlain. I wanted to let you know that if you have any questions, I would be happy to answer them."

I felt my cheeks warm. "Thank you," I replied, hoping his offer of assistance didn't mean that Meredith thought I was mucking everything up.

As if he could read my mind, his face softened. "Meredith has had nothing but high praise for you and your team. If anything, I was hoping myself or my wife might ease your mind a little."

I relaxed and smiled genuinely at Lord Dom. "I would appreciate that," I replied.

"Wonderful," he said. "Maybe we could speak during the afternoon tea this afternoon."

The visiting court had been allotted some time to rest and refresh before an informal garden tea that afternoon.

"That would be perfect." I replied.

I DIDN'T GET to rest, but then I hadn't just travelled halfway across the continent either.

Once the visiting court was settled in their rooms and served some light refreshments in their suites, I made my way down to first my office to grab my iPad, and then down to the kitchens to check on preparations.

I expected to walk into chaos, but instead found the staff working together like a well-oiled machine, with Ethan standing at the helm.

I took a moment just to admire him. He was so...*in charge*. He had everything under control and the staff looked to him as their captain.

He was too good for that steward position he wanted. He was deserving of a position much higher, with far more responsibility than a steward on a super yacht. He was good enough even to take on the position of Lord Chamberlain, just as Meredith had been unsubtly hinting at.

If only he wanted to stay.

If only working here in the palace would be enough for him, but I doubted it would be. He had an incurable case of wanderlust. He wouldn't be happy staying in one place, and daydreaming about it would only make his leaving that much harder to deal with.

I didn't interrupt him. He had everything well in hand, and there were other things I could check up on.

I scurried out of the kitchens and headed up to the function room, where the afternoon tea would be held. It wasn't as large as the ballroom or the formal dining room, but it was still large. It opened out onto one of the garden terraces that had a view of not only the Aegean Sea, but also a sliver of the island as well.

It was only an informal gathering with the guest list being

only the Kabiero court and the Mervielle court, but that meant, combined, there were twenty-six guests, not including the children and their attendants.

I found Callie directing her workers as they put the finishing touches on the decor. Here again was another person who knew who she was and was confident in her skills and abilities, and I once again felt superfluous.

I'd always known my place in the world. I was the pretty porcelain milk jug on the shelf that people looked at and admired but was not really useful. Sure, I made a tea set look good, but a milk jug was either never quite big enough to serve everyone's needs or was too big and was a waste. A milk jug looked pretty sitting on a silver tray, complimenting the sugar bowl and giving a certain air of sophistication to the other pieces on the tray, but it was really quite useless.

Not unlike how I felt.

It hadn't bothered me before. I was happy to be the milk jug, if that meant I was included. Everyone ooh and ahhed over the little milk jug and I wasn't opposed to people admiring me.

Now though, as I was thrust into the world of working royals, I felt even more useless. Why couldn't I have been a teapot? Or even a teacup? Even a saucer had a job more important than the milk jug. It might not be as pretty as the milk jug, but it was useful, and me? I wasn't useful at all.

I looked again at Callie and decided she didn't need my help. Callie knew exactly what she was doing, and I would only get in her way.

I turned on my heel and walked away, heading for my office. I would need to head up to my suite soon and get ready, but I had some time to kill.

Before I could make my escape, one of the village women stopped me.

"Lady Sophia," she said with a passable curtsey.

"Helena," I replied with a smile. "Everything looks amazing."

Helena smiled shyly and then looked over her shoulder to where a few of the other women had gathered. They all came closer and gathered around me.

"We wanted to thank you," Helena said, speaking for the group.

"Thank me? For what?"

"For the opportunity to work here in the palace and for all you've done to help us."

I felt my cheeks warm and looked down, clearing my throat, hoping they wouldn't notice my discomfort. "I didn't do anything," I said. "Not really."

"But you did," Helena insisted. "You've taught us so much and we're all so grateful."

"My Instagram following is up by two hundred percent," another woman, Karissa, said.

"And there's no way any of us could be here in the palace, doing this, if not for all the help you've given us."

"You have all worked hard," I said, speaking the truth. These women had been eager participants in the impromptu classes I'd held at Callie's insistence. "Your success is solely due to your dedication."

"Yes, but without you to teach us, none of us would have known where to even start," Helena said.

I didn't know what to say. I was proud of the way these women had taken control of their lives, but I couldn't take credit for what they had achieved. I'd barely done anything, really. A few pointers about how to style a photo and how to dress for a job interview and how to curtsey and how to address the different ranks of peers. These were things I'd grown up learning and it felt disingenuous to accept praise for things so inconsequential.

I smiled at the women. "I'm so glad things are going well for you all," I said, not wanting to offend them. Even if I couldn't comfortably accept their gratitude, I was touched that they wanted to offer it to me. "If you have any questions or need any help with anything, please come to me. I'll do whatever I can to help."

I said goodbye and scurried off, a weird mix of embarrassment and pride warring inside me.

Locked away in my office, I scrolled through Instagram. I had been obsessed with the social media platform up until a few weeks ago. It was part of my job, and I still scheduled posts to the palace account, but my personal account had dropped off. I scrolled through it now, wincing at the photos of Nico and his lady-love. I wasn't jealous. I hadn't loved Nico. I'd barely liked him—especially toward the end—but I'd felt a sense of accomplishment as I saw him blossom from the shy wallflower into a stylish influencer. I'd felt the same thing working with Ethan, but unlike Nico, Ethan had surpassed what I could teach him. I should probably feel proud of that, but it didn't feel like I'd actually done anything. Ethan had only needed room to grow. I'd given him the right soil, and he'd thrived without me doing much at all.

The same with the group of women Callie had asked me to mentor. All they'd needed was a little bit of direction and some encouragement and they'd flourished. I felt like an imposter, especially when they looked at me with such admiration. Anyone could have done what I'd done for them. I felt guilty for feeling proud of them and what they achieved. They weren't my achievements, after all. Despite the claims I'd made to Frankie about being a fairy godmother who could turn a pumpkin into a prince, it hardly felt like something I should be thanked or congratulated for.

I closed out of the app and tossed my phone on the desk. Leaning back in my chair, I closed my eyes and gave myself one minute only to feel bad for myself. Who was I to sulk when everything I had ever wanted in my life and been handed to me? There were people out there who had to bend and scrape for everything and here I was whining because I didn't feel useful.

My job might not seem useful, but I was responsible for the image of the palace and the king and queen. That was an enormous responsibility, and I was good at my job. No, I was *great* at my job. I should not be sitting in my plush office complaining because I was feeling the thinness of my life. And my life did feel thin, almost transparent. Ethan had a rich tapestry weaving through his life. So did Callie, not that I knew much about her. My life, by comparison, was like looking at a sun catcher. In the right light, I sparkled, but without the sun, I was nothing special.

Phew. I was full of all the metaphors in my melancholia.

I stood and shook the despondency from my body. I needed to snap out of it. I had to sparkle this afternoon and I couldn't do it with this malaise hanging over me.

"You look lovely."

My breath stalled in my chest as I turned to look at Ethan.

I'd seen him walk into the room, but I hadn't noticed when he snuck up behind me. Okay, he didn't 'sneak' but I was doing my best to avoid him and hadn't been paying attention to what was going on behind me.

"T-Thank you," I stammered, and then smiled tremulously.

"You're avoiding me again," he said, looking down at me with a tight smile.

"No," I denied—lied. "I just didn't want to get in your way. You've been busy."

"I have," he replied with a nod. "But I always have time for you, Sophia."

He took my hand and lifted it to his lips, brushing a soft kiss on my skin.

I swallowed thickly. "You've done a magnificent job," I said, dragging my eyes away from him to take in the garden tea.

There was a long buffet table piled high with treats—both savoury and sweet. There was another table set with an assortment of teas and several single-cup teapots waiting to be filled as each person made their request.

"Thank you," he said with a hint of a grin. "But I had help... actually, I hardly did anything."

"Corralling Cirillo and Chef Diakos is not 'doing hardly anything,'" I said, turning to him. I reached out to rest my hand on his suited arm. "You are incredible. I saw you, earlier. You looked like you were directing a play or choreographing a ballet. You were in your element."

His smile warmed, and he laid his hand over mine. "I have to say, I have enjoyed these last few weeks more than I expected to," he said. "Apart from the part where you kept me locked up for fear of embarrassing you."

"I did not," I scoffed, but he laughed, his eyes sparkling. "Ethan, I—"

"Lady Sophia," Lord Dominique said, approaching us with his wife on his arm. "This is wonderful."

"Thank you," I said, "but I can't take credit for it. Lord Ethan has done all the heavy lifting." I turned to Ethan. "Lord Ethan, allow me to introduce Lord Chancellor Dominique Furore, and Lady Priscilla Furore. They are members of the Merveille royal court. Lord Dominique, Lady Priscilla, this is Lord Ethan. He has been helping me out with all the preparations in lieu of a Lord Chamberlain."

Dom reached out his hand and shook Ethan's, and then Priscilla did the same. I'd omitted giving Ethan's last name because...well because this couple knew every single royal family on the continent and if I said the wrong name, they would know we were lying. I swallowed and hoped my palms weren't sweating. Why hadn't I thought this through?

"I don't envy you the job," Priscilla said with a smile.

Dom scoffed. "How can you say such a thing when we both do it on a daily basis?"

Priscilla smiled at her husband, placing her hand on her barely there baby bump. "Yes, *we* do it. Together. Poor Sophia has had to do it on her own."

"Oh no, not really," I said. "I've hardly done anything. It's all Ethan and Callie."

"Don't listen to her," Ethan said. "Without Sophia we would be a rudderless ship."

I blushed, feeling very undeserving of his words.

"I know it is a little late in the game, but if you need any help for the final preparations, don't hesitate to talk to us," Dom said. "Seating arrangements are Priscilla's specialty."

"Really?" I asked, not meaning to speak.

Priscilla smiled and nodded. "I have quite intimate experience with seating tricky peers," she said.

I bit my lip, and Priscilla took my hand. "Find me tomorrow morning and I'll spend some time with you."

"That would be amazing," I said. "I thought I knew all the ins and outs of the peers but…it would be wonderful to get another person's opinion."

"It's a date then. After breakfast?"

While I made arrangements to meet with Priscilla, Ethan and Dom drifted off together, deep in conversation.

"It looks like we lost them," Priscilla said, smiling fondly after her husband. "How about we get some tea and one of those delicious-looking cakes? I know Jeanette was looking forward to chatting with you. She follows your Instagram feed and has questions."

"Of course," I said, crossing the room with Lady Priscilla.

We got our tea and a plate of cakes and joined a circle of comfy chairs where Lady Jeanette was sitting with her baby in her arms.

"Oh, Lady Sophia," Lady Jeanette said. "I'm so glad you came over. I have so much I want to talk to you about."

"Really?" I asked, before sipping my tea.

"Oh, yes. I am such a fan of your social media. Teach me your way, oh wise one," she said with a chuckle.

"Oh wow," I replied, taken aback. "I follow you as well. In fact, I modelled our social media branding after the one you built for the Merveille royal family. You were such an inspiration."

Jeanette blushed prettily, her peaches and cream skin colouring delicately. "I honestly didn't know what I was doing when I started. I had a background in PR and that was about it. But you've built an amazing platform. I know Meredith is thrilled with your work. Tell me, how do you take such gorgeous photos?"

"It's all in the lighting," I replied. "Lighting and styling."

I relaxed as we chatted. I could talk social media stats and strategies until the cows came home, and talking with someone who also took it as seriously as I did felt good. Most people rolled their eyes at me when I started on about it all, but Jeanette was an avid listener and even gave me some ideas I hadn't thought of. I'd been feeling so untethered by being surrounded by so many capable people, but speaking with Jeanette and even Priscilla, had me starting to believe that maybe I wasn't as redundant as I thought. I was good at my job, even if I had moments of self-doubt.

It wasn't long before Lady Margaret and Lady Savannah joined us. I could see just how close these women were, and I envied them. I hoped that one day I would have relationships with the other ladies-in-waiting here in Kalopsia, as these women had. I hadn't realised just how important friendships were until I looked around and realised I didn't have any.

Frankie plopped down beside me and grinned. A little reminder that maybe I did have a little taste of what these women had. I took Frankie's hand and squeezed it, and she squeezed back.

CHAPTER 16

Ethan

There was a lot riding on tonight. Not the ball. That was still a couple of days away. No, tonight was the formal banquet, and it was also the first time I would meet Sophia's parents. I had to make a good showing, that's what the last few weeks had been about.

I allowed Toby to fuss with my tuxedo and my tie and my hair. I was once again wearing the cufflinks Sophia had given me, as well as the aftershave she bought. I didn't know what it said about me that I liked wearing the things she picked for me. I did know that I liked Sophia. I liked her more and more as the days went on, and I found myself trying to make excuses to stay in Kalopsia.

I'd spent a lot of time talking to the Lord Chancellor at the garden tea a week ago and I could see myself in a similar role. I'd found a satisfaction in working at the palace, a satisfaction

I'd never felt before. I enjoyed the work. I liked the staff, and it meant I could stay with Sophia.

Except…it also meant coming clean to the king and queen. I would have to reveal my true identity if I was to seek employment with them, and I didn't think that would go over too well. How would they feel when—*if*—they found out that I'd been lying this whole time? What would they think if they found out I was a nobody from Australia who'd been travelling the world and working in bars for the last decade? They certainly wouldn't be opening their arms or their home to me. I would be lucky if I didn't get away without some sort of legal issue. I'd met Danika, the head of security, and I didn't think she would be very nice to me if she found out who I really was.

None of them would be.

I just had to look to Dorian to see how I would be treated if they knew the truth.

I huffed out a sigh and brushed Toby away. I just had to get through the banquet and then the ball, and then I could leave. I hadn't been doing much research on my next place of employment—the job at the palace had been keeping me too busy—but I was pretty sure Sophia wouldn't kick me out of the villa immediately. I'm sure she would give me a grace period, and if she didn't, then I had enough money saved to get a hotel until I could find a job.

With a nod to Toby, I left the room. I ignored the sick feeling in my stomach. I'd managed to keep up the ruse with Dom, and he seemed to know everyone there was to know in the nobility of Europe. If anyone was going to out me, it would have been him or his wife.

Which meant, if I could fool Dom—and I hated to do so,

considering how nice he'd been to me—then I could fool Sophia's parents, too.

Francis was waiting for me with the car out the front of the villa, and I nodded to him as I climbed inside. I was going to be a bit early, but I wanted to check in with Cirillo before I went into the banquet. If there were any last-minute crises, I could try to sort them out before the palace was inundated with peers.

I didn't go to the main entrance. I had Francis drop me by the servants' entrance and went straight into the scullery area. The staff scurried about, but made time to nod and smile at me. No one seemed to be in panic mode, so I hoped that meant everything was going well.

I cut through the hall and found Cirillo's office, but he wasn't there. I hoped he hadn't gone to the kitchen to hound Chef Diakos. I'd managed to broker a tenuous truce between the two hot-tempered staff members, and the last thing we needed tonight was for them to break the treaty.

Holding my breath, I stepped into the kitchen. Cirillo was indeed in the kitchen, but Chef wasn't yelling at him. It seemed as if Cirillo was actually helping—not with cooking, naturally, but with intercepting the other chefs and wait staff to answer their questions so they wouldn't have to bother Chef Diakos. I didn't know that it was his job to do so, but I wasn't about to interrupt when it seemed to work.

Cirillo caught my gaze and nodded.

"All good?" I asked.

"Yes," he replied after a look at Chef.

Chef nodded, but her face remained stoic, her mouth a thin line as she cut herbs with the speed and precision I could never hope to achieve.

I cocked my eyebrow to see her doing something one of the other chefs could do, and Cirillo shrugged.

"It relaxes her," he said. "Helps her focus."

"Okay," I replied. "Well, if you don't need me, I'll do my last walk through and check everything is ready."

Cirillo nodded again, but he was already turning away to listen to something one of the line chefs was saying.

I smiled as I left. It was extremely satisfying seeing the kitchen working so well. I couldn't take the credit for it. Every member of the palace staff was dedicated and skilled, but I did like to think I played a small part in making the working relationship between the majordomo and the chef better.

"Great minds think alike."

I turned and I'm pretty sure my jaw unhinged as I saw Sophia standing in the doorway of the dining room. She wore a floor-length gown in a pale beige-pink. It was made of layers and layers of some sort of soft, floaty material that swished around her legs as she walked. The bodice wrapped around her torso in multiple layers, leaving her shoulders bare. Her hair was pinned up loosely, leaving soft curls to frame her face, and her lips were painted pale pink to match her dress.

She looked…I swallowed…she looked amazing.

"Wow," I said.

Sophia smiled shyly, her cheeks flushing. "Wow, yourself," she said, stepping toward me.

I tore my gaze from her to look around the dining room. "I was, ah, I was just checking everything was, ah…" I trailed off as she came to stand beside me. I couldn't concentrate with her so close.

"Me too," she replied with a smile. "It looks great. You did a magnificent job."

I shook my head. "I had nothing to do with this," I said. "This was all Callie."

Sophia looked away from me. "You and Callie have been spending a lot of time together," she said softly.

I put a hand on her arm, and she turned to look at me. "We've been working together. That's all."

She searched my eyes for a moment before exhaling and dropping her head again. I was going to say something else, but before I could, she took another breath and straightened her shoulders, beaming a smile at me.

"It's time you met my parents."

I felt the blood drain from my face. "Now?"

"Now is the perfect time," Sophia said. "Before everyone else arrives. They'll be more...approachable without the rest of the peerage around."

I straightened my own shoulders and sucked in a fortifying breath. "Okay," I said, offering her my arm.

Sophia hooked her arm through mine and we exited the dining room.

"Are your parents staying here in the palace?" I asked with a frown. I hadn't actually thought much about where her parents would stay while in Kalopsia. Sophia had said nothing about them staying at the villa.

"No, they have their own place nearby, but they came early to see me and..." Sophia huffed out a breath. "They wanted to see if they could grab some time with the king before everyone else arrived and monopolised his time.

They're hoping to revive their diplomatic roles, but in France."

"Ah," I said with a nod. "They thought doing it tonight would be a good idea? Wouldn't the king be more amenable to the suggestion when he wasn't entertaining a court from another monarchy?"

"I think they hoped that having the Queen of Merveille here would help their cause somehow," she replied. "I really don't know what goes on in their heads sometimes."

We paused before the closed doors of the meeting room, where everyone would gather before the banquet. A footman stood sentry and Sophia held up her hand to stop him from opening the door.

She turned to me. "Are you ready for this?"

I nodded. "Yes," I answered confidently.

"Okay, good," Sophia said, blowing out a slow breath.

She nodded to the footman, and he opened the doors. We stepped into a large room filled with couches arranged in cosy conversational areas. A long bar ran along one wall and was manned with formally attired bar staff, and behind them glittered shelves of alcohol.

There were a few people milling around; networking, I assumed.

"They're over there." Sophia motioned with her head toward a smartly dressed couple, who I recognised from the photographs I'd studied.

"Mother. Father," Sophia said when we approached. "I'd like you to meet Lord Ethan."

I gave them my most charming smile and held out my hand to Sophia's father.

"Mr. Dellis," I said, shaking his hand. "Mrs. Dellis," I said as I offered my hand to her, but instead of shaking my hand like I had assumed, she placed her hand in mine in such a way as if I was to kiss her hand. I had never done that before in my life. It was not something a boy from Oz did. Nevertheless, after a fraction of hesitation, I bowed my head and brushed my lips lightly across the back of her hand. It was weird.

I straightened and smiled. "It's so lovely to meet you. Lady Sophia has told me so much about you."

"Really?" Mrs. Dellis replied. "She hasn't told us anything about you."

It was meant to be an insult, but I let it roll off my back. I smiled and chuckled, as I imagined Dorian would do in such a situation. "Yes, she has been restricted from saying too much with the NDA and all."

Mrs. Dellis' eyebrows popped. It had been a gamble lying like that, but I hoped it sounding intriguing to someone like Sophia's mother.

"Lord Ethan has been staying at the villa," Sophia said.

This time it was Sophia's father who raised his eyebrows. "The villa? Are you here for business or pleasure, Lord Ethan?"

"A little bit of both," I answered vaguely. "I'm here unofficially, but there is a lot to like about this country." I couldn't help looking at Sophia when I said that.

"And will you be staying long?" Mrs. Dellis said, her voice honey smooth as her eyes sized me up.

"Not as long as I would've liked," I replied, sticking to the script instead of blurting out that I would stay indefinitely. I still didn't know when I would leave, but I was leaning toward extending my stay for as long as I could.

"Then it's lucky we got to meet you," Mrs. Dellis said, stepping forward and linking her arm through my free one. "Why don't you get me a drink and tell me all about yourself. If our lovely Sophia hasn't been able to say much, surely you can."

"Mother," Sophia hissed.

"It's fine, dear," Mrs. Dellis said. "I'm sure Lord Ethan wouldn't mind telling me a bit about himself since he has been spending so much time with you."

Mrs. Dellis led me toward the bar. "Now, Lord Ethan, tell me where you call home. Your accent is…interesting."

"I've travelled extensively," I replied. "Sometimes it feels like I don't have a fixed address." Not a lie. "But tell me more about you. Sophia tells me you were ambassadors. That must have been fascinating and very rewarding work."

If I could get Sophia's mother to talk more about herself, then I might avoid an interrogation. That was the plan, anyway.

"YOU DID WELL," Sophia said as we walked out onto the balcony.

The banquet was done, and all the visitors had gone. Sophia and I stayed back to direct the pack-up crew and make sure everything was sorted in the scullery. The next few days would be busy as we prepared for the ball and then…and then my time would be up.

"I got lucky," I replied.

"It was certainly an inspired idea to get my mother to talk about herself," Sophia said with a small grin. "She's her own favourite subject."

I smirked. Mrs. Dellis really did like to talk about herself, but whether or not I'd achieved the goal we set out with— namely, convincing everyone I was a duke—I wasn't sure. I was still waiting for someone to knock on the door of the villa and accuse me of being an imposter.

"I suppose we'll find out over the next couple of days," I said. "If your parents are going to expose me, it will be before the ball, right? They won't want to cause a scene."

We reached the edge of the balcony, and Sophia turned so her back was leaning against the balustrade.

"You're right," she said. "But I don't think you have anything to worry about. If my father had suspected anything he would have said something to me."

"So we've achieved our goal, then," I said, leaning on my elbows and looking out at the night. "You got your parents to believe I'm a duke and proved to Frankie that you're a fairy godmother."

Sophia didn't reply for a long moment. "I suppose we did," she replied quietly.

I wanted to turn and look at her. I wanted to do more than just look at her, but...I didn't. I couldn't. I was afraid that if I did, I would never let go, and as much as I wanted to stay, Sophia had never once asked me to. I didn't know what that meant. Was she waiting for me to say something? Was she waiting for me to tell her I wanted to stay?

What was I waiting for? I'd decided, so why was I still holding back?

I straightened and turned to her. The words were on the tip of my tongue. I would tell her, ask her if she wanted me to stay.

I swallowed. I'd never wanted to stay anywhere before. My feet were always itching to go, to travel to a new place, to experience a new thing. But things were different now. Kalopsia and gotten under my skin...or maybe it was Sophia who had gotten under my skin. Who was I trying to kid? Of course it was Sophia. Of course she was the reason I wanted to stay.

I lifted my hand and tucked a stray strand of hair behind her ear. We'd been here before, maybe not in this very spot, but we'd had moments like this before. Moments that were heavy with potential. I felt like I was in the door of an airplane just waiting to jump out and free fall. Yes, I'd sky dived before, so I knew exactly how both terrifying and exhilarating that moment could be.

"Sophia, I—"

"I suppose I should now turn my talents toward finding you a job," she said, pulling away from me.

"What?"

"You know? A job on a super yacht? That was the whole point of this, right? That was what you wanted? Why you agreed to this ridiculous bet? You've held up your end of the bargain and now it's my turn to do the same."

"Sophia, I—"

"I can't ask my parents, obviously," she said, taking a few steps away from me.

She lifted her hand to tap on her lip with her finger. Her face turned away from me. She was putting space between us, and more than just physical space. Had I read this entire situation wrong? She'd told me she liked me. We'd shared touches and kisses and…and I'd thought we'd also shared ourselves. But maybe it had been one-sided all along?

"Or anybody who was at the banquet tonight," she said.

I sighed. "Or anyone coming to the ball," I added, accepting the truth.

She just wasn't that into me. I was good for a short time, a bit of a lark, a rich girl slumming it with a tourist. Wasn't that what I'd thought when Sophia and Frankie first approached me? Spending time with her, living in the lap of luxury, pretending to be a duke...I'd forgotten who I was and where I came from. I'd begun to believe my own press. I'd almost believed the con. Which was stupid. I wasn't a duke, and I barely had two cents to rub together. I lived pay check to pay check, and I changed jobs almost as often as I changed my underwear. I hadn't stayed in one place longer than a year since I'd left Australia and here I was, contemplating giving up my wanderlust for a woman who didn't even want me to stay.

"It's okay," I said, straightening my jacket and tugging on my cuffs as I'd seen Dorian do a hundred times or more. "If you could just write me a reference, then I'm sure it will go a long way to opening some doors for me. Don't worry about me, I'll be fine. I've been doing this a long time."

She turned and looked at me finally. I couldn't decipher the look on her face. If I thought she was into me, I would think there was a flash of hurt, but that couldn't be right because I knew. I knew she wouldn't even think twice about me once I left. And if she did think of me, it definitely wouldn't be the way I would think of her. It definitely wouldn't be with yearning and the keen regret at having lost something that I never really had in the first place.

"I should go," I said. "It's late."

Sophia opened her mouth to say something, but then closed it without speaking. She nodded, and I turned and walked away. I wanted to look back to see if she watched me go, but I'd been rejected enough tonight, and I didn't want to risk seeing a look of indifference on her face.

I would get over her.

Eventually.

CHAPTER 17

Ethan

"*L*ady Sophia is here," Toby said, coming into the bedroom where I was psyching myself up.

The ball was tonight. Everything we had been working for came down to tonight. As far as Sophia was concerned, we'd already achieved our goal, and I suppose we had. Even so, tonight was the last hurdle. And closure.

Tonight was the last night I would see Sophia. I already had plans. Unexpected plans, but plans nonetheless. Plans I wanted. Plans I'd strived for. I'd finally gotten that job on a super yacht and we were to set sail in a couple of days. My bags were packed and I would move out of the villa first thing in the morning.

It was what I wanted, and yet...

"My lord?" Toby prompted.

"Of course," I replied with a tight smile.

I turned and stepped toward the valet, holding out my hand. "Thank you, Toby. Thank you for everything."

Toby lowered his head in a nod of acknowledgement. "It has been an honour, my lord," he replied, shaking my hand.

I took a deep breath and straightened my shoulders. "Wish me luck," I said.

"You don't need luck, my lord," Toby said.

With one last nod, I left the bedroom and headed toward the sitting room, where I knew Sophia waited for me. I shook off the melancholy and plastered a charming smile on my face, channelling Dorian. I would need to be a Dorian-clone to get through tonight, and not just so I could fool all the peers assembled for the ball. I needed his stoic coldness to stave off my own emotions. I couldn't let Sophia see just how much I wanted to stay.

Charles nodded to me before opening the doors to the sitting room, and I sucked in a breath at the sight that waited for me. Sophia looked...magical. She glowed with an aura that took my breath away. She was always beautiful, and never more so when she let the mask drop and I got to see the real her, but tonight...tonight there was something about her that punched me in the gut.

Sophia stood by the window. The sun was setting, and the sky was aglow with washes of pinks and purples and she—seriously, I kid you not—glowed with gold from the dying rays of the sun. I couldn't even say what she was wearing except it was a long gown that left her shoulders bare and her hair was scooped up off her neck and piled artfully on her head.

"Lady Sophia," I said, my voice rough.

She turned slowly, and my breath hitched. She smiled at me

and I could have gotten lost in her eyes in that moment. I wanted to get lost in her. Forever.

"Lord Ethan," she replied, her voice a breathy whisper.

We stood like that, staring at each other across the room, and I once again felt like I was standing on the precipice of something...I just wasn't sure what. Two paths were laid out before me and I had no idea which was the one I should take.

I didn't want this to be our last night together. I didn't want to leave in a few days and sail away on a yacht, even though it was what I'd been working toward all this time. I did not want to be separated from this woman ever again.

I was so sick of pretending. I was sick of pretending that I was a duke, but more than that, I was sick and tired of pretending not to be completely and totally in love with Sophia. I wanted her to know how I really felt, regardless of whether she felt the same way. The words burned on my tongue. I wanted to blurt them out and damn the consequences. If she didn't feel the same way, then at least I'd spoken my truth and I could leave without the heaviness of them weighing me down.

But that wouldn't be fair to her. At least not if I did it right now before the ball.

Later. After the ball. I would tell her. Lay my heart on the line. I would tell her how I really felt and if she told me she didn't want me to stay, then I would leave and I would go, knowing I hadn't wasted an opportunity. If she asked me to stay, if she told me she wanted me too, I would...I didn't know, but I would figure it out.

"The car is waiting," Charles said, breaking into the suspended moment.

I cleared my throat and stepped forward, offering my arm to Sophia.

"You look exquisite," I murmured.

The corner of her lips turned up in a sweet smile as she looked up at me. "Thank you," she replied.

She slipped her hand into the crook of my elbow and I could feel her touch through the layers of my tuxedo and shirt like a brand...except brand probably wasn't the right words since it didn't hurt.

I breathed in, filling my nose with her delicate scent and making a wish on the first star that appeared out the window. I wasn't one for making wishes, but I was starting to believe in fate. Was it fate that took me all over the world? Was it fate that brought me to Kalopsia? Was it fate that brought me to Sophia? I was beginning to think it was.

THE PALACE WAS LIT up like something from Disneyland (or Disney World...I always got those two mixed up). We joined the line of cars entering the driveway, and I turned to look at Sophia once more. It appeared I would be doing that a lot tonight. I couldn't not look at her and if things didn't go the way I wanted tonight, then I wanted to memorise her face so I would never forget the amazing woman beside me.

She turned to face me and frowned. "Is something wrong?" She asked.

"No, why?"

"You keep looking at me," she said and then her cheeks flushed.

"I am just trying to remember every single part of tonight," I replied truthfully.

She looked down and away, finally turning to look out the

window. "I hope you don't mind that we are arriving with everyone else," she said.

I would have liked to have been onsite early so that I could make sure everything was ready, but Sophia insisted I arrive in the car with everyone else. She even insisted that she come and pick me up. She said it was about making an entrance, making sure everyone saw me as a duke and not as a palace staff member. To be perfectly honest, I didn't mind the whole palace staff member part. I'd felt remarkably at home in the palace working with Cirillo and Chef Diakos. Helping with the preparations for the state visit had fulfilled something in me I hadn't even known I'd been lacking. It was the first time I'd had a job that I wasn't itching to move on from. It was a sad thing to realise I was no longer that person. I no longer had any right to be down amongst the other palace staff. As of earlier that day, my duties had ended, and I had handed over the management of the evening to Cirillo, even as he protested hotly that he was not the person for the job. I assured him he would be fine, and I knew the palace was actively seeking someone to take on the role I had—ever so briefly—held.

Because I was moving on.

Even if I didn't move on, I couldn't apply for the position. That would mean revealing who I really was and then…yeah, that was a can of worms I had no desire to open. There was no way I wanted to put Sophia in a position where she had to admit to lying to the king and queen.

Which left me where? I had determined to bare my heart to Sophia tonight and tell her I wanted to stay, but to what end? Staying would complicate matters, and that was the last thing I wanted to do. I was between the proverbial rock and a hard place. I was damned if I did and damned if I didn't.

Sophia reached for my hand, dragging my thoughts away from the spiral attempting to pull me down.

"We're here," she said moments before the door opened.

One of the palace footmen held out a hand to help her from the car and then she waited for me to alight.

I stood before the palace in all its glittering glory and took a mental snapshot. One day I would write a memoir and I would remember this night fondly. Right now, I felt like I was heading to the gallows.

I smoothed my tuxedo and tugged at my cuffs—the affectation that I'd used to mimic Dorian had now become one of my own tics.

"Stop fussing," Sophia said, slipping her hand through my elbow. "You look amazing and you have nothing to worry about. You have met almost every one of these people before."

"That's a slight exaggeration," I said with a grimace. "I've met probably only a third of them."

She waved her hand in dismissal. "You've met all the important ones. Everyone else is just window dressing."

"Jaded much?" I asked, with a raised eyebrow.

"That's not what I meant, and you know it," she replied. "I just mean, you don't need to impress anyone here. You've already convinced the king and queen, not to mention my own parents. No one else matters."

I took a deep breath and let it out slowly as we climbed the red-carpeted stairs. "You're right," I said. "Dorian wouldn't see these people as anything other than worker ants invited simply to magnify his brilliance."

Sophia giggled softly. "I dare say you're right," she replied, as we approached the doorman standing at the door.

Meredith had decided not to do a receiving line but to

instead have everyone announced as they entered the ballroom. It meant she and Jamie could sit through the entire process, and being as pregnant as she was, nobody disagreed with the decision. It also meant the court was free to arrive with the guests rather than spend the first half of the night standing in a receiving line greeting everyone. No one wanted to do that.

I had already seen the decor, but was once again amazed at how wonderful everything looked. Callie and her team had worked tirelessly to transform the mostly bare palace into something that wouldn't be out of place in any of the monarchies around the world. The Kabiero court may be only newly resurrected, but they were fast regaining respect from the other monarchies around the world. Something that was bolstered by the official visit from the Merveille court.

We stepped up to the ballroom doors and waited for our turn.

"May I present Lady Sophia, Archontissa of Kalon," the crier called. "And Lord Ethan."

I KNEW A BALL MEANT DANCING...OF course it meant that I had to dance and quite honestly; I enjoyed dancing. But I didn't expect to be dancing *the entire night*. And I certainly didn't expect to have my dance card punched by just about every female in the room (okay, I didn't really have a dance card...I think they were outlawed at the turn of the century...maybe not; I don't know; I don't think I even really knew what a dance card was).

I had managed one dance—ONE—with Sophia, and then I was mobbed. Okay, not mobbed because this was a fancy ball at a palace and these people were royalty, or at least royalty-adjacent and they wouldn't do something so crass as mob me BUT I had been handed from one dance partner to another. It wasn't like the women asked me to dance with them; I was simply introduced to one person and of course propriety said I needed to ask them to dance, and then I was introduced to another person, who I again asked to dance, and so on and so forth until the night had nearly ended and I'd barely had two seconds to speak to Sophia, or anyone else for that matter.

If I was a woman and this was the regency era, I'm pretty sure they would have crowned me belle of the ball, or a diamond of the first water (yes, I watched *Bridgerton*, so what?).

It seemed everyone wanted to dance with me, and I wasn't conceited enough to think it was because I was anything exceptional. I knew exactly why everyone was so interested in me. I was an unattached duke of mysterious origin. I was a curiosity.

The music finished, and I bowed to my partner before excusing myself and making my getaway before she could introduce me to anyone else. I needed air and a drink and something to eat and to see Sophia—and not necessarily in that order. I'd only had glimpses of her throughout the night. After our one and only dance, the crowd had swallowed her up, and she appeared to dance as many times as I did and all with different partners.

Jealous? Me? Absolutely. I wanted to be her one and only dance partner, but I could hardly complain when I'd been handed around like a tray of crab puffs. Not that I was complaining. I'd obviously achieved my goal of fooling everyone about my origin. Sophia had godmothered me into a duke, thereby winning her bet with Frankie. I should be happy.

I should be celebrating the triumph, but it didn't feel like much of a victory when it also meant I would be leaving.

I needed to find Sophia. I needed...

There she was. A vision. Standing off to the side looking like she was catching her breath, not dissimilar to me. My feet were moving before I could consciously instruct them to do so. I stepped before her and bowed, holding out my hand.

"May I have this dance?" I asked.

She groaned softly, and I looked up. "My feet are killing me," she hissed.

I grinned. "Same," I whispered back. "But let me have this one dance and then we'll find a place to sit and hide."

"Deal," she replied, putting her hand in mine and letting me lead her to the dance floor.

It was a slow dance, a gentle waltz. I took her in my arms and slowly twirled her before joining the other dancers as they traversed around the dance floor. It felt good to have her in my embrace. The parts of myself that had felt scattered all night snapped back together, and I felt the rightness of it. The rightness of the two of us together.

What had I been thinking? I couldn't walk away. Not now. Not after falling in love for the first time in my life. There was no way I could walk away without at least laying my cards on the table. If that meant going before the king and queen and admitting the truth about everything, then I would do that. I would take the blame entirely and shield Sophia from any consequences, as long as it meant staying by her side.

If she wanted me.

And that was the kicker. I didn't even know if she wanted to be with me. I had no idea if she felt anything remotely like what I felt for her. I was in love with her—even if I didn't even really understand that myself. Could I really let myself believe she loved me back?

Then there was all my baggage—emotional baggage. I'd watched my parents fade, like *actually* fade before my eyes as they stayed in the same place and did the same things and let their lives stagnate. I'd already seen it happening with my brother too, as he also met and married and started a family, never venturing beyond the boundaries of his small life. I didn't want a small life. I didn't want to disappear into the scenery, as I'd seen my family do. I didn't want to become a piece of furniture, bearing the scars of regular wear and tear until eventually I ended up on the rubbish heap. I didn't—

"That's a lot of thinking going on," Sophia said. "Do you really need to concentrate so hard while dancing?"

I took a deep breath and focused on the woman in my arms instead of the anxious thoughts in my head.

"Do you want to get out of here?" I asked.

"God, yes," she replied. "I thought you'd never ask."

I manoeuvred us around the dancers until we could dance ourselves right out the terrace doors. With a soft laugh, Sophia hooked her arm through mine and led me into the gardens. The path was lit with fairy lights and there was a cool breeze coming in off the ocean. We wound our way through the terraces until we came to what I thought of as our place. The little alcove with the amazing view of the sea and a small stone bench where we could sit—where we had sat, where we had kissed for the first time.

Sophia sat with a soft groan. "My feet are on fire," she said as she kicked off the offending footwear.

I sat beside her and leaned back, stretching my legs out in front of me, glad to be off my feet as much as Sophia was.

"The ball is going well, don't you think?" she said, turning to me.

"I couldn't rightly tell you," I said. "I've been too busy dancing."

She laughed softly. "You have been a popular dance partner," she said. "But that's a good thing."

"Is it?" I asked, sitting up and turning to her. This was the moment, wasn't it? We'd achieved our objective and now I could be completely honest with her.

She looked up at me. "What? What do you mean?"

I shrugged, reaching for her hand and twining our fingers together. "It's just…is it really that important if everyone thinks I'm a duke? Would it be so bad if I turned out to be just an ordinary person?"

I was beating around the bush, but I really wanted Sophia to be on the same page. I wanted her to want me to stay and I wanted her to tell me she wanted me to stay without me having to spell it out to her.

"What are you saying, Ethan," she asked, her voice barely above a whisper. Her eyes searched mine as if she was looking for the meaning behind my words. What was she hoping to find?

"I'm asking if it would be so bad for me not to be who everyone thinks I am," I repeated. "You said your parents like me…would they really care so much if I wasn't a duke?"

She searched my eyes again. "I don't understand what you're saying," she said again, her fingers gripping mine.

"I'm saying I—"

"Sophia? Is that you?"

Sophia pulled her hands from mine, and we both turned to see her mother approach. "Oh, I'm so glad I found you. Your father and I haven't had any chance to speak with you tonight. Come, walk with me."

Sophia shot me a quick, apologetic look before slipping her shoes back on and standing. I watched, the words once more unspoken on my tongue, as she walked away.

CHAPTER 18

Sophia

I didn't look back. I wanted to, but I didn't because I wasn't sure what I would see if I did.

We were having a moment...weren't we? I thought we were. I thought maybe Ethan was about to tell me he wanted everyone to know the truth—which should have freaked me right out, but didn't because I thought he was going to say he wanted everyone to know who he really was so he and I could be together.

Or was I just kidding myself?

But what other reason was there for him saying those things or even suggesting that it wouldn't be so bad if people knew the truth?

I think we both knew that it wouldn't be as easy as he was suggesting, but that he was even suggesting it was...well, I didn't even know what it was or what it meant.

"You and Lord Ethan seemed to be getting cosy," my mother said as she walked me toward a different part of the terrace gardens. "Is there something you want to tell me?"

"I'm sure I don't know what you mean," I replied, my heart pounding.

Either my mother knew the truth, and that was why she was dragging me away, or…or what? My head was too muddled to even think of another reason she would interrupt what I thought was going to be a pivotal conversation.

Mother sniffed. "Come now, Sophia. I've heard all about the close working relationship you have developed with Lord Ethan since he has been helping with the preparations for the ball. I want to know what is going on between the two of you and if it is serious."

I stopped, yanking my mother to a halt, since her arm was wrapped around mine.

"Why does it matter if he is serious or not?" I asked.

My mother turned and looked at me with disbelief. "Of course it matters. We know nothing about him, apart from him being a duke. How are we to assure he is a suitable match for you if you can't tell us anything about him?"

"I signed an NDA," I lied.

"Exactly," Mother replied, pointing her finger at me. "And if you two are serious, then obviously that NDA needs to be broken or whatever they do to dissolve it. Your father and I can't approve a match unless we know everything about him."

"You can't approve a match?" I asked incredulously. "Doesn't what I want matter?"

Mother snorted delicately. "We're obviously not going to match you with someone you can't tolerate, but love is blind, Sophia. He could be a scoundrel or a reprobate or a con artist who is only trying to get close to you so that he can infiltrate the royal court."

I blinked owlishly, not quite believing the words coming out of my mother's mouth.

"You think he's a spy?" I hissed.

Mother folded her arms and looked at me shrewdly. "I wouldn't put it past him," she said. "He is very charming and extremely good-looking, I'll give him that, but that accent? That accent is...odd, and why have I never heard of him before? I know everyone in the royal courts of Europe. And why you? Why now?"

I gaped. "Why me?" I asked, my voice barely above a whisper. Could my mother not even believe someone like Ethan would want me just for me? Could he only like me because of what came along with me, namely my title and access to the Kabiero court?

I should have expected this. It was what she had drilled into me from the time I was a small girl. My only value was in what I could do, or how I looked, or the knowledge I had. No one could ever want me for just me because there was nothing under the sugar-coating she had meticulously built around me.

And hadn't it been true all these years? I had been her creature. I learned all the lessons she taught and internalised all of her core beliefs and I'd used that talent to do things like create an image of who I thought everyone else expected me to be. I'd even used those same superpowers to turn Nico into a social media darling. Wasn't it what I was doing with the women from the village? Wasn't it what I had done to Ethan, too?

I had become my mother. I was sugar-coating those around me, just as she had done to me. Even my job as social media manager for the palace was a form of sugar-coating.

The realisation hurt, and more so because in the months I had been away from my mother, I'd started to see myself as something—*someone*—else. But I wasn't. I was the same person she created, wearing the same mask she handed down to me. And just like those porcelain dolls I had always felt like, I was empty inside, too.

"What is wrong with you?" Mother asked, pointing to my face and making a circling motion with her finger. "That look on your face...I don't like it."

I rearranged my features and plastered a pleasant smile on my face. "Lord Ethan is not a spy," I said. "I may not be able to tell you much more about him, but I can tell you that."

"Well, you can never be too careful," she said. "We lost our country once and now that the king is back on the throne, we don't want to lose it again."

"I'm sure the king's security team have that well in hand."

"Okay, so he's not a spy. Can you at least tell me if there is something going on between the two of you?"

How to answer that question? The truth was, I didn't know. The other truth I knew was too complicated to explain, not that I could ever tell my mother the truth of how I met Ethan or the bet. Then there was the pesky feeling of being nothing but an empty shell with a pretty façade. How could Ethan possibly like me enough to stay when there was nothing to like? He'd lived such a full life and I...I hadn't. He'd tire of me before long and end up leaving, anyway. It was just as well I hadn't gotten a chance to tell him how I really felt.

But I couldn't say any of that to my mother. I had to keep up the pretence, because one of the reasons I was doing this was to get her off my back. If she thought there was a chance Ethan and I could be together, she would stop trying to set me up with every eligible peer in Europe.

"It's too early to tell," I lied, making my smile wistful. "But I have high hopes."

~

"Lady Sophia."

"Oh God, not you too," I said as Dorian intercepted me.

Dorian frowned at me, and I sighed.

"What is it?"

"I need to speak to you."

"Right now? Can't it wait?"

"Not unless you want tomorrow's media pages filled with the disaster that is about to befall this event."

I stilled, and my stomach bottomed out. "What disaster?" I asked, my heart once again pounding in my chest.

"If you come with me, I will show you and hopefully you can minimise it."

I followed Dorian as he stalked into the palace and toward the stairs that would take us down to the scullery. I didn't think Dorian even knew where the scullery was, let alone be aware enough to realise there was a problem.

A disaster was the absolute last thing I needed. The visit from the Merveille court had gone so well so far, and this was the last event. They wouldn't be leaving for a couple of days, but those days were going to be spent away from the public eye so that Meredith and Jamie could catch up with their friends in a more private setting. If something happened now, it would sour the entire trip— or so it would look to the press—and it would all be my fault.

My position in court was tenuous enough. I couldn't afford anything to mar the palace's image. It was my one job. There might not be very much else of substance about me, but image was something I was good at. It was my deft hand at creating just the right image that had won me my place in court. I couldn't do anything to jeopardise it.

Which was another reason I couldn't let the truth of Ethan out. How would it look if Ethan was suddenly revealed to be nothing more than I tourist I'd picked up in a bar? I should never have allowed Frankie to talk me into this whole bet. It was reckless and irresponsible. I had jeopardised my life in the palace and here I was considering ruining everything because of a boy...okay, a man, but it was the same sentiment.

Revealing the truth about Ethan would absolutely blow up my life, and then what would I have? I certainly wouldn't have a job anymore. I probably wouldn't even have anywhere to live. My mother would disown me. The king would take my title away from me...I assumed he could do that. He'd had enough authority to take it from my father and give it to me, so there was nothing to say he couldn't take it away from me too.

I wouldn't even have Ethan. Even if he thought he had feelings for me now—which he had never confessed to... not really —they wouldn't last. Ethan's life was like one of those amazing travel books you could buy, with pages and pages of incredible photos and stories. My life was pretty much the equivalent of a travel brochure that only showed the highlights and could be read in five minutes. No man would ever find that life interesting, or me, by extension. The only thing I had to offer was my title and position in court, just as my mother had always told me. The only way I would ever find someone to share my life with was if he needed my connections.

Love was a dream and only for those who had far more interesting lives than I ever would.

Dorian pulled me into Cirillo's office.

"So what is the disaster?" I asked.

"This," Dorian said, motioning with his hand to a stack of napkins on the desk.

I squinted at them, but could see nothing amiss, certainly nothing that would cause the local media to trash the ball.

"Um...you're going to need to help me out here," I said. "What exactly is the problem with the napkins."

"The damask pattern is different," Dorian said. "Look."

I looked, but couldn't see what the problem was. The damask patterns, which were white on white and barely notice-able, looked exactly the same.

"You're being ridiculous," I said, looking back up to Dorian.

"Am I?" he asked, folding his arms and staring me down.

"What is this really about?" I asked, folding my arms in return and looking back at him with my own glare.

"I think it should be obvious," Dorian replied cryptically.

"Maybe to a pretentious jerk like you, but I'm failing to see any 'disaster' here. They're just napkins and in the diffused light in the ballroom, no one is going to notice the difference."

"I beg to differ, but you and I both know I didn't drag you down here to complain about the napkins, although I would like to have it on the record that *I* noticed the difference."

"Yeah well you have some weird over-developed fabric-recognition power that defies explanation."

"Thank you," he said.

"Not a compliment," I replied.

He huffed.

"Okay, so what is this about if it's not about the stupid napkins."

"Ethan."

"Ethan? What about Ethan?"

"I know what you're thinking about doing and I want to discourage you from that course of action."

"Can you maybe talk like a normal human being instead of speaking to me in snob-speak?"

"You were thinking about coming clean about who Ethan really is and I have to say I think that is a terrible idea."

CHAPTER 19

Ethan

It took me a moment after Sophia left to gather myself. It felt like we'd both been about to admit to something life-changing, but the moment had been stolen. I was a little rattled and couldn't immediately gather my wits.

It had been so close...*we* had been so close, and I was more determined than ever to tell her the truth about my feelings.

I wasn't one of those people who shied away from powerful feelings. It was what had taken me around the world, but I'd never felt this strongly about another person before and it knocked me off kilter. I was far too used to not getting close, not investing myself in people, because I was always leaving. The depth of emotions stirred up by getting to know Sophia was unfamiliar and instead of embracing the feeling as I normally did when such feelings were inspired by journeys or destinations, I'd doubted myself.

Watching my mother and father slowly fade into the background as their day-to-day lives sucked the life out of them had instilled a knee-jerk reaction to anything that might have the same effect on me. I was always looking for the next adventure, the next high, the next foreign city. There was nothing I liked better than getting lost in the streets of a place I had never been to before. I know some people thought that crazy, but for me there was something inherently freeing about the experience.

Could falling in love give me the same rush? It was unfamiliar territory. It was a foreign experience and was not unlike being lost in an unknown city. There was an adventure to be had in falling in love, but what then? What happened when that initial rush wore off? Would spending all day every day with the same person dull my senses? Would it rob me of the zest for life like it had my parents?

In an uncharacteristically mature moment, I wondered what my future would look like. Would I continue to wander the earth like a lost soul, not having anyone to share the experiences with? Would I ever get too old for my vagabond lifestyle? Would I become one of those grey nomads who roamed the country-side in their caravans and mobile homes? Or would I be one of those who practically lived on a cruise ship? I knew I couldn't continue to backpack and odd-job my way across different continents. It was fine while I was young and had a charming smile, but who would employ a sixty- or seventy-year-old backpacker to tend bar?

I'd never really stopped to think about my future. Sure, those visions of a sixty-year-old man were still a few decades away, but shouldn't I at least have some sort of plan for my later years? And didn't I want to one day have a wife and family?

Those things hadn't been important to me before. A wife

and a family had felt more like a cage than a life, but now I wasn't so sure. It wasn't so bad spending time in one place and getting to know it and the people who lived there. I'd met hundreds of people and I had thousands of Facebook friends and Instagram followers—not as many as Sophia, but I had my fair share—but how many people could I actually call friends? They were acquaintances at best, and that no longer felt like enough.

I might not like Dorian very much, but I'd spent more time with him in the last few weeks than I spent with any other male acquaintance. As weird as it felt, Dorian was probably my closest male friend...or, not friend but...?

Yeah. There was something seriously wrong with my life when I counted someone like Dorian amongst my closest friends.

And what of Sophia? Regardless of the feelings I had for her, we were friends...she had become my best friend.

What did that say about me? What did it say about the life I led? I wasn't someone who needed hordes of adoring fans, but shouldn't I at least have one true friend amongst the crowds of acquaintances?

Staying in Kalopsia had opened my eyes to an alternative way of life. I'd looked at my parents and taken their experience as the absolute. My parents had let the life leach out of them, so that meant the same thing would happen to every other couple in the world. Looking at it now, I could see the immaturity in the assumption. Looking at Jamie and Meredith and the visiting queen and her consort, for that matter, every member of the visiting court, and Frankie and Lucas...none of them were fading into insignificance. None of them were losing their thirst for life. None of them were just getting through the day.

So maybe...maybe my life didn't have to end up like my parents. Maybe declaring myself to Sophia and joining my life to hers wouldn't be the slow death I had imagined.

Whoa. That was...harsh. Had I really thought getting married and having a family would lead to a long, slow death? That was...overly dramatic and ridiculous. I could choose the path of my future...hadn't I been doing that for the last decade? Choosing to stay in one place and giving my love to one woman didn't mean the end of the adventure. It just might be the start of a new one.

I whirled around. Sophia and her mother had long gone, but I knew I had to find her. I needed to tell Sophia how I felt before the night was out. We would sort out all the logistics of it at a later date. I just needed her to know I loved her and that I wanted to stay with her. Just the thought of leaving left a foul taste in my mouth and a heaviness in my heart.

A lightness flared inside me, not unlike the feeling I had whenever I'd decided on my next destination. This was right. This was my next adventure.

My feet were moving, and I was practically running through the gardens back to the palace. My need to see Sophia, to finish our conversation, was more important than anything else.

I reached the terrace doors, and the music from the ball spilled out into the night. Soft light, and the murmurs and laughter of the guests inside filled the air. But Sophia was nowhere to be found. Or at least I couldn't see her at first glance.

I stepped through the doors into the crowd and craned my

neck to see above the heads of the people milling about the cavernous room. There was a rainbow of colours from swirling gowns interspersed with the stark black of tuxedos. But still no Sophia.

Her mother and father were across the room, but she was not with them. The queen, the two queens, and a few of the court members are dispersed through the crowd. But no Sophia. I spied Frankie and Lucas and headed in their direction. If anyone knew where Sophia was, it would be Frankie.

"Hey," I said, forgoing formalities. "Have you seen Sophia?"

Frankie smiled up at me. "I thought she was with you?"

"She was," I replied, "but then her mother came to have a chat with her and now I can't find her."

Frankie patted my arm comfortingly and then grabbed the sleeve of a passing server. "Do you know where Lady Sophia is?" she asked.

"I saw her with Lord Dorian," the server replied with a small bow. "They were heading downstairs."

I didn't wait for him to finish. I was moving to the corridor leading downstairs before Frankie could voice the surprise on her lips. Why had Dorian taken Sophia downstairs? I might have only been thinking of him as a friend a few minutes ago, but that didn't mean I trusted him. He didn't like me, not that Dorian liked anyone, but I got the feeling he especially didn't like my relationship with Sophia. I couldn't work out if it was because he was interested in her for himself or if he saw her as a sister. It didn't much matter if he was going to talk her out of being with me, and I wouldn't put it past him to try.

I jogged down the stairs, passing servers who were going up with trays of finger food and bottles of wine. I slowed as I reached the ground floor and stalked along the hallway, coming to a stop when I heard voices coming out of Cirillo's office. The door was slightly ajar, and even though I knew it was wrong to eavesdrop, I wanted to know what Dorian was saying and what effect it might have on my future with Sophia.

"Okay, so what is this about if it's not about the stupid napkins," Sophia asked as I shuffled closer to the door.

"Ethan," Dorian replied, and I scowled. I knew it. I knew he was trying to undermine me.

"Ethan? What about Ethan?"

"I know what you're thinking about doing and I want to discourage you from that course of action."

"Can you maybe talk like a normal human being instead of speaking to me in snob-speak?" Sophia said, with a hint of exasperation.

"You were thinking about coming clean about who Ethan really is and I have to say I think that is a terrible idea."

I froze at Dorian's words. Sophia was going to tell everyone who I really was? But why? Unless...unless she felt the same way about me and she wanted to clear the way for us to have a genuine relationship.

"What?" Sophia said. I hated I couldn't see her face. I wanted to watch her eyes while she spoke.

"Don't play dumb," Dorian said, and I could imagine him tugging at his cuffs in the way he did. "It doesn't suit you. You heard what I said. You are thinking about revealing the truth about Ethan."

Sophia scoffed. "Why would I do that? I made a bet with Frankie that I intend to win. The only way for that to happen is to make sure no one else finds out the truth."

Dorian didn't speak, and my heart was pounding so loud in my chest that I was sure they could hear it.

"You have proved yourself," Dorian said, a conciliatory tone in his voice. "You performed well above my expectations."

Sophia made a noise of disbelief. "Your expectations?"

"Of course. I knew you would succeed. You are very good at taking a sow's ear and turning it into a silk purse, but I thought for sure the king would have sniffed out the truth by now."

"You underestimated me," Sophia said.

"You're correct. I won't do it again."

There was another long silence, and my mind was reeling. Was this all just a front to stick it to Dorian, or had I only ever been a project for Sophia after all? Had she only ever seen me as the sow's ear that Dorian described me as?

"Good," she said, with a relieved breath. "Now, can we please get back to the ball before someone notices we're missing?"

"Not until you tell me the truth," Dorian said. "You fell for him, didn't you?"

I held my breath and let it out in a soft hiss when Sophia answered.

"Don't be ridiculous, Dorian," she said. "We have nothing in common. We come from two different worlds that are as different as oil and water. Could you even imagine the look on my mother's face if I told her the truth about him? And I would have to tell her the truth if we were in a relationship. The only thing between us is the bet and now that I've so clearly won, there is nothing left."

I didn't hear the rest of the conversation. I stumbled away from the door, my heart spasming in my chest. It had all been a lie.

I'D BEEN AN IDIOT. I'd allowed myself to get caught up in the lie and fallen for my own con.

I left the palace, calling Francis to come and get me. I couldn't face any of them. I especially couldn't face Sophia. Not after what I heard. Not after knowing how she really felt.

This was what I got for turning my back on the truth I had lived by for the last decade. I'd changed. Being in Kalopsia and letting myself get caught up in the life of a duke had changed me. I hadn't even felt it happening. It was the actual embodiment of the whole boiling water and frog metaphor. The frog gets cooked without even realising what's happening to him. That was me. I was the frog.

I'd turned into my parents—the one thing I'd vowed never to do—and I'd *wanted* it to happen. It horrified me. I'd spent years running from this very eventuality and then BOOM! It happened. It had been stealthy, sneaking up on me, playing a dangerous misdirection game. While the shiny palace and the pretty girl had distracted me, mediocrity had slowly wound its tentacles around me and dragged me under.

I'd been lying to myself. I'd never be happy staying in one place. So what if looking back at the palace as we drove away caused a pang in my heart? So what if the very thought of never seeing Sophia again left me feeling bereft and gasping for air? That was just the lie. It was the carefully woven deception I'd worn as a mask this whole time. I was still in its thrall, under its influence, captivated by its charms...

Or I could just be heartbroken and looking for a way to protect myself.

Telling myself I'd never really wanted a life here in Kalopsia with Sophia was easier than accepting that I was prepared to give up everything for her. Believing I'd just been under the influence of the con hurt less than admitting I'd fallen in love with a woman who didn't want me.

The car pulled up in front of the villa, and it was a bittersweet moment. This would be the last time I'd be coming home to this place. And it *had* felt like home and the staff had become friends. I wasn't just leaving Sophia and the job I loved at the palace; I was leaving these people, too. Over the last ten years, I'd never regretted moving on. Usually by the time I was leaving one place I was ready to go, but not this time. I didn't want to admit the truth, but it felt a lot like I didn't want to leave Kalopsia. It felt a lot like I wanted to stay here for the foreseeable future.

Which meant it was past time to be moving on.

I got out of the car when Francis opened the door and headed inside. I'd planned to leave in the morning, but I couldn't stay another night. If I stayed, I was afraid I wouldn't leave. I needed to go now, while I was still reeling from the hurt of Sophia's rejection. Better to leave now than be the pathetic person who hung around hoping to be thrown some scraps from the table.

Sophia didn't want me. She had never wanted me. It had all been about the bet. Now that she'd won, I was no longer of any use to her. I didn't even know if we were friends or if that had been all a con, too. I didn't want to hang around and find out. The only thing worse than finding out she didn't have feelings for me was finding out everything we'd shared was a lie.

"You're home early," Charles said as I entered the villa.

"Something came up," I lied. "I have to leave earlier than expected."

"Earlier? I thought you were leaving early in the morning?"

"I need to leave now," I said, not stopping as I headed for the stairs to my room. "Tonight."

Toby was waiting for me in the bedroom, but one look at my face made his face fall.

"You're leaving now?" he asked as I opened my bag and started pulling out all the clothes Sophia had bought me. My new job provided a uniform, and I didn't want any reminders of my time here on the island.

"I am," I said.

I shucked my tuxedo, ignoring Toby's disapproving look as I let it fall to the floor. I pulled on my old, faded jeans and a black t-shirt, neither of which I'd worn in the last six weeks. It should have felt like stepping back into my own skin, but it didn't. The jeans that had fit me like a glove felt restrictive and strange. I ignored the feeling of wrongness and finished grabbing my toiletries and shoving them in my duffle.

I fingered the cufflinks Sophia had given me. Part of me wanted to keep them—I could pawn them in the future if I needed money—but I put them down and stepped away. I wouldn't want to be accused of stealing. I didn't think Sophia would do that, but I didn't know what was real and what wasn't at that moment, and I didn't know how far she would go if it ever came out who I really was. Would she claim ignorance and accuse me of duping her, too? Besides, I didn't want any reminders of her or the way I felt about her. Dealing with a broken heart would be enough of a reminder of my time in Kalopsia.

CHAPTER 20

Sophia

"Why would I do that?" I scoffed. "I made a bet with Frankie that I intend to win. The only way for that to happen is to make sure no one else finds out the truth."

Dorian studied me closely, and I tried not to shift uncomfortably under his gaze. I wasn't a good liar...I could *embellish* the truth, but straight up lying was difficult for me. More so when under the intense inspection of Lord Dorian.

"You have proved yourself," Dorian said, and I tried not to let the relief show on my face. "You performed well above my expectations."

"Your expectations?" I spluttered.

"Of course. I knew you would succeed. You are very good at taking a sow's ear and turning it into a silk purse, but I thought for sure the king would have sniffed out the truth by now."

"You underestimated me," I said smugly.

"You're correct. I won't do it again." Dorian said, tugging on his cuffs.

"Good," I said, letting out my breath slowly. "Now, can we please get back to the ball before someone notices we're missing?"

"Not until you tell me the truth," Dorian said. "You fell for him, didn't you?"

"Don't be ridiculous, Dorian," I said, my heart pounding with lies. I thought for sure he could hear it and know the truth. "We have nothing in common. We come from two different worlds that are as different as oil and water. Could you even imagine the look on my mother's face if I told her the truth about him? And I would have to tell her the truth if we were in a relationship. The only thing between us was the bet and now that I've so clearly won, there is nothing left between us."

Dorian said nothing for a really long time and I thought for sure he hadn't bought my lie, but then he inclined his head in acknowledgement.

"I knew you wouldn't fall for him," Dorian said. "I may have even had a side bet on the matter."

"With Frankie?" I asked, my heart pounding.

Dorian made a dignified snorting noise. "Frankie set this whole thing up so you would fall for him," he said. "I thought she needed to see that just because she's fallen in love—" Dorian's nose wrinkled at the words "—didn't mean she could make everyone else fall in love too."

"Well, I guess you won," I said, the words tasting like ash on my tongue.

It felt gross, saying the words and denying what I felt for Ethan, but there was no way I was going to tell Dorian the truth about my feelings. Ethan deserved to be the first one to know, not Lord Dorian. And while it was true we'd come from different worlds and had little common shared experiences, that didn't mean we couldn't build something together. And as for my parents, I was nervous about telling them the truth and I wasn't sure what the fallout would be, but I was realising I didn't care. I'd been the perfect daughter all my life, and I felt… empty. But I didn't feel empty when I was with Ethan.

My emotions were all over the place. Wasn't it only a few minutes ago I was justifying to myself why I should walk away from Ethan and not look back? Now I was trying to find a reason to ask him to stay.

Telling Dorian I had no feelings for Ethan had an unexpected consequence. I realised how wrong the words were. Saying it out loud, denying the strength of the relationship that had grown between Ethan and me, clanged discordantly inside me, and I was suddenly so sick of doing what everyone else wanted me to do. I was sick of painting everything with my fairy godmother wand and turning frogs into princes. I was sick of pretending pumpkins were coaches and rags were ballgowns. The truth was, I was sick and tired of presenting my world as a perfect picture so I could please the people in my life. I wanted to *live* my life, not just paint a pretty picture of it. I no longer wanted to be the doll on the shelf who looked perfect and unmarred.

Ethan had been the only one to really see beyond that mask. He was the only one who bothered to look beneath the sugar coat I wore.

"So are we done here?" I asked, looking back at Dorian.

"We're done," he replied.

I didn't wait for him to escort me back to the ball. I needed to find Ethan. I wanted to tell him the truth about how I felt. I wanted to face my parents together with him and tell them the truth. I wanted to shout the truth from the rooftops.

Cirillo was coming along the hall as I stepped out of the office.

"Have you seen Lord Ethan?" I asked. "I need to speak with him urgently."

Cirillo frowned. "Is there something wrong?"

"No, nothing like that," I assured the poor man, who looked like he was moments away from panicking. "I just need to speak with him on an unrelated manner."

Cirillo frowned. "I'm afraid you're too late," Cirillo said.

"Too late?" I replied, matching his frown.

"Lord Ethan already left. He called his car just moments ago."

I didn't bother to say goodbye. I lifted my skirt and rushed away. If Ethan had only just called for his car, I could possibly catch him before he left. I didn't know why he was leaving so early. I thought for sure he would stay to the end so we could debrief...and finish our conversation.

I jogged up the stairs in a wholly undignified way, not caring about who saw or what they might think if they saw me running. I crossed through the foyer and burst through the open doors in time to see Ethan's car driving away.

I slumped against one of the giant pillars supporting the portico and frowned. Why did he leave? Why hadn't he said goodbye?

SLEEP DIDN'T COME EASILY, and it wasn't just the adrenalin from the ball. Something was wrong with Ethan. It was unlike him to leave like that, and I didn't like it. Not only that, but I still felt the oily guilt of saying all those things to Dorian. I hadn't wanted to lie, but what other choice did I have? Dorian was not a man to tell secrets to. I wasn't worried he would spread rumours. I was more worried that Dorian used secrets as currency. It was bad enough that I'd needed to tell him about the bet in the first place; I didn't also want him to know my innermost heart.

I rose with the sun, even before my lady's maid came to open the curtains. Tossing and turning all night hadn't done me any favours, and I felt like death warmed over, but I had a bad feeling that Ethan was running away and I needed to know why. I needed to know if that moment in the garden was self-projection or if Ethan shared my feelings.

I slipped out of the castle and roused a driver to take me to the villa. The senior chauffeur, Deacon, had the morning off, so I had to use one of the younger ones and I closed the privacy screen after he'd started the drive with far too much chatter. I normally didn't mind talking to my driver, but this morning I was too on edge to be polite.

I fidgeted in my seat, not able to sit still and wished the car would go faster, despite the dangers of the windy and steep road. I couldn't quell the sense of foreboding rising within me. I just hoped I could get to Ethan before he did something stupid.

Finally, we rounded the corner, and the car pulled into the driveway of the villa. The sun glinted off the stonework and limned the building in gold. But it didn't make me feel any better. Usually I felt a sense of peace at the villa. The house was at the centre of some of my very favourite memories. There was no peace this morning as I scrambled from the car, not even waiting for the driver to open the door.

I strode across the courtyard and up the stairs to the patio. The doors opened before I could reach for them, and Charles stood in front of me. His face was stoic—as it always was—but I just knew Ethan had already left.

"Where?" I asked. "When?"

"Last night, my lady," Charles said, closing the door and following me as I headed for the stairs leading to Ethan's room. "As for where, we don't know."

"How can you not know?" I growled as I reached the landing.

"He left on foot," Charles said, apology plain in his tone. "While we were distracted."

I burst through the door to Ethan's room, half-expecting, half-hoping he would be in bed and I could yell at him for scaring me. But the room was empty. The bed made and looking very much like it hadn't been slept in. The mahogany valet stood in the corner with Ethan's tuxedo from last night arranged on it neatly, and on the matching mahogany dresser glinted the cufflinks I'd bought him.

The door on the wall of the room opened and Toby came in, bowing his head when he saw me, and he looked as dejected as I felt.

"He's really gone?" I asked, knowing the truth even before I voiced the words.

"Yes, my lady," Toby replied. "He wouldn't even let me pack his clothes for him. He just put on those awful jeans and t-shirt and grabbed his duffle bag and left without even saying goodbye."

Of course he did, I thought and then followed it by saying, "Of course he did," out loud as I sank onto the wing chair in the corner.

I could still smell his scent in the room. Yes, I'd been the one to buy him the fragrance, but it was different on him than it was on a sample card. The very essence of Ethan changed the scent to make it his own, and it filled the room.

"Francis went after him," Charles said. "Once we were alerted that he'd left, Francis took the car and drove around trying to find him."

"I don't understand what happened," Toby said, looking between me and Charles. "I thought he was happy here. I thought he might stay."

"I thought so too," I said softly. "I'd hoped he would."

But it was a fool's hope. I knew all along Ethan would leave. He never stayed, and I'd been a fool to think I could change him. Any person was a fool to think they could change someone else. Sure, I could make cosmetic changes and craft an image for anyone, but that only changed the outside. Even Cinderella's fairy godmother couldn't change who she was as a person. They said the clothes maketh the man, but it was all just set dressing; an illusion, a meticulously wrought fabrication.

I was very good at those. I had lifelong practise at it.

"Should I fetch Francis?" Charles asked. "Maybe he has some clues as to where Lord Ethan has gone."

I sighed. "No," I said. "Ethan left because he wanted to leave. We won't chase after him."

I took a deep breath, breathing him in—or what was left of him—for the last time, and then I stood, straightening my clothes and throwing my shoulders back. It wouldn't do to show weakness in front of the staff. Sure, they'd known me for a long time, but I was the mistress of the house, and I needed to project a strong façade.

"Have you eaten?" Charles asked gently. "Chef Contos can make you some breakfast—"

"No, thank you. I have a breakfast meeting to attend to at the palace. A debrief from last night," I lied smoothly.

I doubted anyone from the palace would stir before noon. There would be a debrief but not for a couple of days so we could gather data and feedback.

"Is the villa to be closed up again?" Charles asked as he followed me out of the room and back down the stairs.

"No," I replied. "Not yet."

I didn't know why I was hesitating. I didn't live here, and I doubted I could even visit regularly, not with the ghost of Ethan haunting the place in his absence. I just wasn't ready to let go of all hope that he would somehow return.

I wandered through the palace feeling unmoored. I headed for the breakfast room, not because I was hungry but because I needed a coffee at least, and some time to pull myself together. I didn't expect to see anyone there, and very nearly turned around and walked away when I saw Frankie. She didn't give me the chance, though.

"Sophia," she greeted with a smile. "Come and sit. I want to hear everything."

"What are you even doing out of bed?" I asked. Frankie was a notoriously late sleeper and was not the cheeriest morning person.

"Lucas asked me the same question," Frankie said with a

grin. "I don't know, I just feel...energised. Last night was so amazing. I've never experienced anything like it before. You must be pretty proud of yourself."

I looked up from the coffee a server put before me and frowned at her. "What do you mean?"

"I mean, you organised it all. You planned this amazing event, the first of its kind for the new monarchy, and it was spectacular. People will talk about it forever. They will judge every other ball against this one."

I didn't know about that, but I couldn't say that. "It wasn't just me," I said. "I only played a tiny part in the whole thing. I was basically just the air traffic controller. Everyone else did the hard work."

"Don't diminish the work you did," Frankie admonished. "I know you didn't do it alone, but that doesn't negate the role you played."

I nodded and sipped my coffee, hoping Frankie would leave it at that. She didn't, of course. That wasn't Frankie's style.

"Speaking of all the people who helped you, Ethan did well. I think I might owe you something."

"I don't even remember what we bet," I replied woodenly.

"Hmm," Frankie said, tapping her chin with a finger. "I don't believe we set terms. That was a bit of an oversight on your part. Not that it matters. You won fair and square and you now have bragging rights."

"Bragging rights?" I snorted. "Who am I going to brag to? If I tell anyone what we did I'd be tried for treason or something."

"You're being ridiculous," Frankie said with a sniff. "Meredith would get a good laugh out of it." Frankie sipped her coffee. "So what happens now?" she asked. "The two of you are obviously into each other for real, so when do you do the big reveal?"

"Big reveal?" I asked, my stomach churning at what she was suggesting.

Frankie rolled her eyes. "Yes, big reveal. You have to come clean now if you want a future with him. It would be better to do it sooner rather than later. In the next day or two so Meredith is still on a high from the ball."

I couldn't answer. My throat was thick and my eyes stung. The hastily erected battlements I'd put up at the villa came crumbling down, and the raw pain of loss and rejection pierced my heart.

Frankie turned to look at me, and her eyes widened. Nobody had ever seen me so vulnerable, and I knew it was a shock for her.

"What's wrong?" she asked, reaching for my hand. "What happened?"

"He's gone," I croaked. "He left last night. Nobody knows where he is."

"Ethan left? Why? Why would he do that? He's in love with you. This makes no sense whatsoever."

"He wasn't in love with me," I said, even as the words burned my throat. "If he loved me, he would've stayed."

"Are you sure he actually left? I mean, maybe he just went for a walk or wanted to watch the sun rise or—"

"He's gone," I replied dully. "He packed his bag and took off in the night like a thief."

"No. I don't believe he would just up and leave like that for no reason," Frankie said.

"He had a reason," I said. "He wasn't in love with me. It's that simple. Our bet was finished, he got what he wanted, and he didn't need me anymore so he left."

Frankie was already shaking her head before I finished speaking. "No," she said. "Nope. I don't believe it for a second. That man was smitten with you. Everyone could see it."

I scoffed a dark laugh. "He was hardly smitten with me. He didn't even bother to say goodbye. He left everything behind and packed only what he'd brought with him. He obviously had somewhere else to go. I know he didn't go back to the back-packers where he was staying before because I had the car take me by there on my way back from the villa. I just have to face facts. He was a much better actor than any of us gave him credit for. He didn't have feelings for me. It was all fake."

Frankie looked at me with pity, and I hated it. I hated the sad look in her eyes. I knew what she saw when she looked at me; a pathetic idiot. Just like Nico had done, Ethan had taken what he needed from me and then left for greener pastures. Could I blame him? I had nothing more to offer him. I hardly thought he would consider my love anything of value.

"You fell in love with him," Frankie stated.

I snorted and grimaced. "And what a fool I was," I said.

Frankie shook her head and straightened her spine. "No, not a fool, but he is. We have to find him."

"What?"

"We have to find him and find out what is really going on."

"I think it's pretty obvious what is going on," I replied.

"Yeah, miscommunication is what is going on," Frankie said. "Believe me, I know what happens when you take things at face value instead of asking questions. I won't believe he isn't in love with you until I hear it from his own lips."

"I'm sure he was just trying to save me the embarrassment of hearing those words," I said.

"Stop it," Frankie said. "I won't hear any more of your doom and gloom. We are going to find Ethan and we are going to get him to tell us the truth."

"Under pain of death?" I asked sarcastically.

"If need be," she replied, more seriously than I cared to acknowledge.

CHAPTER 21

Ethan

I woke with a groan. The bed I'd slept in was comfortable and the room was the perfect temperature, and even the sun coming in through the slightly parted curtains was gentle and inoffensive. Even so, waking up felt like crawling through a spikey bush. I didn't want to wake up to the new reality of my life. I didn't want to take the first steps into a future where Sophia and I were no longer together. Sure, the entire thing might have been fake, but it felt a whole lot like reality to me.

My phone chimed with another alarm, and I took a fortifying breath before throwing the covers off and standing to my feet. The tide waited for no man, and neither would my new job. I wasn't scheduled to start for another day, but surely it would look good for me to turn up prepared to work earlier than expected? There was a lot I needed to learn before we left the marina, and I intended to get up to speed quickly so the crew would have no reason to fire me.

I showered and dressed and checked out of the hotel room. I hadn't gone back to the backpackers, and I didn't think turning up at the yacht in the middle of the night would have been good form, so I'd spent some of my precious savings to get a room.

Sophia hadn't paid me for the time I spent with her, and even if she'd tried to, I would have rejected it. She had bought clothes and food and paid my expenses for the last six weeks. I couldn't have let her pay me as well. That just felt...wrong.

I headed down the marina walkway to the massive yacht where my new life would begin. The sun was shining brightly, and the sea glinted merrily and by all accounts, it was the perfect day, except all I felt were rain clouds and thunder-storms. I should feel like I was walking on the moon, instead I felt like was walking toward the gallows.

Whoa. That was dark.

I rolled my shoulders and shook my head to try to dislodge the black melancholy hanging around me, and plastered a smile on my face as I approached the gangplank.

I wasn't sure if I was supposed to call out to ask permission to board the boat. I wasn't clued in to all the yacht-etiquette yet, but I didn't have to worry because there was a steward waiting for me at the entrance to the gangplank. I showed him my iden-tification, and he led me aboard.

My interview hadn't been held on the boat. I hadn't even applied for the job, they'd come to me. Apparently someone had recommended me to them. I assumed it was Sophia. The chief steward called me out of the blue and interviewed me in a local cafe. The package she'd offered was one I couldn't disregard out of hand. But I would have walked away if there had been any chance this thing between Sophia and me had any future. Last night proved I'd been right to accept the job.

"I hope you don't mind that I'm a day earlier," I said to the chief steward after I'd greeted her. "My previous employment finished earlier than expected."

"It's not usual," she replied, "but I'll allow it because there is so much for you to learn. Before you get your gear stowed away, the owner would like to have a word with you."

"Of course," I replied, even though my gut tightened with anxiety. The last time an owner had interviewed me, it hadn't gone well. I would be quite happy never interacting with a yacht owner ever again, in all reality.

I followed the chief steward down a narrow hall and she knocked on a closed door before opening it and waving me through. I stepped into the large space and stopped when I saw who was waiting for me. I scowled.

"Lord Dorian," I said, giving him the slightest of bows; barely more than an inclination of my head.

"Lord...no, you're a lord no longer," Dorian said with a smirk. "It's just Ethan now, isn't it?"

"Yes," I replied, taking a quick look over my shoulder to ensure we were alone. It wouldn't do for my deception with Sophia to get out.

He stared at me like he was trying to read my mind, and I tried not to fidget under his gaze.

"I bet you're surprised," Dorian said.

"Not really," I replied.

"You knew I was the owner?" he asked, with the lift of his eyebrows, the only sign I'd caught him off guard.

"No, I didn't know, but it makes sense. You wanted me out of the palace and away from Sophia. What better way to do that than to offer me a job on a yacht that was leaving Kalopsia?"

His lips thinned as he looked at me silently. I could never get a good read on Dorian, no matter how much time we'd spent together—not that we'd spent all that much time in the same space. He always came across as cool and arrogant and as if he was continually looking down his nose at everyone and everything.

Did I want to spend the next few months on a yacht out at sea with this man? I couldn't rightly answer. My initial reaction was *hell no*, but I couldn't walk away from this job just because I didn't like the owner.

"Are you sure this is where you want to be?" Dorian asked, snapping out of my thoughts.

I looked at him curiously. "Do you not want me to work for you?" I asked. "You were the one who recommended me for the position, right?"

He inclined his head in agreement. "I did, but that was before…" His voice faded out and he looked away from me and out the windows at the sparkling sea.

"Before what?"

He shook himself and turned back to smile at me. Not a friendly smile. Dorian didn't do friendly smiles.

"I would've thought they had offered you a place at the palace. You filled the role of Lord Chamberlain well enough and the palace is desperate to fill the position."

I snorted. "I can hardly take the position there without revealing who I really am. I didn't think that would go over so well and it definitely wouldn't be good for Sophia."

"No, I suppose not," Dorian said, tapping his lip with a finger. "So you still want to take the job then, even after…"

"After finding out that you're my boss?" I finished for him. "It's a good job and it will look good on my resume."

"Fine," he said with a bored sigh.

The door opened behind me, and the chief steward appeared without being summoned. I looked back at Dorian once more, but he wasn't looking at me. I followed the chief steward out, wondering what new hell awaited me under the employment of Lord Dorian Stamos.

OVER THE NEXT couple of hours, as I packed away my gear in my shared bunk room and familiarised myself with the layout of the ship, I vacillated over my decision to take the job. I'd taken the job to get away from all things Sophia, but working for Dorian would be a constant reminder of what I'd lost. Not even lost, not really. I couldn't lose what I'd never had, and truth be told, I'd never had Sophia.

The job was supposed to be a new start for me and a way to leave it all behind; the palace, the bet, Sophia. And it was a good job, despite it being employed by Dorian. I didn't like the guy but I couldn't deny having his name on my resume would go a long way to getting me better gigs.

That burned. It really did. I didn't want to be grateful to Dorian for anything. He was a smug, upper-crust jerk, and I hated being beholden to him for anything.

As there were no official duties for me to do, after I'd been introduced to the rest of the crew and given an overview of the duties I would be responsible for, I was given leave to complete any on-shore business before my job would start in earnest the next day.

I left the yacht and headed back into town. Without conscious thought, I headed back to the bar where I'd worked B.S. Before Sophia.

The bar wasn't officially open for another hour, but I went in the back entrance.

"Hey Ethan," Sonny, my previous bartending partner, called to me. "What are you doing here, man?"

"Hey Sonny," I said, pulling myself up onto the bar as he restocked the fridges beneath. "I was hoping to get my old job back."

Sonny laughed. "You're not serious?" he asked when I didn't join in the laughter. "Do you know how annoyed Mr. Lykaios was when you quit out of the blue like that? You left us high and dry right in the middle of the busy season. No way he'll give you your job back."

I sighed. I'd known it was a long shot, but I couldn't just accept Dorian's job without looking at other options.

"Besides," Sonny said. "I heard you were working at the palace."

"I was," I replied, confirming the rumour.

It wasn't a lie, even if it had been when I'd first started it. I had to give some reason for leaving so unexpectedly and I knew there was a possibility people I worked with would still see me around town, so I couldn't use a family emergency or anything like that. I also needed a reason to be seen in the company of Sophia. Telling my ex-boss I'd been offered a job at the palace seemed the best excuse at the time.

"So what happened? You get fired?"

I shook my head. "The job ended," I replied. "It was only a six-week gig."

"That was a risk," Sonny said, standing from where he'd

been kneeling to reach the under bench fridge. "I hope it paid well."

I shrugged. "Yeah, and I have another job lined up, I'm just not sure I want to take it."

"I'd take it if I were you," Sonny said. "It's gotta be better than working here."

"It's on a yacht."

Sonny whistled softly. "That's what you wanted, right? A steward position?"

"Yeah," I replied unenthusiastically.

"So what's the problem?" he asked, crossing his arms and leaning back against the opposite counter.

"Do you know Lord Dorian?"

"The duke? Not personally, but I know him by his reputation. He wouldn't be caught dead in a place like this."

"Yeah, well, the yacht belongs to him."

Sonny whistled softly again. "I bet it's a pretty spectacular yacht," he said. "And the pay would be amazing. He might be a snobby rich jerk, but from what I heard he treats his staff well."

I had to agree with him grudgingly. Dorian was stuck up and a perfectionist, but I had never witnessed him being anything but respectful to any of the palace staff. And the yacht was amazing. It was the largest one in the marina and had every mod-con known to man.

"So what's the problem?" Sonny repeated with a lift of his eyebrow.

I sighed. "None, I guess. I was just keeping my options open."

Sonny snorted. "Take the job," he said. "You've got nothing to lose."

I jumped down from the bar and shook Sonny's hand. "You're right," I said. "Take care, man."

"You too," he replied. "And put in a good word for me. I might apply the next time the yacht is in port."

I grinned. "I will," I replied as I walked away.

I wandered the town, not really taking the sights and sounds of it in. Sonny was right. I had nothing to lose. There was nothing left for me here in Kalopsia, and getting a job on a yacht had been my goal all along. It was pathetic of me to hold out hope Sophia would come looking for me and beg me to stay. She didn't want me, something Dorian had obviously known, otherwise why offer me the job? He was doing me a favour, although admitting it tasted bad. Besides, I didn't have to work for him for the rest of my life. There was this first voyage and I could decide whether a life on the sea agreed with me. When we got back to port, I could decide if I wanted to continue or if it would be time to move on. I was good at moving on, and I needed to stick with what I knew.

CHAPTER 22

Sophia

We had no luck finding Ethan. Frankie dragged me all over the place, even back to the club where we'd first met him, but no luck. The other bartender working the night we made the bet with Ethan wasn't on duty and no one else had any clue where Ethan might be. They all thought he was working at the palace, which was no help to me whatsoever.

Ethan really had disappeared without a trace.

I drew the line at checking every single hotel on the island. Apart from it being a complete invasion of privacy, I'd come to the realisation that Ethan didn't want to be found. If he didn't want to be found, then why was I even bothering to look for him?

"Where's Ethan?" Meredith asked.

I looked up from the food I was pushing around my plate and shrugged.

Meredith quirked an eyebrow at me, but I looked back down at my plate. I didn't want to be here. I wasn't hungry, but Meredith insisted on having a debriefing meeting over lunch and there was no way I could get out of it.

"Shouldn't he be here?" she asked. "This is a debriefing meeting, after all."

"He left before anyone could tell him about the meeting," Frankie said, and I turned my head to glare at her. She pretended to ignore me.

"He left?" Meredith asked. "Why did he leave? I was going to ask him to stay."

So was I, I thought to myself. It looked like both the queen and I were going to be disappointed.

"He left because..." Frankie started, but then stopped, elbowing me in the side. "It's probably better if Sophia tells you."

I felt the entire table look at me, and I sighed. They were not going to let this go. I could continue to lie and tell them he'd left to go back to his country; but what would be the point? They would continue to badger me about contacting him. I knew Meredith, and I knew that glint in her eye. She wanted Ethan for the Lord Chamberlain position and the only way to dissuade her would be to explain to her just how very inappropriate he was for the position.

Besides, at this point I kind of didn't care what happened to me. I knew I would be in trouble for bringing someone like Ethan into the palace, but I just couldn't muster up the energy to give a damn. I hadn't slept the night before and I'd been on a torturous rollercoaster all day and I was just done.

I was sick of the lies. I was sick of being the good girl who did everything she was supposed to do. I was sick of being that perfect little porcelain doll who sat on the shelf and looked pretty. All of that had stopped me from reaching out to Ethan with two hands and holding on for dear life. It's what I should have done. If I'd been honest with him, maybe he wouldn't have left in the middle of the night.

"The truth is," I said, looking up and staring directly at Meredith. The words stuck in my throat and my heart pounded but...but I would not lie again. I was done sugar coating my life. "The truth is," I started again after clearing my throat. "Ethan isn't a duke. He isn't from another royal court. He isn't a peer or from any notable family. He's a bartender. I picked him up in a bar." My blood was whooshing in my ears so loud I couldn't hear anything else. I swallowed and went on, no longer able to hold Meredith's gaze. "After Nico dropped me, Frankie bet me I couldn't godmother another guy and get everyone to believe he was a duke. Ethan was working in the bar that night and we agreed to try to pull off the con. I would get a date to the ball and get my parents off my back and he would get some valuable experience and contacts for his next great adventure. So he's gone. He obviously found his next job, and he left last night without telling me. I have no idea where he is or what he's doing and..." a sob choked my throat and I stopped speaking. Frankie took my hand under the table and squeezed it. I swallowed again and finished what I was going to say. "So, if you want to expel me from court or arrest me for treason or whatever...do it. Just... make it quick."

Silence fell and held for so long that I had to look up. I expected anger and accusations. I even expected Danika to come storming in and handcuff me and drag me out, but none of that happened.

Meredith sighed. "Why do all our courtiers think we're stupid?" she asked Jamie.

He smirked, but didn't answer. I frowned, looking between Meredith and the king, trying to work out what they were talking about.

"You think we didn't know exactly who Ethan was before he set foot in the palace?" Meredith asked. "Did you forget that both Jamie and I were on the security team for Queen Alyssa? Did you forget what a crack team of security experts we have here in the palace? Did you think anyone would get anywhere near us without having a thorough background check?"

I stared at her, open-mouthed. Frankie squeezed my hand again, and I had the distinct impression she was holding back a laugh.

"As for where he is, I'm sure we could find him without too much trouble. The question is, do you want us to find him?" Meredith asked.

I looked up at her in surprise. "What do you mean?"

"Well, I was serious about asking him to stay. I want him to work for me, for the palace. But what about you? Do you want him to stay? Or was it all fake?"

"Was what all fake?" I asked softly.

"The relationship. The feelings between the two of you. Was it all fake or did you mean it?"

I looked around the table at all the others who were staring at me like some exhibit in the zoo. Thank goodness it was just the immediate royal court and not the entire Merveille court as well.

"I meant it," I whispered.

Meredith smiled. "Fabulous. Danika!" she called.

Dorian coughed, and everyone turned to look at him. He picked up his wineglass and took a sip. "I may know where Ethan is," he eventually said.

"You might know?" Meredith asked before I could.

Dorian set his wineglass down and tugged at his cuffs. "I offered him a job on my yacht."

I pushed to my feet. "You what?"

"You told me you weren't interested in him," Dorian said, his tone infuriatingly reasonable. "He did an exceptional job while employed here at the palace, and I needed another crew member. If I had known you had feelings for him, I…"

"You would have offered him the job anyway," I finished for him.

"Probably," he replied.

"So where is he?" Meredith asked.

"On my yacht, I would assume," Dorian said. "We're scheduled to leave tomorrow and there is a lot to do—"

I ran from the room, not waiting to be dismissed.

"WHOA, HOLD UP," Frankie called after me as I reached for the car door. "I'm coming with you."

"Fine," I replied, opening the door and sliding in, not waiting for Frankie or the driver. "But hurry up."

"The marina," I said to the driver when he got in the car.

"And step on it," Frankie said. "I've always wanted to say that," she whispered to me.

I gave her a tight smile. I was too anxious to appreciate her humour. I just wanted to get to the marina, find Ethan, and discover the truth about what had happened between us. All of this could be for nothing. He could have gladly walked away from me and had no intention of ever seeing me again, but I couldn't help hoping that it wasn't the truth. I couldn't help hoping that him leaving behind the clothes and other things I bought him was a sign...a sign that maybe it all meant more to him than his current actions were communicating.

"This is so exciting," Frankie said. "I feel like I'm in a movie."

"It's terrifying," I replied.

Frankie turned to me and cocked her head to the side. "Terrifying?"

"I've never done anything like this before," I said, my legs jumping and my fingers twisting together. "I've never gone into a situation where I didn't have a reasonably good idea of what the outcome was going to be. I've never put my own feelings ahead of what everyone else expects of me." I looked at her then. "What if he laughs in my face? What if everything I feel means nothing to him? How can I ever get over that? How can I ever show my face to anyone at the palace ever again?"

Frankie's expression softened, and she reached for my hands. "First of all, I doubt Ethan would laugh in your face and I really, truly believe that he feels all the things for you and this is not one-sided. But—" I sucked in a breath and Frankie squeezed my hands. "But," she said, her tone softer. "If Ethan doesn't feel the same way about you as you feel about him, then it will hurt, but it won't be the end of the world. You will get over him, even if it doesn't feel like that at the moment. Falling in love—even with the wrong person—isn't anything to be ashamed of. Falling in love makes us all better people, even if that love isn't reciprocated. You will be fine. You will be stronger. And when the perfect man walks into your life, you will be ready to love him and all this will be like a bad dream you had once upon a time."

"That…sounds like you think Ethan is going to walk away from me," I said, my heart pounding even harder in my chest, and the urge to tell the driver to turn around and take us back to the palace was strong. I appreciated what she was trying to do, but I really wanted someone to tell me everything was going to be okay. I wanted her to assure me I was doing the right thing. I wanted her to take the risk out of what I was doing.

Frankie squeezed my hands again. "I suck at motivational speeches," she admitted. "But I will never lie to you. I really believe Ethan and you are meant to be together, otherwise I wouldn't say it. But if he is too stupid to see how amazing you are and what a gift you would be to his life, then he's not worthy of you."

"Okay, but can you lie to me just this once and tell me he is going to tell me he loves me and that he wants to be with me forever and ever and ever? Please?"

Frankie threw her arms around me and hugged me tight, but she didn't tell me what I wanted to hear. She didn't sugar coat the situation for me and I supposed future-Sophia would appreciate it, but present-Sophia could have really done with some well-meaning lies.

The car came to a stop, and I froze. All my energy stalled and I couldn't move. The driver opened the door and Frankie nudged me. When I still didn't move, Frankie physically shoved me along the seat to the door opening. I got out before she pushed me out and then I was standing at the marina and wondering what the actual hell I was doing. I didn't do this. I was frazzled and disheveled and completely out of my element.

There was no Instagram filter that could fix this. There was nothing I could do to make this any easier or less scary.

I swallowed and turned to get back into the car, but Frankie stood there, barring the door.

"I don't even know which yacht belongs to Dorian," I said.

Frankie rolled her eyes. "That's easy," she said. "Just look for the biggest and most obnoxious one."

When I still didn't move, Frankie hooked her arm through mine and led me toward the dock.

"It will be way worse if you let him leave without finding out the truth," she said. "I know you're scared, but honestly, wouldn't it to be better to know definitively? Wouldn't it be better to find out the truth so you're not left wondering for the next however long and wondering if he will just turn up one day and sweep you off your feet?"

"Yes?" I replied tremulously. Would it be better to know? If I didn't know then I also couldn't possibly have my heart crushed into a million tiny, irreparable pieces.

Frankie snorted. "Come on," she said. "I promise to punch him if he's mean to you."

I didn't know if that was any sort of comfort, but I let her lead me along the walkway toward the biggest, and yes, the most obnoxious yacht in the marina...and that was saying something compared with the other very large and very obnoxious yachts surrounding us.

"Ahoy the...what is the name of this dang boat?" Frankie said. "*Seaward Lord?* Are you kidding me?" Frankie rolled her eyes.

"Ahoy, the *Seaward Lord*," she said with less enthusiasm. "Permission to come aboard?"

"What are you doing?" I whispered to her, clinging to her arm.

"Isn't that what you have to do when you want to board a boat?" Frankie asked.

"I don't know," I replied. "I've never had to board a boat uninvited before."

Frankie shrugged and turned back to the massive yacht as someone stepped onto the deck.

"Excuse me! Hello! You up there," Frankie yelled, trying to get the person's attention.

The person turned to look down at us and I sucked in a breath. It was Ethan. It was Ethan, wearing a damned yacht uniform.

"Frankie?" he said. "What are you—"

Our eyes met and…phew. All the feels. It was a rush and so far beyond terrifying I couldn't even begin to articulate.

This was the bit where he walked away or scowled at me or…or disappeared for a moment before reappearing on a lower deck…which was what he did. He was coming to me, not running away. He could just be coming to yell at us to get off their dock, but he could have done that from the upper deck, right? He didn't need to come all the way down just to yell at me.

I tracked his progress as he leaped from the boat to the dock, not bothering with the stairs, and stalked toward me. I swallowed, really hoping the look in his eyes was what I thought it was, and I wasn't just projecting my feelings onto him.

Ethan opened the gate and stepped up to me, his eyes searching mine.

"Sophia," he said, my name a rough rasp.

"Ethan," I replied, my voice just as rough.

"What are you..." he exhaled roughly. "What are you doing here?"

"I needed to know," I said.

"Needed to know?" he asked, tilting his head to the side.

I swallowed and licked my lips. "I needed to know if anything that happened between us was real."

Ethan clenched his jaw and looked away from me for a moment. "You're asking me that after what I heard you say?" He didn't look at me when he spoke.

I frowned. "You heard me say...? What did you hear me say, Ethan?"

He turned back to me then, and the hurt was clear in his eyes. "I heard what you told Dorian."

I searched through my memory, trying to remember what I'd said to Dorian that Ethan could have possibly overheard.

"He asked you if you fell for me and you told him it was all for the bet and that we had nothing in common and there could never be anything between us," Ethan said, his voice tight.

I reached out and gripped his arm. "I lied," I said, desperate for him to understand. "There was no way I was going to tell Dorian the truth."

He didn't pull away from me, and that was good, right? I plunged on. I needed to say it all now, get it out in the open, and be honest with him.

"I did not want Dorian to be the first person to know I had fallen in love with you," I blurted. "I figured you should be the first person I told, not him."

Ethan sucked in a breath.

"But then I went to find you and you were gone. I was going to tell you at the ball. I was going to confess everything and ask you to stay."

My breath was coming in pants and from the rapid rise and fall of Ethan's chest, he wasn't finding the simple act of breathing any easier.

"What about your parents? What about the king and queen and the bet?"

"None of that matters," I said, squeezing his arm. "The king and queen already knew—don't ask me how, or at least, ask me later about how they have the annoying habit of knowing absolutely everything that goes on in the palace. I should have known better than to deceive them. And as for my parents, I don't care what they think. I've based my happiness on their approval all my life and you know what? I've never been happy. You make me happy. Being with you makes me happy and if they can't be happy for me, then I don't care."

His face softened, and I sucked in my first full breath. "You're in love with me?" he asked softly.

I snorted an inelegant laugh. "I'm so in love with you it's making me do crazy things, like confessing everything to the king and queen over breakfast," I admitted.

He lifted his hand and tucked a tendril of hair behind my ear, his hand pausing to cup my cheek. I closed my eyes and leaned into his hand, relishing his touch.

"I love you too," he whispered.

"Kiss her," Frankie whispered from beside us, and Ethan and I laughed, having totally forgotten Frankie was even still there.

Frankie held her hands up and backed away. "I'm going, I'm going. I'll wait for you by the car."

I didn't wait for Ethan to make the first move. I stepped into him, lifting to my toes to place my lips against his. His arms went around my waist and pulled me close, slanting his mouth over mine as he returned my kiss.

It was everything I'd dreamed of and more. Better even than the kisses we'd shared previously. I clutched at him, desperate never to let him go.

All too soon, he lifted his head and gazed down at me. My eyes caught on the blue epaulettes on his white crew shirt, and I frowned.

"I can't believe you took a job with Dorian," I said.

"I didn't know I would be working for Dorian at the time," he replied with a wry smile. "And I very nearly refused the job when I found out."

"Well, you can just quit now," I said.

Ethan raised his eyebrows. "Quit and do what? I can't get my job back at the bar."

"Who said anything about working at the bar? I have a job for you."

He grinned down at me. "Being your boyfriend is not a job," he replied, dropping a kiss on my lips. "As much as I would enjoy doing it full time."

"Do you trust me?" I asked.

"Of course," he replied.

"Great. Then quit your job and come with me...that is...if you want to stay in Kalopsia?"

"If it means staying with you, then yes, I want to stay in Kalopsia," Ethan replied.

CHAPTER 23

Ethan

"You're resigning then?"

I turned from Sophia to look at Dorian. Neither Sophia nor I had even realised he'd arrived. I pulled Sophia into my side and smiled at him.

"I am," I replied.

Dorian rolled his eyes. "I asked both of you if you had feelings for one another and you both denied it. I wouldn't have even bothered with the job offer if I'd known you were going to quit on the second day." He tugged on his cuffs with a forceful jerk. "Now who am I going to get to fill the position?"

"I might know someone," I said, thinking of Sonny. "He's never worked on a yacht before—"

"Neither had you," Dorian pointed out unnecessarily.

"I'm trying to help, here," I snapped.

Dorian huffed out a breath. "Fine. Pass on the details to the Chief Steward before you leave."

Dorian didn't wait for my reply, turning on his heel and stalking away.

"What did you say to Dorian?" Frankie said, approaching us, but looking to where Dorian walked down the dock.

"I resigned," I said.

Frankie grinned. "Good for you. I take it that means you're staying? And you're going to take the job—"

Sophia reached out to cover Frankie's mouth. "We're not telling him about that yet," she said.

Frankie winked and then mimed zipping her lips together.

"Why don't you go and get your stuff and we'll go to the palace."

"The palace?" I asked, trying not to sound as freaked out as I was. "Right now?"

Sophia smiled up at me. "We have to tell the king and queen everything," she replied.

"Right," I said with a swallow.

Sophia pressed up onto her toes and kissed my cheek. "It's going to be fine. Go and get your things. You trust me, right?"

I nodded. "I do," I replied with a sigh. "It doesn't make me any less nervous, though. We basically lied to them this whole time. It's perfectly normal for me to feel a little apprehensive."

"Just go," Frankie said with a roll of her eyes. "The quicker we get there, the quicker we can get it over with."

"Right," I said, and pulled away from Sophia reluctantly.

I wasn't a coward, but facing the king and queen after pretty much conning them for a month and a half definitely had me feeling a touch of anxiety...maybe more than a touch.

I boarded the yacht and headed to my bunk. It didn't take

long to packed my stuff. I changed out of my uniform and grabbed my toiletries from the bathroom, stuffing them into my duffle bag. I swung it over my shoulder and didn't even spare the room a glance as I left.

The yacht was everything I had expected it to be and more, but I no longer felt the desire to sail the seas on it. My wanderlust felt...cured, if that was even the right word. I didn't think it would be the end of my travels, but I no longer felt the overwhelming need to keep moving. I was no longer running from a life of stagnation and mediocrity. Just because I stayed in one place didn't mean my life had to also stay still. That's not how life worked. Stagnation was a choice...or rather the failure to choose...which was still a choice, paradoxically.

My parents had chosen to stay still. That might be a bit too harsh, because I don't think they actually consciously decided to stand still. I think it was an easier choice at first and then it was just easier to keep making the choice repeatedly. And they weren't *unhappy* with their life, which was the most important distinction to make. It wasn't something that would make *me* happy, but that didn't make it the wrong choice for them.

Travelling the world had been a choice for me too, even if it was because I was trying to escape an imaginary noose. That wasn't the sole reason I wanted to travel...life was far too complex to distill motivations down to a single reason. Wanderlust had been part of me from a very young age, even if I couldn't articulate it. Wanderlust, combined with the fear of turning into my parents, had kept me moving because I couldn't conceive that there was another way. I'd never really believed I would fall in love or that falling in love would be just as adventurous as travelling the world had been.

And now I had the opportunity to travel *with* someone, and

share all those experiences with someone who could appreciate them along with me. My wandering no longer needed to be a lonely experience. I looked forward to showing Sophia some of my most favourite places in the world and discovering new ones with her by my side.

I stepped onto the gangplank and looked up at the island of Kalopsia. It was beautiful and as small as it was, there were still undiscovered places I was yet to explore. Never before had I wanted to stay and get to know a place as much as I wanted to get to know my new home. And strangely, it did feel like home. I wasn't quite sure how my immigration would work, or if the king and queen would even let me stay, but I was willing to try everything and agree to anything in order to stay here with Sophia.

"Ready?" Sophia asked when I joined her and Frankie on the dock.

"Ready," I replied, taking her hand.

Sophia twined her fingers through mine and we walked down the dock toward a waiting palace car.

I was still nervous. I had to convince the king and queen to let me stay, and then I had to convince them I was good enough for Sophia. I didn't know how we were going to navigate my lack of title and what that would mean for my future relationship with Sophia, but I trusted her. I trusted she knew what was best in this situation, even if my knees knocked at the thought of the coming confrontation.

"THE THRONE ROOM?" Frankie muttered under her breath beside me as we entered the palace. "Seriously?"

"Shh," Sophia hissed.

"What's going on?" I asked out of the corner of my mouth as we followed one of the palace staff down the hall toward the 'throne room.'

I'd only ever ducked my head in the room once when I was familiarising myself with the palace, but I'd never actually seen Jamie and Meredith sitting on their thrones.

Frankie made a 'pfft,' sound and rolled her eyes. "Meredith is being melodramatic," she replied in a hissed whisper. "Don't let the stage fool you, they are not going to behead you."

I swung my head toward Frankie, my mouth agape. I hadn't even considered beheading. Logically, I knew it was ridiculous. Jamie and Meredith wouldn't behead anyone, but now that Frankie had put the thought in my head, I couldn't get it out. How Mary Queen of Scots had been so poised on the chopping block, I would never understand.

Sophia elbowed me. "Don't listen to her. We will not be beheaded," she said, the voice of reason calming my jumping nerves.

"That's what I said," Frankie huffed. "All I said was that Meredith was being melodramatic and that Ethan shouldn't feel like he's on trial or—"

"I'm on trial?" I squeaked.

I wasn't too manly to admit to squeaking. This entire thing was playing havoc with my nervous system. Even the long walk down the corridor had the effect of raising my blood pressure as the doors loomed closer. I'm sure they built the palace this way on purpose—the whole 'intimidation' aspect. It was working. If this was Meredith being melodramatic, then I would hate to see her in a really bad mood.

"I take it she knows about the…bet?" I asked.

Frankie snorted. "Understatement."

"She knows, and she's a little tetchy about it."

Frankie snorted again. "She's more tetchy about not being included in the betting pool than the fact that we were trying to con the entire palace."

I reached up to tug at my collar. I wasn't even wearing a suit and tie. I was in jeans and a t-shirt, but my shirt felt like it was choking me.

"I don't think that makes it any better," I said.

Frankie waved my concern away with her hand and made a dismissive noise. "Seriously, she's just trying to scare you."

"Yeah, well, she's doing a fantastic job," I replied.

"She did spend a decade as Queen Alyssa's personal body-guard," Sophia said. "She knows all the intimidation tactics."

"Jamie too," Frankie agreed. "He has that whole scary stoic-king-face going on."

"Yeah, I'd prefer not to be on either's hit list," I said. "I want to stay in Kalopsia and if the king and queen are mad at me, I don't know how that is going to be possible."

Sophia stopped and grabbed my hand, turning me to face her.

"Trust me," she said, grinning up at me. "This is all theatre and entertainment for Meredith. You're not in trouble, and I have no doubt you will be allowed to stay in Kalopsia. In fact, I guarantee it."

I relaxed only slightly at her reassurance that all would be well. I trusted Sophia, but I was still an outsider and an untitled no one from a foreign country. They had no reason to want me to stay, especially when my first introduction to them had been under false circumstances.

The doors opened, and I took a deep breath as I entered.

"Oh crap," Sophia muttered beside me and I tracked her gaze to see her parents standing with the assembled court.

"I have to give it to Meredith," Frankie murmured. "She really commits to a role."

My eyes moved off Sophia's parents to where Meredith and Jamie sat on their thrones. They were on a raised platform above the rest of us and Meredith was wearing her crown. So was Jamie, but he paled compared to the sight Meredith made. Frankie was correct. When Meredith committed, she *really* committed. Not only was she wearing her crown, but she was decked out in all the jewels and silk and finery that she could fit on her body. She looked every inch the avenging queen, and I swallowed, eyeing the six-foot sceptre she held at her side. That would pack quite a punch if she decided to hit me with it. I barely registered the sword leaning against Jamie's throne. I did not miss the black-clad security team arraying themselves around the room, nor the diminutive head of security, Danika, as she stood beside the king—diminutive but deadly.

"I thought you said they weren't mad," I whispered.

Before anyone could answer me, Meredith spoke.

"So nice of you to join us," she said with an evil smirk. "I believe there needs to be some formal introductions made."

Frankie groaned softly, and I imagined she was rolling her eyes, but I wasn't game to take my eyes off Meredith to look.

"Of course, Your Majesty," Sophia said, stepping forward and curtsying. "May I please introduce Mr. Ethan Samuels, a visitor to our country from Australia."

Meredith pursed her lips. "A backpacker, yes?" she asked.

Someone in the crowd—possibly Sophia's mother—gasped.

I stepped forward and bowed. "Yes, your majesty," I replied. I straightened and looked her directly in the eye. "I apologise for the deception."

Meredith turned to Jamie. "Why do these people think they can get anything past us?" she asked.

The corner of Jamie's mouth curled up. "It's not exactly a terrible thing if they underestimate us," he replied. "Right?" he asked, looking at Danika.

"Makes my job easier," Danika replied with a smirk.

"Wait...you knew?" I blurted out, forgetting I was addressing royalty. "You knew this whole time?"

"Of course we knew," Meredith said with a dramatic sigh and roll of her eyes.

"Danika wouldn't have let you into the palace without knowing everything about you," Jamie added.

I turned to Sophia. "Did you know they knew?"

She shook her head. "Not until this morning."

"So this was all for intimidation purposes?" I asked, confirming what Frankie had been saying all along.

Meredith rolled her eyes again. "I have to have fun somehow," she replied. "And you could have let me drag it out a bit longer." She sighed and then smiled. "But it's not all about that...there is another matter we need to talk about."

"O-kay," I said slowly. "Is this the bit where you throw me out of the country?"

Meredith grinned. "No, this is the bit where we offer you a job."

I LIFTED my wineglass and took a sip, still not quite sure how I survived the 'throne room.'

"Lord Ethan," Dorian said, raising his glass at me.

I smirked as I raised my glass in return. I was a lord now. An actual lord. Not a duke or a viscount or an earl, but a lord nonetheless. Lord Chamberlain to be exact, which came with the 'lord' honorific and address, plus a generous salary, and a suite in the palace.

"How does it feel to be a titled gentleman?" Frankie asked, grinning at me.

"Not much different from when I was pretending to be one," I admitted ruefully.

"It will start to feel a little different once everyone starts bowing and scraping to you," she said with a grimace. "Trust me, I know."

Frankie was the only other non-peer in the court—and yes, I was now part of the royal court—not that she would stay that way for long. As Lucas' fiancée, she would take on the title of marchioness (or whatever the Kalopsian equivalent was, which I was still trying to get straight in my mind) when they married.

"I think our situations are a little different," I remarked. "I'm not actually...anything."

"Yes, you are," she argued. "You're the Lord Chamberlain. That's just as legitimate a title as any other."

"You know, there is something we could do to make it more legitimate, if you're worried," Dorian said, studying the wine in his glass.

"Oh?" I asked, raising my eyebrows.

"Well, in times past, the Lord Chamberlain was a eunuch..."

The chatter around the table fell silent as everyone looked first at me and then at Dorian.

He put his wineglass to his lips and took a sip.

"Pardon?" I asked, not sure just how serious he was.

Frankie elbowed Dorian and laughed. "Oh my God, Dorian," she said with a cackle. "Don't listen to him. That was back in the day when the Lord Chamberlain was responsible for the royal bedchambers." She shook her head. "I'm sure Meredith and Jamie wouldn't require that much of a sacrifice of you."

"No," Jamie said, a horrified look on his face. "And we don't need anyone else in our bed chamber either."

There was a shocked silence and then giggles around the table, led by Meredith. Jamie rolled his eyes. "You all know what I mean," he grouched with a shake of his head.

I smiled, but looked over my shoulder distractedly. Sophia was taking a long time to rejoin the table, and I was beginning to worry. She'd left to talk to her parents, and I'd wanted to go with her, but...

"Go and find her," Frankie said. "She doesn't need rescuing, if that's what you're thinking, but it would be good for her parents to see you supporting her decision. She's lived her entire life trying to please them. Now that she is making decisions about her future on her own, it would be good for them to see others will support her choices."

"I don't want to undermine what she's trying to do," I said. "They need to see her standing on her own two feet and not needing anyone else to prop her up."

Frankie cocked her head to look at me. "You're right," she said. "But maybe go and wait outside the door, so you are the first thing she sees when she walks out. She's going to need reassurance after dealing with them."

I stood, but I didn't need to. Sophia walked into the dining room, her eyes unerringly finding me as she walked in my direction. She looked...good; confident and happy. Sophia walked right into my arms and kissed me.

"It went well, then?" I asked as I held out her chair for her.

"They were not over the moon pleased, but it went better than expected. It helped that Jamie and Meredith approved of our relationship."

"And you're okay?"

She grinned up at me. "I'm better than okay," she said. "I won't deny it was hard, but I feel liberated."

"Here," Frankie said, handing Sophia a full glass of wine. "Drink this."

"What should we drink to?" Sophia asked, turning to me.

"A new adventure," I replied, clinking my glass with hers.

"I like the sound of that," she replied, before taking a drink. "As long as that means we're going on an adventure together."

"I wouldn't have it any other way," I replied, dropping a kiss on her upturned lips.

EPILOGUE

Sophia

I fidgeted in my seat as the cab wound its way through the traffic. I had travelled extensively through Europe and even visited the United States and Canada, but I'd never been to Australia and I didn't exactly know what to expect.

Ethan reached across the seat and placed his hand on mine, giving me an encouraging smile.

"They're going to love you," he said.

Yeah, it wasn't visiting Australia that made me nervous. It was meeting Ethan's family.

It had been an eventful few months since we revealed our deception to the royal court. Ethan had taken to his position as Lord Chamberlain like a duck to water, and even Dorian had complimented him on the job he was doing—grudgingly, but it was still a compliment.

Meredith had given birth to a bouncing baby boy. Prince Alesandro Ferdinand Christophe Kostopolous, named for Jamie's father, the previous king. Both mother and baby—and father—were doing well. Of course Prince Alesandro was the most perfect and intelligent and adorable baby to have ever been born...according to Meredith, at any rate. Not that I disagreed. The entire court doted on him and he was bound to grow up spoiled rotten by all his 'aunts' and 'uncles.' I was pretty sure Meredith was already in talks with Queen Alyssa about an arranged marriage between him and the young princess...although, I don't think either queen had come to the realisation that both children were the heirs to their respective thrones...so...

The cab pulled to a stop, and Ethan squeezed my hand before getting out. I looked at the small, brick, suburban house and swallowed. Ethan had gone through so much to finally win my parents' approval, and I was willing to do whatever it took to do the same except...Ethan had a natural likability that I just didn't possess. Everybody liked Ethan;even Dorian, and he didn't like anyone. Not to mention Elena, who was just as hard to please as Dorian was, had nothing but praise for the new Lord Chamberlain.

I was not so fortunately blessed and I was petrified I would not measure up to who Ethan's parents wanted for their son, no matter how many times Ethan had tried to reassure me.

I got out of the cab and joined Ethan at the boot, where he was removing the luggage. As he shook the cab driver's hand, the front door of the house opened and a woman came out, a wide smile splitting her face. There could be no mistaking this woman for anyone other than Ethan's mother.

I had spoken to Colleen before. We'd met over Skype, but

this was the first time we would meet in person. There was something a lot less confronting about talking to someone over an internet connection. The in-person meet and greet removed that layer of protection and as much as I had been getting better at not relying on my porcelain doll sugar-coating, meeting new people still made it tempting to fall back onto old habits.

She waited for us to approach before she came down the stairs of the porch and flung her arms around Ethan. He dropped the bags with a laugh and picked her up in a hug. I smiled at their display of affection—it was not something I had experienced with my own family, although I wished hugs had been a more frequent occurrence while I was growing up.

"Mum, I want to introduce you to Lady Sophia," Ethan said when he put his mother back on her feet. "Sophia, this is my mum, Colleen."

Colleen smiled shyly at me and then tried to curtsy. Ethan barked a laugh, and I rolled my lips together to try not to laugh —not at Colleen, but at the expression on Ethan's face. Colleen scowled at her son and backhanded him on the arm before turning back to me.

"I probably didn't do that right, but I've been practising ever since Ethan told us you were coming and—"

I reached out to grasp her hand. "It was perfect, but you don't need to curtsy to me."

Ethan put his arm around his mother. "I said you didn't have to do that," he said.

"Yeah, well, you and your brother tell me a lot of things and I'm never sure whether to believe you or not."

Ethan chuckled. "I'm sure all Sophia wants is to try your famous carrot cake. You did make it, didn't you?"

"Of course I did," she replied, as if any other answer would be madness. "Come on inside and I'll put the kettle on. I dare say that after such a long trip you're dying for a cuppa."

Colleen headed up the path to the house and Ethan hung back, turning his eyes on me and searching my face. "Are you okay?"

I sucked in a breath and nodded. "Nervous," I replied.

He smiled gently. "You don't need to be nervous," he said. "If anyone has anything to worry about, it's me. You are getting to see the house I grew up in and I can assure you it is nowhere near the standard to which you would have grown up in." We both turned to look at the house. It was a redbrick bungalow that looked like it was built in the seventies, but it was neat and tidy if a bit dated.

"I think it looks wonderful," I said truthfully.

Ethan drew me in close to his side and kissed my temple. "I'm glad you're here," he said. "I can't wait to introduce you to everyone."

"Are you sure we shouldn't have stayed in a hotel...or at least booked a room for me?" I asked, as we headed toward the house.

"My mother would never forgive me if we'd stayed in a hotel."

Jet lag was real, and it was kicking my butt. The last few days felt like swimming through molasses, and I didn't see any light at the end of the tunnel. I was convinced this was now my new reality. I would forever be this lethargic blob who found it hard to wake up in the morning but couldn't sleep in the middle of the night. Ethan didn't seem to suffer from the same affliction. Or maybe he was better at masking it.

I hadn't let the jet lag stop me from sight-seeing, though. Ethan had taken me on day trips into the city of Brisbane and we'd gone to the Gold Coast and the Sunshine Coast respectively—one was south of the city and the other north.

I'd met his father, Trevor, his brother, Shane, his sister-in-law, Patricia, and their two kids. Ethan was meeting his newest nephew for the first time and I couldn't deny melting at the sight of him holding baby Andrew. It was the same when I watched him with Prince Alesandro, despite me cautioning myself not to get too far ahead in our relationship. Unhelpful thought patterns were hard to change and so, despite coming a long way, there was still a part of me waiting for Ethan to tell me he was leaving. There was no evidence that he was ready to move on. If anything, he seemed to make Kalopsia his home more and more each day. I knew it was all in my head, so I tried really hard not to listen when the thoughts came, but I still wouldn't let myself get too carried away with my dreams for the future. Ethan was it for me. Now I just had to believe I was it for him, too.

"Are you doing okay?" Ethan asked me as we stepped out into the backyard, where the Samuels were hosting a barbecue.

I smiled at him. "Still struggling with jet lag," I replied, "but I'm okay."

I was. I'd enjoyed my time in Australia so far, and I loved Ethan's family. They seemed to accept me too, and they forgot about my title and just treated me like part of the family, which I adored.

"Are you ready to eat some barbecued sausages?" Ethan asked with a grin.

"I've eaten sausages before," I replied.

"I guarantee you haven't eaten sausages like this," Ethan said with a chuckle. "I think Aussie sausages are a food group all on their own."

"Lead the way," I said.

Ethan wove his fingers through mine and tugged me into the yard where everyone gathered.

"Are the snags ready, dad?" Ethan asked.

"Just about," Trevor replied.

"Excellent," Ethan said, rubbing his hands together. "Now this is how to eat a real Aussie sausage," he said, handing me a piece of white bread.

"What am I supposed to do with this?" I asked.

"I'm about to show you," he replied. "The sausage sizzle has some quite rigid rules. There was recent controversy about the onions being put underneath the sausage, but everyone knows the sausage goes first, then the tomato sauce, and then topped off with the onion."

"Sauce is last," Ethan's dad said.

"I disagree," Ethan said. "Putting the sauce on last means it goes all over your nose when you take a bite."

"I thought you said these rules were rigid," I observed. "They seem rather fluid to me."

"Maybe, but we all agree it has to be white bread," Ethan replied with a grin. "I don't like my bread buttered but mum insists on butter. My brother likes barbecue sauce on his—"

"Blasphemy," Trevor grunted as he turned the sausages once more. "It's tomato sauce or nothing."

"And Patricia likes fat sausages rather than thin ones. We blame her upbringing in New South Wales for that fault in her character."

"I had no idea there was so much cultural division over a sausage in bread," I said, biting my lip to stop myself from laughing.

"You think wrangling the royal peers of Europe is a tricky job, that's nothing compared to running a sausage sizzle at Bunnings on a Saturday," Colleen said.

Bunnings was a large warehouse-style hardware store, which Ethan had insisted on taking me to as part of our sightseeing. It hadn't been a Saturday, so there hadn't been a sausage sizzle. I counted myself lucky after the way the Samuels' family talked about it. They made it seem like a Black Friday Sale smash and grab.

I watched as Ethan loaded my white bread to his exacting specifications. He placed the sausage diagonally across the bread with a generous squirt of tomato sauce and topped with cooked onions. I waited for Ethan to load his own and then watched as he folded the bread around the sausage like a taco.

"Okay," he said, moving us away from the barbecue.

"Don't I need a plate?" I asked, looking helplessly at the meal in my hand.

"It won't last long enough for you to need a plate," he replied. He nodded to me and smiled. "Go on. Take a bite and prepare yourself for a flavour revolution."

I rolled my eyes, but lifted the sausage and bread to my lips. I had to open my mouth wider than was lady-like to fit the first bite in my mouth. I chomped down and then opened my mouth and blew out a steamy breath.

"Hot, hot," I mumbled around my mouthful, but Ethan just laughed.

"It's not an authentic experience if you don't burn the roof of your mouth with the first bite," he said before taking his own giant bite.

$$\sim$$

"WHERE ARE WE GOING?" I grumbled as we drove through the pre-dawn darkness.

"It's a surprise," Ethan replied, turning to grin at me.

"Couldn't this surprise happen at a more reasonable hour?" I asked with a yawn.

"Nope," he replied.

I sipped the coffee Ethan had so thoughtfully supplied as we drove south...or at least I thought it was south. We'd been in the country for nearly two weeks and I still got lost if I walked out the front door without a guide. Ethan had an unbelievably honed sense of direction that came in handy for all his travels... it also helped he'd grown up in the area. I, on the other hand, got lost in the local shopping centre.

We travelled in companionable silence and I dozed, content to be with the man I loved and to not have anywhere I needed to be or anything I needed to do. I hadn't even looked at my emails since touching down in the country. At first it was because I was so jet-lagged, but now it was because I didn't want to. I loved my job, but it was also nice to be away from it. I'd handed over my social media duties to my new assistant for the duration of my stay and I didn't miss it. I probably would, eventually, but it had been so long since I hadn't had an agenda, I was enjoying being off-grid...not that I was completely off-grid. I still posted photos to my personal accounts, but that was for fun, not business.

Once we got back to Kalopsia, our lives would once again be

filled with the busyness of palace life, and mine more so now thanks to Frankie and Callie. After the success of the mentoring program I'd participated in prior to the state visit, we'd decided to keep it running and even expand it. Finally I had a practical use for my weird god mothering skills. Not only was I helping others, but it helped me too. Slowly, slowly I was discovering who I really was beneath the façade I'd built around my life... and I liked the new Sophia...a lot.

"We're here," Ethan said, rousing me from my daydreams.

I looked curiously out the window to see we'd arrived at a large field with people milling about. It wasn't immediately obvious what they were doing or why we were there.

"Come on," he said, excitement infusing his voice.

I got out of the car, rugged up against the cool morning air. Ethan came around to clasp his hand around mine, and then we were heading for the clump of people. It was only then I saw the reason we were there.

"Is that...is that a hot-air balloon?" I asked.

"Yep," he said proudly, turning to grin at me. "You're not afraid of heights, are you?"

I bit my lip. "No," I replied. "I don't think so."

The next little bit was busy as they briefed us on what we had to do and what we couldn't do, and then we were tasked with helping to get the balloon filled and the gondola upright, and then we were in the air.

The gondola was a lot bigger than I'd expected it to be. There were twenty-four people in our group, which was a lot more than I'd envisioned...when I'd envisioned flying in a hot-air balloon, which wasn't often.

"Look at that," Ethan said, pointing to the mountain range

and the first rays of the sun peeking over the top, gilding the range with gold.

Ethan stood behind me, his arms around my waist as I leaned back against him. "It's beautiful," I said.

"Are you glad I woke you up so early now?" he asked.

I snuggled back against him. "I'm happy to get up at any time if it means spending time with you."

When he didn't say anything, I tilted my head back to look at him.

"Was that too cheesy?" I asked uncertainly.

"No, it was perfect," he replied.

He pulled away from me, and I turned to face him. He lowered himself to one knee, and I gasped, my hands covering my mouth as I looked at the open ring box he held in his hands.

"I love you, Lady Sophia Dellis," he said, "and I want to spend the rest of my life with you. Will you marry me?"

The entire hot-air balloon basket held its breath as everyone waited for my answer. I nodded, tears leaking from my eyes, my throat clogged with emotion.

"Yes," I managed to croak. "Yes," I said again after clearing my throat.

Ethan's smile was brighter than the rising sun as he slipped the diamond ring on my finger. He stood and scooped me up in his arms, being careful not to disturb the balance of the gondola too much. The people around us cheered and clapped and I dare say a few people took photos too. I didn't mind. Hopefully, I could find some of those photos on Instagram later and keep them for myself.

"I love you," I whispered to him.

"I love you too," he said right before he kissed me.

The End

Do you want to know what was going on behind the scenes of Sophia and Ethan's love story?
Sign up for my newsletter using the URL below to get a FREE bonus Epilogue:
https://mailchi.mp/emmaleaauthor.com/royal-refinement-bonus-story

DISCOVER THE YOUNG ROYALS UNIVERSE

Are you curious about the Merveille Royal Court?
They have their own series called The Young Royals and it
starts with...

Book 1 - A Royal Engagement

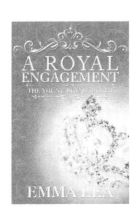

Despite being the second child of the King and Queen of Merveille, Alyssabeth thought that if she kept a low profile she could stay out of the media's glaring spotlight and live a relatively normal life. That was until her father, the King, and her brother, the Crown Prince, was both killed in a hunting accident.

Her dream of joining the UN was no more and instead she needed to return to the small European country of her birth to pick up where her father and brother left off. Her Harvard degree in International Relations is forfeit and in it's place she must become Queen, that was if the misogynistic Parliament can see past their prejudices.

Not much had changed in the small country in her four year absence, but there are two noticeable differences. Her brother's two best friends Will Darkly and Jordan Wicks have grown up into two very intriguing men. Jordan practically swept her off her feet from the moment she stepped off the plane, but Will's more reserved, darkly intense interest in her gave her tingles.

Alyssa wasn't sure she was cut out to be Queen, but she knew that she wanted to do her father and brother proud, so she was willing to give it her best shot, even if it meant going toe to toe with Parliament. And then there was the small matter of her needing to be married in order to fulfil her birthright and take her place as the Head of State.

Buy A Royal Engagement Now

Book 2 - A Royal Entanglement

On the day of the new Queen's coronation, a man from Lady Alexandra's past turns up unannounced in Merveille. Lord Frédéric intercepts him and discovers that Alex had left this man at the altar six months ago and now he was here to claim her.

Alex hasn't told anyone the real

reason she left everything she had worked so hard for in the States to move to Merveille and take up the position of Queen Alyssa's personal assistant. But now the main reason for her flight from the US has turned up on the palace's doorstep and she is backed into a corner. The only person that she can think of to help her is Freddie, but she's worried that getting too close to him might just do more harm than good.

The last thing Freddie wants is to get entangled with a woman. He liked to keep his options open, but now that he has returned to Merveille for good, his mother is trying her damnedest to get him married off and producing the next Bingham heir. When Alex asks for his help, he is only too eager to help her and maybe get his mother off his back in the process. He never expected to fall for her.

Buy A Royal Entanglement Now

Book 3 - A Royal Entrapment

The Queen is getting married and Priscilla is required to work alongside the Lord Chancellor, Dominique, to ensure that the whole affair goes off without a hitch and that they don't, unwittingly, start World War Three. The only problem is that Priscilla finds Dominique insufferable

and Dom isn't all that enamoured with Priscilla either.

When Priscilla's sister, Bianca, falls for Dominique's brother, Louis, the two young lovers hatch a plot to ensure that they can spend time together, but it means that Dom has to pretend to be interested in Priscilla and get her to date him.

The more time they spend together, the more Dom and Priscilla start to like each other, except that now Dom is caught in a difficult spot...should he tell Priscilla that he only asked her out because his brother wanted to date her sister, or should he keep quiet and hope she doesn't find out?

Buy A Royal Entrapment Now

Book 4 - A Royal Expectation

Lady Jeanette Bower had always known what her life was going to look like. It had been drummed into her since she was a little girl. She would marry a titled gentleman and make him a splendid wife who was above reproach. It was what her mother had always wanted for her and Lady Jeanette always did what her mother wanted her to do. She was a good girl. The only problem was, Lady Jeanette didn't expect a six foot four Australian with sparkling tawny

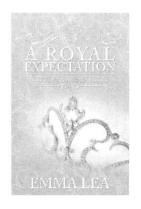

coloured eyes and a mischievous grin to walk into her life and show her that there was perhaps another path for her to take.

Drew Taylor had just landed his dream job and the fact that it was half way around the world from his meddling mother was just icing on the cake. He never expected to be swept off his feet by a woman on a hot pink Ducati. A woman who also happened to be one of the queen's ladies in waiting. And then there was the complication of the viscount she was supposed to marry. How could a cane farmer's son from tropical Queensland compete with a man who could give Lady Jeanette the title she had always wanted? He couldn't, but that wouldn't stop him from trying.

Buy A Royal Expectation Now

Book 5 - A Royal Elopement

Lady Meredith Bingham thought that she had her life sorted. She was a member of the royal guard - an elite security team tasked with protecting the queen of Merveille. She was also close personal friends with the queen and part of her inner circle - the ladies in waiting. But then her mother had to go and ruin it all. Lady Caroline Bingham was sick of her daughter fooling around and playing

soldier. She thought it was high time her daughter got serious about her future and found herself a suitable husband. With the duke pulling double duty as the country's prime minister, it was only right that his daughter start acting like a proper daughter of nobility. Much to Meredith's chagrin, the queen agrees that Meredith must step down from her post.

Prince Christophe Kostopolous was a prince in exile. For the last ten years he had been living under the pseudonym of Jamie Kosta, and for the last seven years he has been part of the royal guard. Very few people knew his true identity, but that was all about to change. The people he had been hiding from all these years have found him and he may finally have his chance to reclaim his rightful place on the throne of his small island nation of Kalopsia. The only problem is, he has fallen for a certain duke's daughter and she has no idea who he really is.

Buy A Royal Elopement Now

Book 6 - A Royal Embarrassment

Savannah has a secret...a secret that could cost her everything she's been working for.

Coming to Merveille and taking up a position as one of Queen Alyssa's ladies in waiting hadn't

been part of Savannah Rousseau's plan, but she wasn't going to turn down the opportunity when it came her way. The daughter of an impoverished viscount, Savannah had nothing to lose and everything to gain by being included amongst the new queen's entourage...as long as no one found out about her secret.

Savannah loved her son. Archer was the sun and moon of her life, but being a single mother would mean instant disqualification from the ladies in waiting. So she hid him from the queen and her new friends...for two years. Now someone had stumbled upon her secret and Savannah would do anything to ensure that she didn't become a royal embarrassment.

Jed Fairchild came to Merveille to escape his own scandal and the last thing he wanted was to be embroiled in another. Finding out about the young boy and impoverished viscount that Savannah had stashed in the abandoned hunting cabins was a complication that he didn't need. Being attracted to the hot-tempered lady in waiting was another. All Jed wanted was to live a simple life working with his horses and ignoring the rest of the world, but with Savannah in his life and the inquisitive Archer following him like his very own shadow, the quiet life was the last thing Jed had...and maybe it wasn't really what he wanted after all.

Buy A Royal Embarrassment Now

Book 6.5 - A Very Royal Christmas

Lady Georgina Darkly, the newly titled Duchess of Pemberton, did not need one more thing to deal with the week before Christmas. The temperature was dropping alarmingly, a snow storm had been predicted, the milk tanks in the dairy were close to freezing and there was a leak in her bedroom roof. To top it all off Clarabelle, the cow that had a mischievous streak a mile wide, had escaped the confines of the barn and could very well freeze to death if Georgie didn't find her soon. The absolute very last thing she needed was an arrogant, stubborn, wealthy, and undeniably *gorgeous* Italian to turn up on her doorstep in need of rescuing.

Leonardo Ricci, youngest son of one of Italy's wealthiest families did not want to be stuck in the middle of a snow storm in a country barely more than the size of a postage stamp. He wanted to be with his friends in Milan not suffering through a stilted family Christmas with his parents. When a cow appeared in the middle of the road and caused his beautiful Ferrari to career out of control into a snow bank, he honestly didn't think his day could get any worse...and then he met the Duchess. She was opinionated, stubborn, far too capable for her own good, stunningly beautiful, and immune to his charms. They had nothing in common and if she hadn't rescued him then he probably would never have given her another thought. But then they got stuck together in her rundown mansion with no electricity and no phones...and that's when the sparks really started to fly.

Buy A Very Royal Christmas Now

Book 7 - A Royal Enticement

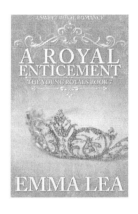

Lady Margaret de la Fontaine was the forgotten lady in waiting. She didn't mind...most of the time. She liked working with Lady Savannah and the others and believed whole-heartedly in what the queen was trying to achieve in their small country of Merveille. She just wished that someone would notice her, just once.

Queen Alyssa's ladies in waiting had, one by one, met and fallen in love with their dream partners, all except Margaret, not that anybody had given her single status another thought. That didn't mean she didn't also wish for someone to love, but she wasn't holding her breath, especially since her best friend, Lady Hadley Winchester, was now part of the ladies in waiting. It seemed the newest member of the group was a hit with everyone, including the queen, which was great but once again left Margaret as the wallflower.

Until Brín.

Brín noticed the sweet wee Maggie standing against the wall while everyone else at the ball danced and chatted. He felt a kinship with her, even across the room and sought her out for a little bit of harmless flirting. He was supposed to be checking out the candidates for his arranged marriage, but he really wasn't keen on the whole idea. He understood his responsibility as the lost heir of a broken down estate that was haemorrhaging money, but he didn't really see himself as the marrying kind...and even if he did, he'd want to do it for love, not money.

Brín was immediately taken with Lady Margaret, but alas, she was not the debutante his advisors had picked out for him. That honour went to Maggie's best friend, Lady Hadley. But what was a newly minted earl to do when he had the livelihoods of several staff and families to look after? Not to mention, if he didn't find a solution he may very well lose the estate and the title that went with it.

Buy A Royal Enticement Now

ACKNOWLEDGMENTS

The initial idea for this story was to do a gender-swapped retelling of *My Fair Lady*. I love that movie but...I hate the ending. I always thought Eliza should have ended up with Freddie. The professor, in my opinion, did not deserve Eliza's heart.

When it came to write my version, I asked myself if I really wanted Sophia's character to be as unlikeable as the professor was in *My Fair Lady*, and the answer was, of course, no.

So where Professor Higgins was unbearably arrogant, I made Sophia the opposite. I found her insecurities and the crushing self-doubt she suffered so incredibly relatable to my own life. I was inspired by a song by *Little Big Town* called 'Sugar Coat.' While the song doesn't describe the same situation, I think the sentiment is applicable.

The last eighteen months have been awful for all of us but slowly, slowly things seem to be getting better. I don't think anything will be the same as it was pre-2020 and hopefully the changes will be for the best. *fingers crossed*

I know I couldn't have gotten through it all without the support of my family, and especially my husband. He is...*nonpareil.*

This book would not have even been finished if not for Kathryn. I had a serious attack of the doubts in the middle of this book and if not for her continued encouragement I would have stuck it, unfinished, in a drawer. Thank you Kathryn for having faith in me that I could do it.

Big thanks and love for Brooke (and her new kitten Lucy). I am forever grateful for you. You have become the editor in my head as I write and I know that I am a better writer because of you.

Thank you to every reader who has picked up this book (and any of my other books). Your continued support makes this possible and I hope you enjoyed your little vacation into my fictional world.

ABOUT THE AUTHOR

Emma loves to read. Reading has been her escape and safe place for as long as she can remember. Her earliest memories are of reading (or making up stories to go along with the pictures in her books) and it is the one thing that has always brought her happiness when nothing else could. Now she write stories and hopes that when people read them, they can find an escape, a safe place and a little moment of happiness when they need it.

She lives on the beautiful Sunshine Coast in Queensland, Australia with her wonderful husband. She has two beautiful, grown-up sons, two daughters-in-law, and a new baby grand-daughter, and a cat who is supposedly her co-worker (but she doesn't really contribute much).

Emma is a ferocious reader with eclectic tastes and has always wanted to write, but never had the opportunity due to one reason or another (excuses, really) until finally taking the bullet between her teeth in 2014 and just making herself do it.

THANKS

Thank you for reviewing this book and recommending it to
your friends and family.
Honest reviews are important for authors and I appreciate the
time you have taken to share your thoughts.

OTHER BOOKS BY EMMA LEA

This is Emma Lea's complete book library at time of publication, but more books are coming out all the time. Find out every time Emma releases a book by going to her website (www.emmaleaauthor.com) and signing up for her Newsletter.

SWEET ROMANCES

These are romantic tales without the bedroom scenes and the swearing, but that doesn't mean they're boring!

The Young Royals

A Royal Engagement

Lord Darkly

A Royal Entanglement

A Royal Entrapment

A Royal Expectation

A Royal Elopement

A Royal Embarrassment

A Very Royal Christmas

A Royal Enticement

The Kabiero Royals

Royal Ruse

Royal Refinement

Bookish Book Club Novellas

Meeting Prince Charming

Meeting the Wizard of Oz

Meeting Santa Claus

SWEET & SEXY ROMANCES

In my Sweet & Sexy Romances I turn up the heat with a little bit of sexy. No swearing, or very minimal swearing, and brief, tasteful and not too graphic bedroom scenes.

Love, Money & Shoes Series

Walk of Shame

Standalone Novels

Amnesia

HOT & SEXY ROMANCES

Hot & Spicy Romances turn the heat way up. They contain swearing and sexy scenes and the characters get hot under the collar.

Recommended for 18+ readers

Brisbane City Hearts (formerly TGIF)

Love to Hate You

Want to Date You

Hate to Want You (coming soon)

Collins Bay Series

Last Call

The Christmas Stand-Off

Game Changer

Made in the USA
Columbia, SC
04 February 2022

55344121R10195